FROZEN BUTTERFLIES

A NOVEL

SIMONA GROSSI

PIPES & CLOUDS

FIRST EDITION PUBLISHED IN 2018.

ISBN: 978-0-9998825-2-8

Original cover artwork by Hazel Lam
Author Photo by Marco Paonessa

A GIFT TO MY READERS

Dear Reader,

Thank you for purchasing *Frozen Butterflies*. I hope you'll enjoy it and hope you will continue to read my stories. As a small token of my gratitude, I would like to give you a copy of my novella, *Like Still Water*.

Check the section at the end of this book to learn how to get it for free.

simona

If I could only warm my hands and
make them fly again . . .
                                    S. B.

NIGHT ONE

I don't know why I keep waking up in the middle of the night. I've tried every possible remedy. Pills, therapy, pills again, meditation, hypnosis. Nothing seems to work. One of my teachers used to say that "everything happens for a reason." Well, I've yet to find that reason.

During the day I teach. Sometimes it's hard to stand in front of my class after a sleepless night. My legs shake, my vision blurs, I can't hear students' questions and have to ask them to repeat themselves two, three times . . .

I wear heavy glasses and I don't like them. They cover my face. But I haven't been able to wear contacts for a long time. My eyes are too tired after nights spent reading and writing, and so I've given in. And after all, the glasses hide the bags under my eyes and help hide my misery.

I could wear makeup, but makeup has never been my thing. It would make me look like a scary clown.

Am I sad? I don't know. I feel lost. The therapist I saw last year called it depression. He said we should meet twice a week for six months. If we were lucky, we would find the right dose of this or that drug, and I would be cured. Wasn't that easy? I felt so empty in that room as he was talking to me. Empty and lost. Yes, that's how I felt. I left thinking I would never let him treat me. Then I met with two other therapists. They were also useless, so I eventually gave up. After all I should know how to treat myself, as that is what I do. For a living.

I teach psychology at a university in Los Angeles. I wrote a book on midlife development that was praised as one of the most innovative works of the year when it came out. It's about midlife transitions: Boredom with a life or lifestyle that no longer provides fulfillment. Feeling restless and wanting to do something completely different. Questioning decisions already made and the meaning of life. Daydreaming. Persistent sadness. Increased sexual desire and sexual affairs. Increased or decreased ambition.

I don't know why I chose this topic. I was only twenty-six at the time. What did I know about these things? The book was a success.

Recently I have started reviewing my book. At night the hours feel endless, so I had to find something to do, and I thought about my book. I didn't read it to help me sleep. I knew that would have not worked. In fact, hardly anything does.

I do sleep sometimes though, but mostly during the day, and only for a few hours at a time. And that is what I did today. My class was at noon. I taught for two hours, collected my things from the office, took the bus, and returned home.

I live by myself, and I'm not in a relationship with anyone at the moment. Or, I should say, I haven't been in a relationship for the past four years. I turned thirty-five this year, and I think I must be going through some sort of crisis. But I can't say exactly what it is, when it started, or why. And I don't think my problem would technically fall within the categories I describe in my book.

As soon as I got home, I looked for something to eat and poured some scotch into my glass, but before I ate anything, the scotch kicked in, my head started spinning, and I crashed on the sofa. At five p.m. I woke up, and I haven't been able to go back to sleep since then. My stomach is craving food or sleep. I'm not sure. It's one a.m.

My book is open to the chapter on "Boredom with Life or Lifestyle." The topic seems perfect at the moment. I leaf through the pages but feel uninspired. I'm bored by my analysis of boredom, and this is unexpected. I still have six hours before getting ready for school. What will I do now?

I open the window in my living room and look outside. It's dark. In my neighborhood there are no street lights. That should help people sleep, but it doesn't help me. If my street were illuminated and there were a few stores and bars open, I could perhaps go out, meet someone. I'm sure there must be other people like me who can't sleep and would appreciate street lights, street life, at this time. Yes, that's a shame.

I wander around the house with no precise idea or plan. I make some coffee, go to the living room, and push my big couch close to the window. I start sipping my coffee and look outside. I'm not sure what I'm hoping to see in the darkness. In fact, I'm probably not even looking outside. Who knows what I'm looking at?

A taxi catches my attention as it pulls up on the other side of the street. I expect someone to get out. Instead someone gets in, and the car leaves. It's a woman, but I can't see who she is. It's the third night this happens. For no reason, I feel I should follow her, but now it's too late; she has disappeared.

NIGHT TWO

I had no doubt I would be awake tonight too. I used to get surprised when, two years ago, I would wake up at two or three in the morning. But at that time, insomnia wasn't the routine that it now is for me. And I feared it. I remember waking up in the middle of the night and being scared. Hard to say why. Now, I've somehow surrendered.

It's almost two a.m. I go to the bathroom, and rather than the usual routine—mirror, sigh, toilette, mirror—I take a shower, avoid the mirror, go back to my room, and get dressed. I'm not sure I know what I'm doing. My instinct is controlling my actions, and I let it.

I make coffee, place my wallet and my coat on the kitchen table, and prepare to leave as soon as I hear the taxi. Before my coffee is ready, I see the car. It came again. I turn off the stove, and I'm dragged to the door by an inexplicable euphoria. The taxi's still there. The woman is late. She sees me waiting across the street but doesn't acknowledge me. She enters the car, and it leaves.

I remain motionless for a while, considering options. I could take my car and follow the taxi. I could call a taxi. But I don't do any of these things. Instead I turn and go home. I wonder what she could be doing at night, always at the same time. And now I'm curious to see when she comes back.

I turn on the stove again and finally make the coffee I didn't make before. I'll sip it close to the window, read something, and wait for her to return. I push my couch closer to the window, take a soft blanket, some photography books, my coffee, and lay back. At five a.m. she hasn't returned, but I might have fallen asleep at some point, and now I'm not sure. I'm mad at myself for falling asleep. I should have stayed awake. And I'm mad at myself for not sleeping, and for seeking stupid ways to get through the night. Who cares what she does or doesn't do with her own life? Who cares whether she comes back late? It's none of my business, and certainly it won't help me sleep again. I have a problem, and she has nothing to do with it.

NIGHT THREE

I woke up again. This time a little after two a.m. I have no intention whatsoever of following anyone. But, again, I witness the same scene. The taxi arrives, she gets in, and the car leaves.

I leave the window open, not to check on her, just to let the fresh air enter the room and maybe slowly put me asleep. After an hour or so, I hear another car approaching. I return to the window. It's a taxi. It stops across the street. And it's her again. She pays the driver and walks to her door. I can see her. She's crying.

It's after six, and although the sun is about to rise, I close my eyes. In less than thirty minutes, the alarm will go off and I'll have to prepare for class.

DAWN ONE

It's one thirty in the morning, and I'm wide awake. I browse the internet looking for ideas, places that might be open now. I go on Yelp and filter the clubs by "open now," but nothing comes up. I keep looking and finally find a place called the Red Moon. It seems like a jazz club or a bar that stays open all night, but the information I find is not clear, and the photos on the website don't help either. I call. The place is open. A woman answers but is dismissive. She says they'll be open until 5 a.m. I hang up and stare outside my window, trying to decide whether I am brave enough to go. The woman I keep seeing would go. I know she would. I'm home, wondering about her and the Red Moon.

I get dressed and call a taxi.

It arrives before I can think things through. After I give the driver the address, he turns to check me, and that makes me once again question my choice. What am I doing? Before I change my mind, we are on our way.

We drive through unfamiliar streets and alleys. The city is deserted.

"Do you know the Red Moon?" I ask the man, wondering whether I might have dreamed the call, the whole thing.

He looks at me through his rearview mirror and smiles. Before I decide that what I'm doing is not completely stupid, that everything will be fine, the car stops.

"Here you are," he says. "Good luck and be safe."

I want to ask him to wait for me, tell him I will pay for his time, but I don't. I pay for the ride and just go.

There is only one building on the street, but there is no name on it, no sign of a club or a bar or anything like that. The building looks like an old factory and takes up the entire block on the fringe of the art district. From the outside, you would never guess that the factory could host a nightclub—assuming that is where I'm going. The place is made of old, fired bricks. I stop to look at them. The night is crisp and warm and bitter and inviting. It tastes like scotch. No, I am not afraid. I know that taste and like it. It is somehow familiar.

I go closer to the bricks and press my nose into them. They smell like the past, I can almost touch it.

I can see two floors, but the top one looks empty, as there's no light coming from the big windows, one of which is broken. But the ground floor seems deserted too. I can hear no music or noise coming from there. It's silent all over, as if something is trapped in those bricks, perhaps the present too.

I walk around the building. There's no one there. After some wandering, I am in front of what looks like a door beneath a tangle of ivy. I knock, and a man wearing a black suit and tie appears. It's hard to say whether he's from the present or the past. He looks elegant. His demeanor does. I am in a safe place. I will be fine.

He asks me if I need help. I say I'm looking for the Red Moon. He asks for my ID.

"Susan?"

I like the sound of my name, it also feels familiar. But then he gives me a smile similar to the one the driver gave me before, and that smile turns him into an untrustworthy stranger. What is it that I am missing?

He asks me to follow him, and we go down the stairs, perhaps two floors. I'm still confused or maybe still inebriated from the bricks.

He doesn't speak, and I feel more uncomfortable. But talking to him seems inappropriate, so I don't.

We reach a room lit by a few feeble candles. He's standing in front of the entrance, so I can barely see anything. But then he moves to show me the place and says, "Welcome to the Red Moon, Susan."

After I watch him disappear up the stairway, I turn to the room, and I can finally hear some music.

There's a jazz trio in the left corner. I try to see who is playing, but I can't. I can only see the instruments, and they seem to be playing on their own.

I enter the room and sit at the bar. The bartender asks me what I want, and I order scotch, trying to make the place taste more familiar. A stranger seated not far from me starts staring at me. I take my glass and look around in search of another, more comfortable, place to sit.

There are a few couples that seem intimate with each other, others that seem to have just met. And there's a woman sitting on her own, wearing a minimal, dark mask. Odd—or perhaps not so much. I look around more, and now it seems that everyone is wearing invisible masks. It's the way they move and talk that gives me that impression. The man who was staring at me before has disappeared, so I return to the bar and take my old place.

"Do you like it here?"

I turn and see a man wearing a dark-blue shirt, the collar opened, the sleeves rolled up.

I like what I see.

"Let's drink together. I'll order another one of these if you finish yours."

I smile, and he comes closer to offer his hand.

"I'm Nick."

"Susan."

"Are you a regular?"

I pause and look at him. "No, this is my first time," I say. "You?"

"I'd like to say the same, but, no. I'm pretty much a regular."

"Are you by yourself?"

"Yes," I say, while it looks like he's examining me, his eyes piercing mine. I feel uncomfortable, almost naked in front of him, and I look elsewhere to catch my breath. But yes, I like what I see.

"What do you do?" I then ask.

"I'm a writer. Actually, a blogger."

"Isn't a blogger a writer?"

"Not everyone thinks so." He looks down at his drink, forces a smile, and then looks at me, questioning something—me. I must look out of place, and perhaps I am—or maybe I just came unprepared.

"You? What do you do?"

"I teach."

"What do you teach?"

"Psychology. Personality and cognition."

He remains silent for a while, and I feel even more uncomfortable.

"What do you write about?" I ask.

"Stories."

"Stories of what?"

"Of people. Stories that I find interesting, hoping my readers will agree with me."

"That's why you come here? To find stories?"

He laughs and sips his drink.

"I do come here for inspiration. Idea hunting, that's what I call it. But it doesn't always work. When it does, then I go home and write."

"So that means you write at night?"

"Preferably. I don't have to. I could write during the day, but I prefer the night."

"Why?"

"The night is more intimate. You dare, you wander. There's silence, no distraction. Your entire body craves any sort of creation."

I look at him. I can hardly speak, and I fear he could leave at any moment. *Please don't leave. I can do better than this.* I try to push some questions out of my mouth, but my mind seems disabled, not responding. He's magnetic, hypnotic. His eyes are dark, deep. I feel I can reach him, reach deeply into him, through them, and that distracts me even more, almost nullifying my efforts. That is unusual. It scares me, and it scares me to think that he might be doing the same thing to me, just better. And if he is, what does he see? Does he like what he sees?

His hair is dark. Wavy, slightly covering his eyes. He's tall, thin, and a bit round shouldered. He seems almost consumed by something, someone—or maybe just himself. In his forties, I would say, early or late forties. Or maybe I'm wrong. It's too dark to see things clearly. It's truly too dark.

"If you write at night, then when do you sleep?"

"During the day, a bit now and then."

"And do you feel OK?"

"What do you mean?"

"Don't you feel tired, exhausted, after being up all night?"

Are we similar? It feels like we are.

He smiles.

"After I finish my piece, I go to bed, and when I wake up I feel rested and ready for a new night."

He looks more deeply into my eyes, and I start shaking. And then I feel almost frozen, trapped in him or by him, as if he can control my mind, my movements.

"You know, we're breaking the rules here," he then says.

"Which rules?"

"If we want to have sex, we shouldn't talk about ourselves so much."

Did I hear that right? Did I really? I swallow my excitement to hide it, but I can't stop the sweat that drops from my forehead onto my lip. He notices and follows the drop with his eyes. I should turn, say something, but I can't.

"I think I'd better go home."

"I'll give you a ride."

"No, thanks. I'll take a taxi."

"Here's my card. Call or email me if you feel like it."

I take the card, free my eyes from his, and leave.

It's almost seven, and I should probably try to get one hour of sleep or at least some rest before getting ready for class, but I can't. I keep thinking about his eyes. I'm obsessing about them. It's like they're gripping my stomach. I feel so stupid. I don't know him, but my entire body craves him. I take a long, hot shower and masturbate thinking about him.

DAY ONE

I called him after work. He didn't seem surprised, but he did his best to make me comfortable.

"How was your day?" he asked, as if we were old friends or had been dating for a while. I told him about my class, the struggle to keep my eyes open, and my losing both focus and the thread of my lecture at some point.

"Do you think you'll be able to have dinner with me tonight? I'd like to take you to dinner." His voice was as deep as I recalled.

"I'd like you to."

I could sense his smile, but I wished I could see it. After I hung up, I made some tea, turned on the radio, and started daydreaming about the night. Finally, exhausted, I gave up and fell asleep. When I opened my eyes a little before nine, I rushed through a shower, shaved, and with my hair still wet, put on a simple black dress and left. Only once I was out of the house did I realize I had a long, thin cut on my right upper thigh. My dress covered most, but not all, of it.

"Susan," Nick called from across the street. He must have been waiting for a while when he saw me. "I thought you might have fallen asleep."

"I actually did," I said, when I entered his car. "I'm sorry if I made you wait. I didn't mean to."

"That explains it," he said, running his hand through my wet hair as if he wanted to examine it. I attempted a smile, but a rush of warmth that was too strong to control turned that smile into something else.

There was something about him that felt familiar and something that made me uncomfortable. But it wasn't the comfort that I found most attractive.

I hadn't asked him where we were going. When I realized that, I was surprised. I had always been in control. It seemed like I needed to. And now I didn't care. He was in control, and I liked it.

"Don't you want to know where we're going?"

"I . . ."

No, I didn't.

"I don't go out that often," I confessed, not sure why.

"Why's that? Are you a broken heart or something?"

"No, definitely not. I'm just, I've been . . . on pause, I guess." I had not been "on pause." Actually, it felt more like stalling, with a destination I knew I was not going to reach, because I couldn't. I was broken, perhaps bound to crash. But now it felt like I was moving. He was *moving* me, and he could take me anywhere really. Or was I just crashing?

He smiled and continued to drive. We didn't say much. He was studying me, and I was studying him. From time to time he would turn toward me and penetrate me with his eyes. It seemed as if he were trying to go deeper and deeper, as if he were testing his ability— or mine to resist. I liked the test. And so there was mostly silence, but somehow we were communicating. Then his phone rang. He glanced at it and pulled over to answer.

"Any problem?" I asked when he hung up.

"Yes. No, well . . . Jack, my partner, asked me to write a piece for tomorrow. He was going to, but can't."

"I'll understand if you have to go."

"I have a couple of hours, but then I'll have to work. I'll have to find a hook, something to write about."

"I see. Do you absolutely have to post something tonight or tomorrow?"

"Yes. It's the agreement we have with our sponsors . . . anyhow . . ."

"Can I help?"

"You? No. I don't think so. How would you help?"

"I don't know. I might help you come up with ideas, write the piece. I've written before."

"Blog posts?"

"No, psychology pieces, a book on adult . . ."

He remained silent for a while and didn't seem convinced, but then he said, "Fine. Let's cancel our reservation. We'll order pizza and go to my place to work, if that's fine with you." I nodded that it was.

His place was close by.

"This is where I live."

He pointed to a tall building that looked old and charming, with big windows that somehow reminded me of the nightclub of the night before. In fact, his building also reminded me of an abandoned factory. I told him that, and he agreed but said that the building was in fact an old bank.

"This building must have witnessed a thousand interesting stories. When I write, I'm inspired. Perhaps it talks to me. I thought this could happen when I bought my apartment. I chose it because of that."

The apartment was a loft, with little furniture. There was an old, brownish sofa with coffee stains all over it, a large coffee table piled with books and newspapers, ashtrays filled with butts everywhere, a large desk that seemed like the desk of an architect, two computers, an old typewriter, a big TV against the wall, and a messy kitchen on the left.

"This is how I'd always imagined the apartment of a writer," I thought and said aloud.

"Chaos?"

"An artistic one."

"Pizza should be here soon. Would you like a beer?" he asked.

"Sure." I sat on the sofa while he went for the beers and returned.

"Do you read blogs?"

"No, not really."

"Why not?"

"No offense, but I often find them boring, with no story in the stories."

"What type of stories do you like?"

"Stories about people like me. Real stories, not ones made up to capture audiences, advertising. Unlikely stories, stories that might not sell. Real." As I was thinking about what I had just said, I looked at the books on his shelves, searching for ideas, and noticed a worn notebook with a dark-blue cover. That looked different.

"What's this?" I asked.

"Oh, that . . . I completely forgot about it. It's a journal. I took the bus one day when my car was down for repair, and . . ."

"A journal?"

"Yes, a journal someone, a guy, lost. I like the story. It's somehow familiar. His girlfriend reminds me of someone I knew. And I like the writing. It's good, but a bit depressing. I asked the bus driver whether they had a lost-and-found department. He said they did, but he didn't seem to trust it much. He said if I wanted to return the journal to its owner, I'd better try to find him myself."

"Is there a name on it?"

"On the journal? Yeah. The author's name is Andrew. But no last name. And the journal contained an envelope that seemed ready to be mailed. There's no sender's name, but there's an address on it. I thought I might go and check the place out, but haven't had a chance." He sipped his drink and added, "I didn't feel like opening the envelope. Although, of course, I did read his journal, so . . ."

I opened the journal. The date I read on top of the first page was July 2 of last year.

When the delivery guy arrived, Nick went to the door, and I started reading.

July 2

Today the city seems more dirty than usual. I had to run some errands downtown and so I spent an hour there. It was awful. It felt as if there was asphalt everywhere, and the asphalt felt like black, dirty, hopeless tar, like I always imagined you could find in the lungs of a dying smoker. In fact, the city looked like giant lungs filled with death. I never took you downtown when you asked me to. You said you might want to live there one day. You said there is art, profound art, hidden in the filthy corners of the city. That you needed to be brave and explore it to find it. I said you would also need to hold your nose not to smell the urine and the alcohol and the crap. And when I said that, you looked discouraged and sad that I couldn't see what you saw. I just saw ugliness everywhere. I still do. I still see the same, ugly scene every time I go downtown. I wish you had told me what you saw and explained to me how to see it myself. I wish you had taught me how to look at things to capture their essences, to capture what I seemed to be missing. Why did you choose me in the first place if you knew we were so different? Didn't you want to teach me what you knew, take me into your world? You know, Emily, people are humans. You are different, you are not of this world. But I am. And, still, you chose me. But then you gave up. And it was probably my fault, 'cause I should have begged you, I should have begged you to give me another chance. My stupid pride. I miss you. My life is so miserable now that you're no longer with me. It feels empty and miserable. And my apartment stinks. It stinks more than skid row that time you dragged me there. It stinks since the day you left.

"What do you think?" Nick asked.

"I like it. Is it all like this?"

"Pretty much."

I leafed through more passages. What I read pulled me in. It was hard to stop. And then there were drawings. I loved those too. They seemed to be part of the story. Yes, there was a story. One I wanted to read.

"So you were saying ... you wanted to find him ... The address on the envelope must be his address."

"It probably isn't. He seems to be the sender." He pulled the envelope from the diary and handed it to me. "Yeah, there's just an address, no name."

"I see a story here. Don't you?"

"Maybe ... So what?"

"Well, I would want to read this."

He remained silent, looking at me, perhaps thinking what I was thinking.

"What if we looked for the author while posting some excerpts from his journal?" I asked. "That'd be a story too. A story within a story."

"We can't. We shouldn't ..."

"Really? Even if we hid his identity?"

"Why would we want to do this?"

"'Cause it's interesting, the search would be intriguing. And maybe it'll lead us nowhere. But what if it leads us somewhere? You never know what you might find before you start searching. Right?" I looked at him, hoping he would say yes, although I had no idea why I suddenly cared so much.

He pulled the journal from my hands and started leafing through its pages.

"Have you read the entire journal?" I asked.

"More or less."

"Is there a theme?"

"He seems depressed and disoriented after breaking up with his girlfriend. He talks about his relationship with her, tries to understand why he lost her. And ..."

"And?"

"I'm not sure. He seems manic. That's your field though, so I don't know."

"I think the journal, this author, might attract readers."

"Hmm ... I don't know. I'll have to think about this more. Let's eat our pizza."

We ate in silence. Two strangers sitting at a kitchen table, dining as two old friends and perfectly comfortable in that silence. Nick was immersed in his thoughts, and I observed him. He looked like an intellectual, a heavy smoker, heavy drinker, extremely thin. His fingers were long and slender. He could have been a pianist, I thought. I loved his fingers, but I loved his eyes the most, and I loved watching him lost in his thoughts. He would place his chin on his right hand and turn his face slightly to look nowhere, to be nowhere but in his mind. I could observe him without him even noticing. I felt hungry for him, I wanted to know him.

"You know what?" he then said, interrupting the flow of my thoughts. "This might work."

"Are you serious?"

"You made it sound reasonably interesting."

"I would read those posts. They somehow remind me of myself."

"Of you? How so?"

Why did I say that?

"Sometimes I obsess about things perhaps for no reason. Sometimes I feel bored, lost, like I am stalling, waiting to crash."

And so this is me. Would you like to see more?

"Is it the boredom or feeling lost that causes the stalling? Those are two different things."

He seemed to.

I'm lost. Would he like my answer, me?

"Anyhow, I don't think he's bored."

I felt relieved for what he didn't see.

"But clearly lost," he added.

"What? Who?"

"Andrew. What are we talking about?"

"Right. Sorry."

He finished his pizza, went to the window, and for a few moments stared out in silence.

"L.A. looks magic at night, almost another city, don't you think? Sometimes it looks like New York."

"Do you like New York?" I asked.

"I lived there until my late twenties. I got my journalism degree from Columbia, worked for a local newspaper for a few years, and then got a job with the *Los Angeles Times* and moved here. The pay was better, the stories I wrote were more interesting, plus I had a chance to move to the West Coast. I'd always wanted to do that. Although, I must admit, sometimes I miss New York. I'm a New Yorker, will always be."

"What happened to the job with the *Times*?" I asked.

"Oh, yes, that's a long story. I'm much happier doing the job I do now."

There was some silence, and then he talked more about New York and New Yorkers.

"I don't know if I'm a New Yorker," I said, "but that's where I grew up and went to grad school. Sometimes I miss it too."

"Well . . . to New York!" he said, touching my first beer with his third one. Or fourth. I had lost count. "You have a nice smile, Susan."

I felt some heat coming from inside. I wanted to move away from him, hide it, but he was staring at me. I felt his desire. It felt so strong that it seemed to have expanded and occupied every corner of the space around me. What if I was wrong though? I might have been. But if I wasn't, I knew his desire would have no mercy for me this time. So I surrendered myself to it or whatever I had imagined. Did he like what he saw? When he finally turned away to clean up, I was free. From his desire or my imagination.

"Do you want to write this together?" he asked, as he sat at the computer. "We could be coauthors."

"Me? You mean, with my name visible on the blog?"

"Yes, I'd like that. Besides . . . I like you."

Could he hear my questions? Had he just answered? I looked for his eyes, hoping they would tell me more, but they had left after turning my soul around and around so fast that it, my selves, my questions, my voices, had multiplied like in a myriad of mirrors, their loudness so strong I could barely sustain it, there, on the floor, drained, waiting to understand what had just happened, waiting to return to reality, heavier or lighter, I couldn't say.

"Do you mind if I smoke?"

Yes, he had gone.

I said it was fine. He lit a cigarette, stared at the blank page for a few seconds, and then started typing very fast, pronouncing the words he was typing as if he were reading a script.

"I always read out loud when I write," he said. "I need to hear the sound of it."

And so he played his piece for me:

Our everyday life is chaos. We no longer have time to read, let alone write. Everything moves so fast, too fast to even stop and think, to see things, to be part of this life we are in. Yet a man, we'll call him "J.N.," found the time to write a journal, which he then lost, or perhaps abandoned. We found the journal on a bus. There was no name on it and so we couldn't return it to him, but what we read was too beautiful to leave it to chance. So we decided to start looking for him, share excerpts of the journal with you, have you join in our search, seeking your insights on his art, his world, yours.

He wrote and played more, copied parts of the July 2 pages, the ones I had read, and then signed with his name and mine. I liked his music. I watched him going over our piece, looking for typos, changing a word here and there, adding a phrase enthusiastically, and then erasing it with the same resolution. Yes, I still liked what I saw.

"You seem a bit tired. I'll take you home," he suddenly said, perhaps reading or misreading my trance.

"Oh no, no need. I'll call a taxi," I said, looking elsewhere to hide it.

"I insist," he said, looking like he wanted to take me home.

I agreed to accept his ride.

As he was driving I pressed my head against the passenger seat and closed my eyes. And then I opened them a bit and saw that he was looking at me, staring at my legs, which my dress had left uncovered. I closed my eyes again and pretended to sleep. When we arrived at my place I thanked him for the ride.

"You should be careful not to hurt yourself."

"Huh?"

"Your cut. You have a cut on your right leg."

"Oh right, I know. It's nothing. I'll be fine," I said, and I hoped so.

DAY TWO

I slept last night, and I feel different today.

Nick called and asked me to go back to his place to continue working on Andrew's diary, and I agreed. I took a taxi to get there. I would have driven, but I haven't driven in such a long time, and sometimes I'm not even sure I still can. When I got to his place, Nick was cooking, making something he said he'd learned from an Italian chef he had once interviewed.

As he was chopping garlic, he cut his left index finger. He stared at it for a few seconds, almost hypnotized. I thought he might be scared or something, so I took a napkin and went closer to stop the blood, but he pushed me away.

"Don't..."

"I'm sorry, I was just..."

I looked at him, silent, not sure of what to say. He washed away the blood and continued to chop, looking down, and without varying his gaze for a while. Then he looked at me as if he wanted to say something, maybe apologize, but he didn't. He brushed his fingers against some ground red pepper he had placed close to him, ready to be used, and then came closer and pushed his fingers onto my lips.

"Does it hurt?"

What? The pepper? You?

"I need to know if you can take it."

What?

"Can I use this one?"

I looked at him, waiting for him to ask his question—the one he really wanted to ask—but he didn't, and I did not respond.

"What do you think about the blog?"

I turned, trying to decide what I should say, the person I was going to be for him, what I wanted him to see.

"Why are you biting your lips? Does it hurt?"

I turned toward him but didn't answer. He took an ice cube, came close to me, and pressed the ice against my lips.

"Does it help?"

I looked at him, straight into his eyes, and said nothing. He didn't look away. Was he finally asking his question? Were my eyes answering?

"I like it," I then said. "I like the blog." If I couldn't see him, then he shouldn't see me.

"I write for myself, that's the truth." He seemed to be fine with whatever we had. "I do need money," he continued. "That's also true. So if I can make money with my writing, I'm happy, and I can continue . . . writing for myself."

He looked at me to check my reaction. I wasn't thinking about the blog, and I didn't taste the food, as I felt almost anesthetized. The pepper or something had been too strong.

As Nick was clearing the table, I wandered around the living room. There were photos on the walls, some on the coffee table, a few on his desk. I wondered who those people were. Friends? People he had interviewed? And then there was a photo of a boy with what might have been his father. Was it Nick with his father? He returned too soon for me to figure that out.

"This will help the writing," he said, handing me a glass of wine. I thanked him and sat at the computer close to him, holding my glass.

"I'll read from where we left yesterday," I said.

July 3

I'm glad you didn't take your clothes and your books with you when you left. Today the cleaning lady asked me what she should do with them. Obviously nothing. If you come back, you might want them back. I told her to collect them and place them in a suitcase, ready for you to pick up if and when you decide that you need them. It'd be easier for me to give them to you, I thought. But then, after she did that, I asked her to undo it. If you come and all I have to do is hand you that suitcase, we'll only have a few minutes to talk. If you have to collect your things scattered around, it'll take you hours. So, after the cleaning lady placed the clothes back on the clothes rack, and the books on the shelves, I misplaced them, and put them in random places so you'll have to stay longer when you come to retrieve them. Your ballet shoes are still on my desk. I had actually never looked at them as closely as I did today. They must have been painful to wear. At times, I felt they were in fact your feet, and that was easy to believe since you often walked as if you were dancing en pointe, and I would not notice any break between your feet and the shoes. In fact, was there any? The shoes truly seemed your feet. And how painful it must have been to be living your life en pointe, carrying with you that soft, continuous pain. Did you want that? Did that help? Was there a worse pain you were trying to silence? I wish I had thought about it, considered that. I viewed your continuous dancing and walking en pointe as a way to put some distance between you and the world, between your world and mine, between you and me. You were probably just trying to protect yourself and perhaps me from something else. I wish I had thought about it. I went to a ballet last night. Swan Lake. Remember? You wanted me to see it but I resisted. I thought I wouldn't like it. But I did. I felt their pain, the lightness, I saw beauty. Is that what attracted you to ballet? Was it the beauty and the lightness, or was it the pain? I went for a bike ride the other day, along the L.A. river. The road was not that easy. I started riding fast, I fell, and had to go to the hospital to get some stitches. Nothing major. But that pain helped, it was good, as it distracted me from you. And it was good as it got me closer to you, it made me feel what you could have felt sometimes. That pain made me think about you and ballet yesterday, as I was watching the dancers dancing en pointe, their feet pressed into their ballet flats. I wondered if their feet were actually bleeding, and for a few seconds I almost felt their blood in my throat. I thought about the flats you left on my desk. And for the first time, I felt your pain. I think my toes even ached. You were so disciplined in your exercises and diet. Sometimes I had the feeling you hated my attitude toward sleep and food. I slept more than you did, ate more than you did, and ate junk food, which you seemed to fear so badly. I never managed to make you try those wonderful truffle fries I loved, not to mention my favorite hamburger. And I understand ballerinas need to be thin, but . . . You never compromise, do you? Doesn't that make you sad? Do you have to be sad? Why didn't you try the fries once, just once, why didn't you even taste one? You know, that would have made me so happy. And I'd have been so happy if we had talked about you, what you believed, what your fears were. We never did. And was that because you thought I could not understand, or rather because I never showed you any interest? I hope that's not the reason, because I was, I am interested in you. I just didn't know how to show that to you. I should have tried harder, I know. And now I can only talk to your friends and try to understand you better. Is it too late? I met with Sarah yesterday. She didn't want to talk to me. I had to call her three times to convince her. She was surprised by my request and continued to examine me during our conversation, somehow looking for answers to questions she didn't ask. Why did I want to talk about you? What was wrong with me? What's wrong? I'm a moron who lost his girlfriend after four years without even trying to get to know her. Sarah told me about your ambition, your desire to dance Tchaikovsky as a prima ballerina around the world. She said you were obsessed by perfection. I told her I knew that. She described the hours of practice, the time Madam Guillem criticized a move you had made and insisted you repeat it over and over and over again. She said she made you repeat it fifty times. She described the time Madam Guillem said you looked like a clumsy clown and you cried, not because you were hurt, she said, or mortified, but because you were tired after having repeated that same move a thousand times. She also told me that you never complained about anything, and even when you were tired, you tried your best to smile and keep going. She said you knew Madam Guillem and the others were just doing their best to make you succeed. And so, no, you never complained. She remembered you lowering your head when they said they didn't like something you had just done, and saying that you would try again and again until they would say it was OK. Not a single complaint. She remembered your serious expression during rehearsals, and then your smiles on stage. She said you were an actress, that you truly became absorbed in your roles. And when you were on stage, you were that role, and the ballet seemed to have been written for you, if not about you. Yes, you worked hard and never complained. I wonder what you thought when I complained about my job whenever they asked me to change my drawings, to prepare a few more strips. I wonder what you thought when I did that. Did I lose your respect then? Is that when you stopped loving me? Was I too human for you, Emily? I asked Sarah if she thought you were happy. "When she danced," she said. So you were not happy with me. Of course you weren't. Otherwise you would have not left me. "I don't think it was her choice, Andrew," she said. "Of course, it was," I replied. And then Sarah left. She left me in the café where we had met, without saying another word.

Nick typed parts of the pages as I read. And when I finished reading the last line, we remained silent for a while, perhaps thinking about Andrew and Emily, or about ourselves.

"While you were reading, I almost had the feeling that you had written those words," he said out of the blue.

"Why do you say so?"

"I don't know. The way you read. Your voice."

I didn't expect that, and I lost myself in his eyes.

"What do you think?"

"About?"

"About this, Andrew . . ."

Right.

"I don't know," I said, trying to recover my balance and hide my temporary absence. "Too early to say."

He left his chair to get another beer, and I continued.

"Might be obsessive-compulsive."

"Explain."

"He definitely obsesses about Emily."

"We got an email from a reader," Nick said, and he read it. The reader described his relationship with his girlfriend and their breaking up after seven years. He said it was his fault. He did not understand her, did not see her. He said he understood what J.N. was going through: it was "like going through hell."

I watched Nick read and got distracted, lost in the wine I was sipping and the trails its warmth was tracing for me. But I did capture a few lines of that email, and I thought the comparison with hell perfectly fit Andrew's pages. Yes, we should post it.

Nick noticed I had been wandering somewhere. He lit a cigarette and went to the balcony to smoke.

"Do you want to join me?" he asked, perhaps trying to join me. Could he see where I was?

"No, I don't smoke. What does it do for you?"

"Nicotine?"

"Yes, nicotine."

"Works like painkillers, like morphine. Try." He handed me a cigarette, and I tried it but didn't like it and gave it back to him.

"Smoking is addictive," he said, "and there are no good addictions. Once you become addicted to something, it's very hard to stop. So it's better not to start."

"What addiction scares you the most?" I asked.

"My addiction to adrenaline. And fear. I crave fear."

I was hoping he would share more, but he stopped.

When I checked the time, it was one in the morning. I called a taxi and returned home.

I slept for four hours and woke up at six again, but again with the alarm, since I had to get ready for work.

It's interesting how the scenarios I had been contemplating from my window, the cars coming and leaving, that woman and her tears, have lost their appeal to me. Now I enjoy watching the sun rise, the trees' intense green in the morning dew, the changing colors of the sky. And they almost hurt me, as I feel more vulnerable but strangely like I have a direction, something I'm looking for. I look forward to seeing him, and I look forward to him hurting me, because I know he'll then take care of me the way he does. It is as if he can't make me happy without hurting me. So I let him do it, and I look forward to it.

I slept last night, and I was alone, but didn't feel so.

DAY THREE

I arrived at school at 8:05 a.m. though my class was supposed to start at 8:00. In the past that would have bothered me a lot. Not today though. I didn't use my notes and instead improvised. I didn't want to be trapped in a script. Class was rewarding but intense, and once I was done, I sought refuge in my office.

It was raining, and I felt cold. It was probably the dress, which left my legs partly uncovered, or perhaps the fact that I was tired. After half an hour, no student had shown up for office hours. I left the chair to close the door and take a nap, but as I pushed the door closed, someone knocked.

"Professor Blanc? Hi. May I come in? I'm John. I was in your personality and cognition class."

"Oh, yes, sure . . . John . . . I remember you." Actually, I didn't.

He was tall, pale, and had red hair a bit longer than the usual man's haircut and a broken smile. His hands were thin, and they were slightly shaking as he spoke. He seemed nervous.

"I just came to say that I enjoyed your lecture today."

I was surprised to hear that. I couldn't recall a student stopping by to tell me that they had enjoyed my class. Ever. Most of my students seemed to live in their own heads. They rarely showed any particular enthusiasm or affection. And, true, I didn't do that either.

As I was still trying to understand the reason for his reaction, or why I hadn't heard anything like that from a student before, he asked, "Why did you study psychology?"

He wanted to know more about his teacher. That would be typical of students. Not of my students though.

"I always wanted to know how the mind works, how we think and process information, how life experiences change our response to the world."

"And now that you've learned how it works, why do you teach rather than practice?"

Right. Why did I teach?

"I'm not sure," I said. "Perhaps I haven't learned how it works yet, and teaching is a way of searching."

I should have filtered my answer, but I wasn't sure I could. So I asked him why he had decided to take my class.

"Psychology seems fascinating. I'd love to study personality disorders one day." He turned toward the window and stared out somewhere beyond where I could see. "I read a lot about personality disorders," he then added. "I remember someone arguing that they might be extraordinary manifestations of brain power and creativity that people can't understand and dismiss as anomalies. I wish I could make up my mind on what the truth is."

He stopped to check my reaction, but before I said anything, he spoke again.

"I'm sorry, I didn't intend to take much of your time."

"Oh, no. Of course."

He collected his things and shook my hand.

"Good luck," he said. He stood up and walked out the door.

That was unusual too. I wished he had stayed. I liked listening to him. He definitely seemed more mature than his age, although I couldn't actually say what his age was.

When he closed the door, I suddenly felt exhausted. I checked my office for food. I didn't have any, and although there was a restaurant just across the street, I didn't feel like walking there. It was raining, and I was colder than before. I pressed my shoulders against the old chair, started following the rain drops staining my windows, and slowly lost contact with the present.

Why did I study psychology? Really?

Since I was young, I had always felt isolated from the world. I didn't like being with people and preferred to be alone. I remember my father getting ready for a party or family event, and me on the sofa, reading my books or watching old movies or cartoons, trying to come up with any possible excuse not to go. I hated those events. The conversations were not interesting. They sounded empty. I had the feeling that adults were all engaged in finding ways to "kill time," to deceive each other. To me they seemed to be dragging their souls and lives in nonsensical circles. I wanted to be left out.

When my efforts failed and my father managed to drag me to those events, I sat on a chair, my plate filled with food on my lap and a book I had brought with me underneath it. I was only waiting to leave and read. I loved reading. The stories appeared to me as possibilities in life that I could experience. One day I would. I had so many dreams, and at that time the only impediment to them seemed to be my age. The more realistic the story, the more it felt like something that could happen to me, the more interested I became. I didn't like comics, but I liked graphic novels, especially those in black and white.

"Why don't you like colors? What's wrong with you?" asked my father one day at a bookstore. He had pulled a colored graphic novel from the shelf and wanted to buy it for me, but I refused.

"That's not interesting," I said.

"How do you know? Have you read it?"

"This story doesn't look real."

"Why?"

"Life is not colored. Life is black and white and gray."

I was only eight, but I had already concluded that life was not colored, that adults had not captured the essence of it, and I didn't want to be part of their misery. I didn't want to, and I would not fake it. I just wanted to be left alone.

My attitude didn't change over the years. And so, when it was time to go to college, I didn't hesitate when my father asked me if I wanted to rent a studio or a room in an apartment with other students. Of course I wanted a studio.

My studio was close to the university. A small apartment in a not too fancy area of the city filled with cheap and sticky Thai and Chinese restaurants, thrift shops, and some travel agencies to remind you that, after all, the world could be better than the neighborhood. My studio was an old garage that the owners had turned into an apartment, clearly without using much effort or taste. What made it look like a deal to me was that I got a small house for the price of a studio. The downside, though, was that the house was in fact a garage, and it still looked like one. It was old, with the remnants of some cheap paint on the walls and on the carpet that almost seemed to lay on dirt. The bathroom was full of rust around the knobs, and the kitchen always looked dirty, despite my stubborn attempts to clean the brownish stove that must have been white once—or maybe it never was.

But even if it was old, it was my place, a refuge I could turn into everything I wanted it to be, even a romantic, intimate space. And so I bought candles, placed them on the floor and on the chests of drawers, and mostly used them instead of electricity for the first two years. I had only a little lamp close to my bed, which I used when I felt like reading at night before falling asleep. Other than that, I just had my books, milk and cereal, some chocolate, chips, ice cream.

My bedroom was basically the living room of the studio. I had a sofa bed that, if pulled out, would take up the entire room. And so for a while, to keep the house neat and clean (as much as I could), I slept on the sofa. But then, still unhappy with the result, I started sleeping on the floor, using my bed's duvet as a sleeping bag. The candles and the sleeping bag sometimes made it feel as if the ceiling disappeared, giving me the illusion of being outside under the stars on a summer camping trip. But mostly they gave me a feeling of intimacy and proximity to my soul. If forced to articulate it, I would have probably said that something was hurting me. But with the same candor, I would have admitted that I didn't know what it was. Was it my relationship with my classmates? My relationship with my family? The fact that I didn't have a boyfriend? I really didn't know. But I remember some mild feelings of dissatisfaction and doubts about whether the direction I was heading in—assuming there was one—made any sense.

I didn't spend time with my classmates. And when they asked me whether I liked the school, the program, or LA, I replied that I loved being there, and that I wished I had more time to spend with them. But, obviously, that wasn't true. I just wanted to be left alone.

I probably should have looked more carefully to see if there was anyone interesting in my class, if anyone, like me, preferred shades to colors. Someone like John might have been a good classmate, maybe even a friend. Someone like him or like Nick could have explained to me why I preferred candlelight to electricity, and someone like Emily could have explained what discipline, pain, and pleasure have in common.

I felt sad for having wasted time and wondered if, in college, I was in fact already a full member of the group of adults whose lives were empty and filled with nonsense. A rush of sadness sucked the last spark of energy from my day, and I fell asleep. When Nick called to take me to dinner, I was dreaming dreams that could turn true. We were seated on the seashore, and he was playing with my hair. I could see two glasses of wine touching each other on the sand, very close to the water. What would the impediment be this time?

When I awoke, we went to a nice Spanish restaurant for dinner. The restaurant was on the corner of an outdoor market, with some cute tables outside. A group of young men and women were sitting there, drinking beer and singing.

"Whenever I come here I think about a trip to Madrid that was wonderful. I had no time or will to plan. Almost everything was improvised. Still, everything was perfect."

"Improvisation sometimes may work better than plans." I thought about my class.

"Yes. You're more truthful if you improvise. But that's hard to do," Nick said, and sipped his beer.

What was hard? To be truthful or to improvise?

We talked about instinct and analysis. His ideas about the interaction between the two were fascinating, but they left me wondering how much of what he described actually applied to him, and whether his choices had been more the product of his instinct or his plans.

"You are so beautiful," he suddenly said, opening the door of the car for me after we left the restaurant. His eyes were sad though, as if his words were hurting him. But why would they? He attempted a smile, but his eyes cloaked it. I looked at him and didn't know what to say. Should I be happy? Thankful? I was confused.

Once at his apartment, he opened a bottle of wine and looked eager to resume our work. At that point, I was almost sure I had dreamed the whole evening up to that very moment, and that thought hurt.

I'm attracted to you, you seem to be attracted to me. Can we talk about this? This is what I or he should have said. But neither of us did. Instead, he asked me to read, and I did.

July 12

I was in the hospital for a few days. Again in the hospital, I know. I tried your ballet flats and tried to walk on my toes as you used to do for a few hours. True, the flats were not my size, but they were not that small either. I pushed my feet into them and finally made it, I was wearing your ballerina flats. My toes started bleeding but I didn't notice and continued to walk. But then I lost balance and I smashed my left toes against the living room skirting. The pain was excruciating, but I didn't want to see a doctor. So I waited, but the infection got worse, I got a fever, and I had a minor surgery. Now I have metal pins in my foot, and I will have to use crutches for a month or two. That sucks, considering that sports were keeping me busy and distracted. I've not worked on my novels and sketches in a long time. My agent called me at least three times in the past two weeks to ask me if any of my "new projects" were finalized and ready to be submitted. He said that this time my graphic novel should be "lighter" than my other stories. What does that even mean? When I asked him, he said, "you know, something that would make people laugh." I told him I had stopped laughing too long ago to even remember when that happened. He insisted that I move on with my life, that I think about my job and try to preserve it. The problem is, my novels were all inspired by us, our silences, our routines, our fights, your successes, my failures. They were all fragments of a life that I knew. True, they were not "light." There was a whispered line of sorrow in my characters. But that's what I knew. And that feeling still belongs to me and defines me. It's real. Why would I write about something that's not real? Something I don't know? For the sake of it? It would make a wonderful, plastic, sterile literary and graphic exercise. But bookstores and libraries are full of that shit. They don't need mine. I wonder if you truly liked what I drew, my stories. You said you did, but you might have said that not to hurt me. Did you do that? That would be awful. I don't think I could stand it. Is this what you did, Emily? Just the thought of it makes me sick. What did I lose? What did we lose? We probably lied to each other day after day. Didn't we? Why did we do it? We were in love, weren't we? Did I ever resist your truths? Did you try to be honest with me and I wouldn't listen? Did I try to be honest with you and it didn't work? I feel ready to write and draw again, and I think the title of my novel might be Lies We Tell. *And it won't be light, and it won't make people laugh, but it'll probably make people think about the lies on which everyone's life is built.*

As soon as I finished reading, I started shaking. I felt cold and almost stopped breathing. It was Nick's look before, me before that moment, the love stories that never happened, the one that never happened to me, and perhaps something else—so much cold, so much emptiness, nonsense. I pressed my hands against the stained paper of Andrew's diary. My eyes cried, and I hated them for that.

"Are you OK?"

I looked at him but couldn't answer. He poured some wine for me and put "Summertime" on the stereo.

"Would you dance with me?" he asked.

I abandoned myself on his shoulders, and the alcohol, the bass, or his warmth started warming my tears, the ones that he could or could not see. It felt too good to be true. But then he stopped, turned, made a joke, and went to his desk. The music stopped too. What had just happened?

"They were lying to each other," he said and looked at me. No, he couldn't see me. Anything. Or he did and had just lied to me. Or I had lied.

"Nietzsche said that lying is a condition of life." He checked my eyes, seeking their approval, but I wasn't there. "What do you think?"

"I'm not sure," I said, and I wasn't, truly, of anything.

We didn't talk much more. He wrote, I read, and when it was two in the morning, he gave me a stack of readers' emails. I called a taxi and went home. I needed to close my eyes and just disappear for a while. Something was hurting, and I needed that feeling to be mine. Just mine.

DAY FOUR

Today I called in sick and stayed home, but I wasn't sick or tired. I just wanted to have some time for myself on an ordinary weekday. I woke up at six, called the office, put on my old jeans, placed the emails Nick gave me last night in a bag, and left.

I live downtown. The city is a mess up here. There are a few peaceful blocks adjacent to hell, but hell accounts for most of downtown. Fancy hotels close to homeless camps, sophisticated restaurants squeezed between kiosks where exotic things are all sold for two dollars. Los Angeles is a city of contradictions. But it is also a city full of surprises. Hidden alleys with nice little restaurants; an authentic bakery a Mexican family has owned for generations; old theaters, most of which are now closed; a magical bookstore that hosts art exhibitions on its top floor and has a bunch of couches spread all over the other floors, where customers and non-customers can sit and leaf through the books before buying them. Or stealing them.

That bookstore is close to my place, walking distance. I used to go there on the weekends, and I had always told myself that I should return on a weekday to work there, although the bookstore is not thought of as a work space. But who would notice if I snuck in some emails?

I grabbed a coffee at the café on the corner and walked to the bookstore. A guard at the entrance asked me to leave my bag with him. I explained that I had some papers I needed to check to find the right books for my research. I don't think he bought it, but perhaps because it was early and I was the second, if not the first, customer of the day, he decided to let me and my bag in.

The bookstore was empty at nine-thirty a.m. on a weekday. I climbed the stairs to the second floor and walked toward the door that lead to the art collections through a narrow passage. On the right of that passage there are wide windows. The glass is dirty, as nobody ever cleans it. The bookstore stands amid tall and wide skyscrapers that hide the sun. So the clouds from the glass and those from the skyscrapers make it always dark up there, even on a bright, sunny day. You can't see much from those windows, and you're shielded, from the chaos of the city—and sometimes from your own too. It's peaceful. Sometimes.

The city seems distant, and it is enveloped in a thick fog. You could sit on the wide windowsill of one of those windows and stay there for hours just looking at people passing by. It's interesting, that diverse group seems to have been assembled by a divine experiment intended to study human reactions to the unknown and unexpected. And it's the same scene every time I watch it. Just different people. Sometimes. This time too.

The upstairs was only half-illuminated when I arrived, and some cleaning personnel were trying to get rid of the trash, customers' leftovers from the day before. I sat on the farthest windowsill, sipped a bit of my coffee, and started reading.

The emails I read were empty. Mostly nice compliments for the choice of this series of posts, although there were some angry ones too, and for apparently no reason, questions for J.N., questions about me, questions about my relationship with Nick . . . And then I found something, a letter written with a typewriter that had been sent as a PDF attached to an email.

Dear Susan and Nick,

The passages from the journal you published made me think of my relationship with my wife. Or ex-wife I should say. Megan and I grew up together. We started dating when we were fifteen, went to college together, then grad school. At some point, though, our paths diverged. I accepted a job as a pharmaceutical representative and she decided to do research. She spent hours in her lab, sometimes coming home late at night. I was traveling three days a week but the rest of the week I was home, and I remember waiting for her in front of the TV until I couldn't keep my eyes open. A full day wasted waiting for her to return. I rarely saw her. We had sex once a month, if that often, and every time it felt like a concession to me for my good behavior, for waiting without complaining. At that point, I don't even know why I was looking for it, looking forward to it. I felt her disinterest. It was clear. But perhaps I was hoping each time would be different, that I could finally bring us back to where we started. I wanted to ask her if she was seeing anyone, but I feared that she would say yes, and leave me. I loved her, but did not tell her that often. In fact, I can't even remember the last time I did. Slowly I got used to a life on my own and when, one day, she asked me if I wanted to make love to her, I realized that I didn't. My feelings for her were swallowed by my resentment and contempt for a woman who no longer cared for me and, in fact, perhaps at that point, not even for herself. Megan is not like Emily. But I'm worried I might have made mistakes with her as J.N. did with Emily. I feel he was missing something, and I fear I might be doing the same. I've started asking myself questions, revisiting my past with her, my memories. I leafed through our photo book, the photos of our wedding. Megan looked sad. As I was trying to remember why that could be, I remembered our arguments around that time. When we decided to get married, she was happy but I wasn't. I didn't feel ready. She was. I loved her, but she may have doubted that I did. I wonder whether this is when I started losing her. I don't know what I'll do, but I'll do something. What I don't like about J.N. is his doing nothing. He seems to be fighting against himself rather than fighting to get her back. Is loving someone a search for ourselves? If so, I wouldn't fight against myself to find me. Perhaps that doesn't make any sense. If so, just ignore my outburst. I was actually going to do that myself, trash what I had written. But then I thought I should give my thoughts a chance. Maybe you'll get what I don't. In any event, thanks for sharing the diary. It helped.

Ashton

"Is loving someone a search for ourselves?" That put a cold breeze into my stomach. Hard to explain why.

I sipped my coffee to warm me up, stretched my legs along the windowsill, and looked down the street. There were more people now, and they seemed to be walking faster. I felt so far from the ground. The sun had risen a bit. I could spot more of it from where I was. As people were waking up and the sun was rising, I felt I needed to sleep, and that wasn't unusual given my irregular sleeping habits, my search for shadows, silence, and spaces that could be mine and mine only. I looked around and realized I was sharing the room with too many people now, so I collected my things and left in search of food.

After some wandering, I stopped in front of a café. It looked cheap from the outside, but I was so hungry and tired from the walking that I decided to stop in. The café wasn't bad. It was dark, intimate, simple. The music was an interesting mix from the 80s. The waitress smiled at me as I read the menu. There wasn't much to read. I ordered an omelet, and she said I could go upstairs if I wanted. She would bring me my order. I looked around—there were tables available on the ground floor, but I took her suggestion and headed upstairs.

The second floor was a discovery. There were worn and comfortable couches against the walls, a beautiful wide coffee table with worn-out novels and magazines that seemed to have been thrown there randomly. Yet there was an artistic logic. I could see it. The music was filling the atmosphere, and it was soft enough to let you take whatever journey you wanted to take. The table I chose was on the left side of the room, just above the stairs. It looked like a desk, and on it there was a small, unlit lamp. From where I sat, I could see people passing by on the street, a few cars. Everything seemed to move so slowly. Maybe it was the time of the day, maybe it was the street. Maybe what I saw wasn't real. In fact, the same people had passed two or three times in front of the café's windows. I noticed their jackets, so colorful and striking in the dimness of the corner. A red one was particularly loud. Then I saw three cars going in reverse. All of them, slowly, at the same time. I thought I was daydreaming. But then I spotted a camera. So they were shooting a movie or a commercial or something. The sky seemed cloudier now, but at times I could see the sun, although its light seemed to reach me as from another time, filtered by the café.

When the waitress arrived with my order, she bent to turn on the lamp on my table. I said I was fine in the shadows. She smiled, placed the plate on the table, and left. I had not noticed, but I was alone on the second floor, and that felt good. I could barely see the food in my plate, but the shadows made me relax and release any tension left from the night before, the time before.

After I finished my meal, I moved to a sofa in the corner of the room to write notes on the margins of Ashton's email and drift more deeply into myself. The room was still empty. I took off my shoes, extended my legs, lay my head on one of the small pillows, and once I was done writing, I freed my mind and fell asleep. I dreamed about Nick. It was a strange dream, but it felt real. We made love, and it was our first time, but it felt natural as if we had known each other for a long time and had made love many times before. After a short while of us dancing on each other, he pushed my head down. I looked at him and something felt wrong, sad, empty.

"Susan? What are you doing here?"

Nick was standing in front of me. I had to catch my breath. I was dreaming. Something. But he was there, right in front of me. I took some time to sift my dream from what I was actually living. It happened too fast. The dream got mixed with reality, or the other way around. But he was there.

"Shouldn't you be working?"

"I . . . yes."

He didn't say much more and sat close to me. Just looked at me for a while. At another time I'd have tried to fill in the silence between us, but I wasn't fully awake, so I just looked at him looking at me. What did he see? And did he like what he saw? I liked what I saw. Still did.

"What are you doing here?" I asked.

"I like this place. I come here often. The music, the lighting." He seemed not surprised to find me there, as if our meeting had been planned. "Did you find any clue in the emails?"

"No, no clues."

The waitress came with his order.

"The usual," she said, placing the drink on the table.

"What's the usual?" I asked.

"Ginger tea with cognac." I thought it was too early for alcohol, but when he offered it to me for me to try it, I did. I took one sip of his drink and felt warm. I returned the drink to him, but then stole another sip.

"Suzy, can you bring us another one?" Nick asked the waitress, before I could even try to stop him. When the waitress returned with my ginger cognac, I drank it all.

"Why don't we go to my place? We have work to do."

My memories of our walk to his place are confused. I don't remember how we got there. It happened so fast. I feel we got to his place through a back door in that café, but that is not possible. We walked. We must have. The transition was so quick and soft though. I didn't feel any break between us at the café and us in the apartment. Perhaps it was my dream, that soft, almost silent music, the cognac, and the shadows that gave me that impression. Or just the fact that by then I could see only Nick, as everything else had disappeared. And Nick was all of those things. My dream, the silence, the cognac, the shadows.

His apartment was almost completely dark. He had left the curtains down, and they did a great job shielding the room from the sun.

"And from the world," he added. "I like to have my own space, my shadows. I love shadows."

"Really? I do too."

"Of course you do." He dragged me to the sofa.

"You never talk about yourself, do you?"

I felt warm again.

"Why do you like shadows?"

I wanted this. I had dreamed this. I saw this.

"Shadows take you closer to yourself," I said. "You can see things more clearly. There's no noise. No artificial light. Just the contours. The essence. You see what you can touch."

"And so I see you more clearly now. Your lines, essence . . . can I touch you?"

He came closer to me and almost touched my neck with his lips. But he stopped to check my eyes. Then he came closer and lightly pressed his lips against my neck and breathed heavily. I felt warm. His lips seemed to control me. He then went down and almost touched my breasts. But he stopped, slowly rolled up my T-shirt, freed my breasts from it, and then looked at them. I was shaking. When I opened my mouth to get more oxygen, he sucked and bit my lip. And then when I was dying with desire, he stopped. He looked at me and seemed sad again. The same look I had seen before.

"What's wrong?" I asked.

He looked more deeply into me but did not respond.

"What?"

"I'm not sure this is . . . I'm not . . ."

"You're not what?"

"I don't know what to say. I'm not used to this."

I pulled my shirt down and walked to the door.

"Susan wait, come back. Let's talk," he said, looking down, his hands holding his head, which seemed too heavy to stay still on its own. "I need time."

"Time for what? To decide whether fucking me is a good idea? Whether you'll like it? Whether I'm hot enough for you? Am I?"

I turned to leave, but he grabbed me, put his arms around me, my shoulder against his chest. He pulled my hair up and kissed my neck. Then he turned me toward him, undressed me, and pulled me up, pressing me against the wall. He took me in his arms and made love to me. The silence became louder and louder. And louder. And then the silence became silent again.

When I opened my eyes I saw him seated on the couch, staring at a photograph. I would have given anything to know what he was thinking, what he had been thinking before. Yes, I would have.

"Hey," I called.

"Hi," he said, and placed the photo back in its place. "How are you?"

"I'm good," I said, and looked at him to ask his eyes the same question, but they turned away too quickly for me to do so.

"What time is it?" I then asked.

"Six," he said, and handed me a cup of coffee. "Jack called. They need our post in one hour. Do you feel like reading what I wrote? I could read it to you."

His eyes—what I found and what I didn't find in them—made me forget what I was thinking and feeling, my doubts. It was clear to me that my relationship with him was not going to be like any I had had before. And it was clear that, no matter what, it would be hard, almost impossible, to resist him.

"Are you OK?" he asked again.

"Yes, I'm fine."

No, I am not.

"Do you want me to read?"

No. Can we talk about what happened before?

"Yes," I said, and closed my eyes. We had just made love.

He sat close to me and read.

July 14

I've started drawing Lies We Tell. *I have thought about whether you might get mad at me for using your real name and almost changed the name of the main character to make sure nobody would understand it's* you. But then I figured I couldn't do that. I had to see your name, and your body on the pages. I spent hours drawing your face. I'm usually good at portraits, but I couldn't get your eyes and your lips quite right. I tried and tried again, drew and erased, softened, shaded off, drew again, erased one more time. I pierced the canvass and had to start over. Do you remember the time I showed you some of my early drafts? You were in there. I thought you were. I showed you the sketch and you laughed. You said it wasn't you. I said it was a sketch, a cartoon version of you. You didn't like it, and then got mad. I didn't understand why. My sketch of you looked nice to me. Fun. I leafed through the pages of that novel and I think I get it now. You were right. It wasn't you. There were no wrinkles on your face, you were empty, just the contours of a person, with no content in it. How could I do that to you?

"A cartoon version of you"—what was I even thinking? There can't be a cartoon version of you. This time I used charcoal. I didn't use any picture of you, just my memories. I drew your face's lines, your nose, the contours of your eyes, and your lips, your hair. I almost felt as if I were passing my hands through it. So soft and thick, wild, wide. And then I spent hours on your eyes and on your lips. I had not thought about whether I wanted you to be happy or sad. I thought the drawing itself would decide that. But I had a very hard time getting your eyes and lips right. Your eyes were never actually smiling, even when they tried to. They smiled only on stage. Although I knew that wasn't a real smile. That was perfect acting. The audience would never guess. They didn't know you. Did I? And your lips . . . they too hid struggles, and a deep passion, conflicts, doubts. How was I going to render that with the charcoal? I tried and tried again. I couldn't get enough of it, could not get enough of you. Moving my fingers on your eyes and your lips felt good. I felt I could give you life, I could draw you so well that you would become real. I wanted to touch you, to own you, keep you here with me. I tried, and tried again, and at some point I even pretended I had come close to having you on the paper. But it wasn't you. It wasn't even close. I showed my sketch to Joe and he said it was great. "Emily, wow, man, this is awesome," he said, patting me on my back. I felt cheated, and left. I stared at that portrait for a long time, and I knew it was a long time only because I checked the clock and couldn't believe what

I saw. I had been there for hours. I thought I should do better. So I bought some clay and tried to make a sculpture of you. A three-dimensional you might be more truthful, it might capture you better, I thought. But my result wasn't any better. I was ready to give up the idea of my novel, but then I thought I shouldn't. I thought I should try harder, at least this time. So I kept working on it, I kept working on you. I haven't come close to capturing your beauty and sadness yet, but I will try harder. I took a break from the drawings and moved to the narrative. I remembered some of the happiest moments we had together. The picnic in the Malibu hills, the walks on the beach, that vegan restaurant you liked, the movies you watched for ten minutes at the most before falling asleep, your getting sick, me getting sick, our cooking together, me at your debut with the Julliard ballet in New York, you with flowers and fans, me standing behind, lost somewhere, wearing that big, old suit that you said looked like it came from Goodwill. And I never told you this, but that is precisely where I got it. Your hours of practice, my empty afternoons watching porn, my attempts to find inspiration in cocaine, my failures. We were so in love the first year. It seems that my best memories belong there. What happened next? I've chosen to use black and light-blue-purple for the drawings. This color is sedate and seems to slow down the time so I've more time with you. I've made only a few drawings. The hardest part was trying to get as close as I could to the truth. I know I'll never own the truth, but it'll be nice to get as close to it as I can. Will I be healed if I do that? I hope so. Lies starts when we met. Do you remember? It was the afternoon, and it was raining. I was sketching a story at the café close to our favorite bookstore, and you entered, ordered a coffee, and sat just across from me. I'll be forever grateful to that big table where perfect strangers sit close to one another. I could not take my eyes off you. Your elegance and beauty were overwhelming. You were holding your coffee with both hands, trying to warm yourself up. You seemed frightened, and that made you look more charming, if that was even possible. And your legs were moving frenetically. Your thin, long, beautiful legs. You were wearing your tights and legwarmers, and I thought you should be a ballerina. Your whole persona was that of a dancer. Your hair was tied in a chignon, your face was pale, so much that I thought it must have been the makeup that made you look like a pierrot. But that was your skin color, and you were a pierrot. Your snow-white face, and your red lips like rose petals on white ceramic. You kept moving your big green eyes, sometimes checking the people around you, sometimes just following your thoughts. And while you were immersed in your journeys, your eyes met mine for what seemed forever. But then you returned from your wanderings and nervously looked away. "Are you a ballerina?" I asked, trying to bring your eyes back to where they had been before. You looked at me again, then around, then back to me, and said, "Yes, I am." You hesitated a bit, and then you added "Sometimes I wish I were something else." I was so thankful for that unexpected sharing. Why would you, such a beautiful creature, share a bit of yourself with me? "Why do you say so?" I asked. You lowered your head, turned, and left. I followed you outside, and stopped you. "I'm sorry. I don't usually stop strangers. I know that's impolite." You laughed, but then cried. "Would you like to share some cake?" "I don't eat sweets," you said, and looked so sad that I wanted to hug you and take your sadness with me. "What about a tea, with no sugar, then?" You smiled, and we found a precious little tea place and . . . us. I've drawn this. All of it.

I closed my eyes and tried to retain what he had just read as much as I could. Somehow it was as if Andrew's words were melding with my thoughts, my story, our story, and as they did, they added clouds to what I was living, making it more foggy, confusing, and at times darker.

"So Andrew wrote *Lies We Tell*. I wonder if it's been released," Nick said. Then he turned to his computer and started doing research. "No, there's nothing under that title."

He browsed on the internet for a while, and then said he wanted to take me somewhere but didn't say where. We left shortly after. It was seven. The city was more crowded and noisy and somehow felt dirtier. We walked for a while, both silent, until we reached his destination.

The place he wanted to show me was a bookstore that looked almost like a mountain hat. Quite strange for a California setting, I thought. There was a ground floor and a mezzanine, which you accessed through a little wooden stair, and in the corner of the mezzanine, near the ceiling, a handwritten sign said "Graphic Novels." The graphic-novel bookshelf was not huge, but some of the novels captured my interest. Nick pointed to a chair close to the wall and asked me to sit there and leaf through the pages of a few books he selected for me. The drawings were simple and complex at the same time. They looked like sketches, but the characters had depth, life. They looked real.

"I'll get these three," I said, showing Nick my choice.

"Great," he said, but seemed absent now. I had lost him again, who knows to what or whom. I paid for the novels, and we left.

"I think I should call a taxi and go home," I then said, as I felt I needed some time on my own. He seemed disappointed.

"I was hoping we could work on the readers' emails. You didn't like this?"

What was *this*? If *this* was his attempt to expand what we had before, what had just happened, *this* was a lame attempt. I needed to know more about his eyes before, his resistance, what made him change his mind and make love to me, what the impediment to our love story was—I knew there was one. I needed to know how he felt. I needed him. But he had made love to me and then left. So no, I didn't like *this*.

"Didn't we say we were going to post one today?"

"Use the one I gave you at the café. There are my notes on it. I liked it."

He looked as if he wanted to say or ask something, but he didn't.

"OK." He stopped a taxi that was approaching, opened the door to let me in, and before closing it, said, "It was beautiful. Before, I mean. It was . . . beautiful."

I felt my hands and legs shaking, and I did not respond. Nick tapped on the side of the car, and it took off. And that was all I needed. Right there.

DAY FIVE

I didn't sleep as well as the previous nights. I continued to think about Nick and what had happened yesterday, my head spinning, dragged, and pushed by my instinct and my urge to rationalize. I thought I needed a break from him, and I worried that he would call and ask me to meet again too soon.

I went to school, taught my classes with even less energy than usual, and checked my phone a thousand times to see whether he had called, but nothing. At three p.m., I fell asleep on my sofa. The phone woke me up at five. It was Nick.

When I saw his name on the display of my phone, I tried to make up my mind as to what I'd say to him, but the answering machine was faster.

"Susan, it's Nick. I was checking in to see how you were doing. I was thinking that with this whole thing, our posts, I'm probably taking too much of your time. Maybe we shouldn't work tonight. I'll take care of the journal and see if there are emails we might want to post. I'll send you a draft as soon as I'm done. Enjoy the rest of your day. I hope . . . I hope I'll see you soon."

I should have felt relieved, but in fact, I felt empty.

I wandered around the house, thought about calling him back, dialed his number and hung up three or four times, and then decided to take a cold shower, hoping it would shut my head down. I did feel a little better after that but realized I shouldn't stay home. I got dressed, took the graphic novels with me, and went to the bookstore I had been to the day before. I sat in the same spot, and as soon as I did a man in his late thirties came and sat close to me.

"It's my favorite spot," he said. "I should have come earlier."

"It's my favorite spot too. But I'll be happy to leave it to you if you like. I can definitely find other nice spots."

"No, no need. I'll sit here if you don't mind."

Before I said anything, he spoke again.

"Do you like graphic novels?"

"Some."

He smiled and started reading his book, but it was clear he wanted to talk more.

"I fell in love with graphic novels when I was six or seven," he added. "When I found out I could draw, I wanted to write my own stories and drawings, make them into graphic novels. And I've been doing that ever since."

"Have you published any of your work?"

"Yes, a few."

Could it be him?

"I'm Susan. Nice to meet you."

"Matt."

I lost myself in my thoughts again. Interesting coincidence. I was working on Andrew's journal and was sitting close to someone who was also a graphic novelist. Was the world truly small, or had I made it so with my own choices? I must have stared at the same page for quite a while, thinking about my questions, which had something to do with the novel but were not exactly about it.

"That might not be the best novel for you," the stranger said.

"Why?"

"You've been staring at the same page for a long time. I'm sorry, I shouldn't . . . but if you don't like that novel, I can help you find a better one."

"That'd be nice," I said. I felt dragged by what I wanted to believe was a coincidence in the small world of graphic novels I had accidentally entered—a world I had otherwise nothing to do with—curious to see where it would lead me.

"What type of stories do you like?" he asked, trying to figure me out.

"Real stories or stories that feel real."

"Then what you're reading is not right for you. For a start, I'd choose a story in black and white. Colors distract from reality, make the story appear fake, like a cartoon."

I agreed with that. My coincidence and I had something in common.

"Follow me," he said, and started walking without turning back to see if I had followed. "We'll look at a couple of novels you might like."

We walked toward the center of the room, where cluttered bookshelves were hiding another room filled with graphic novels and some old books on various topics, treatises, maps.

"This is my world," he said. "I come here almost every day, sometimes just to touch the books, taste them, their scent."

"Taste them?"

"Yes, books have a distinct scent. After leafing through so many books, sometimes I feel I might recognize the date of the book from its scent."

He looked at me, then back at the shelves.

"Some of these books are from the nineteenth century, but you can get them for a buck or two. Every time I come here I notice one or more gems and take them home with me."

I thought the combination of graphic novels and old books in the room was odd. But maybe I was missing something.

"Why do you like old books so much? Do they have anything in common with graphic novels?"

"Oh, yes, they do. Their pace is similar. Their stories are interesting, silent, and powerful at the same time. Or at least, that is how I feel about them."

"The maps and treatises too?" I asked, not sure I was following. What were the stories in there?

"Yes, especially those. They're filled with stories, just not the conventional ones. They're different. Takes time to find them, but they're there. And their pace is similar too."

He pressed his fingers against some of those books, pulled one from the shelves, opened it, pressed his nose against the pages, and then continued.

"My apartment is filled with books. I had to get rid of furniture to make space for them. No kidding. Now I've only got a desk and a chair, a small couch, a coffee table, and my bed. And, of course, books spread everywhere across the apartment."

"That sounds interesting. I should do the same."

He saw a graphic novel abandoned on a tall shelf in front of us, climbed on the lower shelves, and grabbed it for me.

"I think you might like this one. It's the story of an Iranian girl growing up during and after the Islamic revolution. Take a look at the drawings. What do you think?"

I leafed through the pages.

"Yes, this novel looks more interesting than the one I was reading. I like the drawings. They pull me in. Thanks, Matt."

He smiled and walked away.

"Matt? Would you like to get a cup of coffee?"

He turned and examined me for a few moments.

"Sure," he then said, but sounded uncertain, probably still trying to figure out the reason behind my offer.

"There's this nice café I discovered yesterday," I said. "It's close to here. Just two or three blocks."

When we arrived at the café, we ordered two small coffees, and I suggested we go upstairs. He followed me and was as surprised as I had been the day before.

"Isn't this something?" I asked.

"Very. I've walked by this place a thousand times, but never stopped. To be honest, from the outside, this place is not that inviting."

"I know."

"Why did you want to have coffee with me?" he suddenly asked.

"Why not?"

"I feel there's something you want to ask me. Am I right?"

"Maybe," I said. "I'm curious about your art, what you do."

"Why?"

I thought about mentioning Andrew, his journal, the posts, but I didn't know the stranger, had too many questions in my head, and felt like I just wanted to discover my coincidence slowly, without rushing it.

"What do you want to know?" he asked.

Somehow I had to convince him to share something.

"What does it mean to be a graphic novelist? How different do you think graphic novels are from regular, words-only novels?"

He smiled.

"The stories are built mostly through drawings, and the dialogues cannot be as developed as they would be in a regular novel. You need to be concise, choose the words and interactions carefully. Words play a part, but they don't carry the story. The drawings do. They hold the story together. Imagine something like . . . close to . . . silent movies. The short dialogues are only there to fill in the gaps left by the drawings. And there shouldn't be too many. You have to show, draw what's happening."

He sipped his coffee, and then added, "I do think, though, that a good novel is also visual. It just draws the pictures with words."

I had never thought about it that way, but the stranger was right.

"I'd love to read your novels," I said.

He smiled.

We chatted more, exchanged contact information, and agreed to meet again. When I returned home, it was only nine, so I called Nick.

"You're never going to believe who I met at my favorite bookstore today?"

"Who did you meet?"

"Guess."

"I have no idea."

"A graphic novelist."

"Andrew?"

"That would be crazy. No. Not Andrew. His name's Matt. He's published a few graphic novels. We talked about that, and he helped me pick one that I can't wait to read."

"What about the ones we bought yesterday?"

"They're nice. But this one seems more like me."

"Well, then great."

I waited for him to say something. He seemed to be distracted.

"By the way, I've finished working on parts of the July 15 pages," he then said. "I'll send you an email with the text soon. I just need a few minutes to review what I wrote."

"OK," I said, and felt I should let him go.

"Talk to you later, or tomorrow?"

Yes, he definitely wanted to go.

"If I don't hear from you by eleven, I'll post the piece and go to bed. I wasn't able to sleep last night and I'm tired."

He sounded sad. But maybe he was just tired, as he said. I agreed to talk to him the next day, and after a short while, he sent me an email with the text of our next piece attached. Andrew's words drew the story beautifully. I thought Matt would like that:

I went out last night. Joe and Ed wanted to take me to a bar and introduce me to a woman they both knew. I told them I wasn't interested. You know I hate arranged dates. But they pushed and I didn't want to fight, so I decided to go, but I told myself I'd stay just an hour or so. Getting ready for the night was hard, and comparing that arranged date to our first date was painful. I hated myself for agreeing to go, and I hated every minute of it. She was blond, buxom, and loud. Her laughs were so loud I could barely stand them or the sound of her voice. Even her demeanor was loud. I tried to focus on my friends and talk to them, I tried to think that, after all, it was an opportunity for the three of us to be together. But she dominated and controlled the conversations, and Joe and Ed let her do so. I was disgusted. I Could not understand what I was doing there. I asked them to excuse me. I said I had to make a phone call, left, and never went back.

Perhaps I should have tried to make up a better excuse, but I couldn't wait any longer, I needed to leave. You said I couldn't cry. Apparently, I can. But I'm not sure why I did it. I wasn't sad. I was just angry at myself for a long list of reasons. And then I stopped at a bar where I knew I could find someone to have sex with, and I did. I chose a woman with no face, I asked her not to say a word, just to fuck me, and so she did. I paid her and left. I don't know which of the two things was more painful. Paying for sex or meeting a woman on an arranged date. I had never done either of those things before, and I'm wondering whether this will be my life from now on. I feel trapped in a labyrinth, Emily, and it's a dark one. I know you still love me. You can't let this happen.

The passage was powerful, and yet it didn't do to me what the other passages had done, the ones Nick and I had read together, talked about. Was Nick part of Andrew's story for me? Of its intensity? Did I need him to understand what I was reading, Andrew's feelings, mine as I was reading? Whatever the answers to my questions were, at about midnight I jumped into a taxi and went to Nick's. I didn't think it through. What if he was sleeping? He said he was tired. What if he wasn't there? I needed to see him.

Once I got there, I saw the light of his desk lamp from the street. I pushed the intercom button and waited. He must be there, I thought. But I got no answer. And so I called him on his cellphone.

"Nick. It's me. I'm downstairs. Can you open the door?"

"Susan?"

"Yes."

"What are you doing here? It's not a good time."

"Why not?"

He didn't respond.

"Are you with someone?"

He remained silent. I should have left.

"Are you with a woman, Nick?"

"Yeah. I am," he said. "Sorry."

I felt sick. I didn't add a word, and I left.

When I returned home, I poured some wine and grabbed a bag of popcorn. I had not sealed the popcorn properly while it cooked, and now it was too chewy and tasted of plastic. I tried to pull a blanket over myself but I lost balance, and the popcorn spilled on the floor. I thought about cleaning the mess, fixing myself a sandwich or something. But I didn't clean or make that sandwich. I wasn't hungry or thirsty. Just miserable. I started watching an old movie in black and white. The movie was fun. I cried.

DAY SIX

I woke up to a rainy Friday morning. I had fallen asleep on the sofa, and the first thing I saw when I opened my eyes was my empty glass and the popcorn on the floor. And then I thought about Nick and the night before and felt sick to my stomach and hopeless. I looked for hope, but the things that could offer some were not there. Or I couldn't see them. Except for the rain. I opened the window wide and went back to the sofa to watch the rain and the green coming back to life through its drops. I felt shivers. Somehow the green and the trees in the rain had always had that effect on me. Yes, there was hope in there.

After a while I rose from the sofa and took a shower. My body felt so heavy, almost impossible to move. Maybe the shower's rain would breathe some life into me. I stayed there for a while, and then I remembered Matt. He seemed to have some peace to share. Maybe he could share it with me. And I needed to get out of the apartment, get out of my head. I searched for his number and called.

"I was thinking of going out for a walk and was wondering if you'd like to join me."

"Sure. Where?"

"Maybe the beach. Some place not too far."

"It's raining here."

"Here too."

"Are you sure the beach is where you want to go?"

"Yes. This is when I like it the most."

"Fine. I don't have a car, but I can bike."

We agreed that he'd bike to my place, and then we would use my car to get to the beach.

When Matt arrived, he was carrying a small backpack. "For my sketches," he said. "I always carry it with me."

We walked to my car and drove to the beach.

"I haven't been to the beach in a long time," he said, as I was driving. "Such an unusual day to go there."

"I know. It should be beautiful. There won't be people around, and the light will be perfect."

"You mean, the no-light will be perfect."

"Cloudy, yes, perfect," I said, and smiled.

I wondered what he might be thinking of my choice, of me, but I wasn't worried about his judgment. I couldn't worry about being judged. Not then.

"Why the bike?" I asked.

"Why?"

"Yes. Why not a car?"

"Do you want an honest answer, or a cool one?"

Right, what did I want?

"I can't afford it. Too expensive. Down payment, installments, insurance, gas. Biking is free, and the bike is not even mine. It's my friend's. I don't make much with my novels, and so I need to be careful."

"Do you do anything else besides your novels?"

"Sometimes I work as a colorist, but I don't like it. It's just to make money. Although I don't make much with that either."

"Is it hard? I mean . . . being an artist when you have a small income? Do you ever feel frustrated?"

"Of course. But working nine to five would suck any creative energy from me. I might have to do it one day though. Sometimes when I visit the bookstores where I sell my novels and find them in a little box on the floor, in one or another corner, abandoned there, forgotten, I ask myself what am I doing, why I continue drawing. I guess the answer is I have stories to tell, a voice that wants to be heard. But it's not happening for me. Not the way I'd need it to survive."

A voice calling to be heard. I liked that. I never heard the authors' voices calling to be heard when I entered a bookstore and browsed for books. I closed my eyes and imagined what would happen if I could.

"What are you thinking?"

"I never thought about it."

"About what?"

"I'm sorry for the times I didn't hear your voice and the other authors' voices. I wish I had."

"There would be too many voices for you to handle," he said. "It'd be hell. You should be glad you can't hear them."

I wasn't.

"But it's true, I'm free now. I don't have to report to anyone for my choices and mistakes, and I don't need much to be happy. People talk about needs all the times. Need to go on vacation, need to have a luxury car. I don't have any of those."

I liked his approach to life. I envied his freedom. Mostly though, I liked hearing his voice. It was calming. And I was right. He had peace to share, and he was sharing it with me.

We arrived at the beach, parked the car on the side of the promenade, and walked to the seashore. The sand was wet and cold, so we kept our shoes on. We sat very close to the water, I could almost touch it.

"We might get wet," he said.

"I think I'd like that."

He smiled, pulled his notepad from his backpack, and started drawing. He drew the ocean and the clouds, and then me.

"How do you come up with your stories?" I asked.

He smiled, looked at his sketch, and without moving his eyes from it, said, "I see something inspiring, draw a first sketch, and then imagine a story for it. But I'd say I often start with a sketch of reality. It's life, beauty, that inspires me."

I remained still as he finished his sketch, and I looked at him as he was drawing. He had big blue eyes, dark-blond hair as unattended as his beard, and when he looked at me, at times I felt I saw the face of a boy. And sometimes I liked it.

"This is for you," he said when he was done. The drawing was beautiful, and I felt bad keeping it.

"Don't you want to use it for a story?"

"Oh, I will, but I don't need this. It's in my head. You can have it. Consider it my thank-you note for inspiring my new story."

"What story?"

"I don't know it yet. But it'll certainly be about a girl, a beach, the rain."

I looked at the drawing and smiled.

The sky looked sad. I took off my shoes, freeing my feet, and letting the water touch them, again and again. We stayed there for a while without talking. I felt as comfortable with him as with an old friend. Being with him distracted me, calmed me down, but it did not make me happy. I thought about Nick and what he might be doing, whether that woman was still with him, and whether they were flirting, having lunch somewhere.

"Do you have many friends?" I asked, trying to push those thoughts as far from me as I could.

"No, not many, just a few. Mostly graphic novelists."

"Why is that?"

"We're similar, feel comfortable with each other, don't question each other's choices, beliefs." He looked around, and then added, "Writing, drawing, is isolating. We don't see each other that often, and we respect each other's spaces. Yeah, we're solitary people, although some of us are in committed relationships."

"Are you?"

"Are you what?"

"In a relationship?"

"No, I'm not. And you?"

I hesitated a bit, thought about Nick, and bit my lip.

"No, I'm not," I said, and I felt anger. I was angry at Nick, for my life, and more than I could even be aware of.

"What are your dreams?" he asked.

"My . . . dreams?"

"Yes, your dreams."

"I . . . I haven't thought about it."

"What do you mean you haven't *thought* about it. You don't *think* about dreams. You just have them."

"Well, I don't think I have . . . dreams. At least not at the moment."

"What about wishes? Hopes?"

Right, what about them?

"I don't know, Matt. It'd be nice to be excited about something again, trust people. Meet people that can be trusted." Yes, I was angry.

"That's all? When I think about dreams, I think big, I think of things that seem hard to achieve. None of the things you mentioned are hard to achieve if you work on them."

How would he understand? I turned my eyes away from him and didn't comment.

"What about you? What are your dreams?" I asked instead.

"Write the most beautiful graphic novel I can write. And then be inspired, and write more, and maybe write one that will inspire a producer to make a movie out of it. Maybe I've got something good in my hands already," he said, pointing to his sketch of me.

"Oh, yes, a girl and the beach," I said.

"And the rain."

"Right, that's important."

"Yes, it is. It's part of the story."

And indeed it was.

I checked my phone and noticed that Nick had called. I hated him for calling as much as I would have hated him if he had not called. I was confused.

We sat silently for a while. When I started feeling tired I told him I had to go, and we headed back.

"I had a great time," he said when we parked the car in front of my place. "You were right about the rain."

I waved as I watched him leave. I turned to my door, and before I opened it, the phone rang again. It was Nick. I didn't pick up. But then the phone rang again. And again it was Nick.

"Sorry to bother you. I was hoping you could . . ."

There was some silence.

"Are you free tonight? I've been invited to a movie premiere."

I thought of saying I was busy, but I wanted to see him. After he had slept with another woman. Yes, I needed to see him.

"The producer is an old friend," he continued, "and asked me to write a review, post something on the blog."

So I swallowed any self-esteem and dignity I had left and said I would go.

"About yesterday . . .," he then added.

"I'm not interested, sorry," I said. "We are not together, you don't have to explain."

Was I playing a game with him? His game? Did I want to? Whatever it was, I didn't want him to know I was hurt. But I was.

"Fair enough," he said, and told me he would come pick me up later.

I checked the time. It was only four p.m. I had a few hours to go shopping, and I wanted to look stunning that night. I did a search on the internet to see where I could buy something elegant and sexy. I wanted him to want me and not have me.

I found a couple of stores that seemed interesting and went to check them out. I was used to buying clothes online, and after what perhaps was years, I was finally back in a store, changing clothes in front of a mirror, and imagining Nick's reaction. Was that hope? One thing I was sure of: I desired him.

I bought three dresses, one short, one over the knees, and another longer one, since I couldn't make up my mind as to which would work best. And I even bought new underwear at a store I had never dared visiting before. I thought it looked cheap, but now it seemed perfect. Black lace underwear.

I chose to wear the over-the-knees dress, black heels, and pearls. That would do, I thought. But before I could even try to put makeup on, Nick called.

"I'm here."

I looked at myself in the mirror and decided to skip makeup, except for some red lipstick. The contrast between the color of my skin, my wet hair, and the lipstick was . . . interesting.

I grabbed my purse, turned off the light, and left.

"So . . . where have you been all day? I tried to call you three times."

"I was with Matt."

"Oh . . . your graphic-novelist friend."

I smiled and said nothing. He turned to look out the window, and then he looked at me for a while.

"I might have found something interesting on Andrew," he said.

"What do you mean?"

"An email I received. The guy says he knows Andrew. Says his full name's Andrew Pratt. He disappeared over a year ago and nobody knows where he is."

"Do you believe this?"

"Yeah. I think so. We should meet him. Maybe tomorrow if you're free."

We didn't speak for the rest of the ride, and we soon arrived at the movie theater. There was a group of men wearing tuxedos at the entrance, so I wondered whether we were dressed properly for the occasion.

"You certainly are, my dear. And I don't care. I'm a just a blogger," Nick said, offering me his arm. "Shall we?"

By then, somehow my memory of the night before had temporary left me. All I could see was him, and I still liked what I saw.

The theater was packed, and the film was interesting. A love story between an orchestra director and a violinist. The violinist was fragile and insecure; the director, self-confident and extroverted. The two fell in love, but then started fighting and hurting each other, and then separated. When the movie ended, I was left with a sense of emptiness, but I liked it. I liked it because it was brutal and honest, not like those happily-ever-after, nonsense Hollywood movies I hated. I also loved the photography. In fact, that is what I liked the most—the drawings rather than the words that accompanied it. They were powerful. More than the dialogues.

"Are you hungry? Can I take you somewhere for dinner?" Nick asked, as I was rewinding some of those photographs in my mind.

"Yes, that'd be good."

"I know where we could go."

"I trust you," I said, and sought his eyes but missed them. The word *trust* wasn't a conscious choice. I just said it. But then I realized that I did trust him and his feelings for me. I trusted the man who had just cheated on me.

We drove to the restaurant, but there was no table available.

"The wait is an hour."

"That's long."

"Yes," he said, and suggested we drive to a liquor store, buy some red wine, and arrange a meal at his place. I nodded that it was fine.

He came out of the store with a bottle of Merlot and two glasses. I laughed.

"Why the glasses?"

"I was thirsty, and I thought you might be too."

"How are we going to open the bottle?" I asked.

He reached over my knees and pulled a corkscrew from the glove compartment.

"So you're used to celebrating in your car?"

"Celebrating?" he smiled again. "Yeah, in a way . . . sometimes."

As I watched him pour the wine into my glass, I thought about him and my attraction to him. What did I know about him really? Was my attraction just an idea? I felt hopeless and lost, and I sought relief in the wine.

"Shouldn't we toast first?" he asked.

"A toast? To what?"

"To lies."

"Lies?"

"Yes, to lies."

I didn't understand that. What lies was he talking about? Andrew's novel? The journal? Andrew's lies? His own? Mine?

When we arrived at Nick's place I was drunk, and he noticed.

"I could take advantage of you, but I don't want to."

"Why?"

"Because I care about you."

"Really? That wasn't clear."

"Why do you say that?"

"I'd say having sex with someone after having sex with me is a weird way of showing that you care about me."

"That didn't mean anything. It was just sex."

"And so what was it with me?"

He looked at me, and I just wanted to kiss him.

"I'm sorry," he then said. "I told you I'm not into this type of thing. I can't commit."

"And so you fuck around to make sure women understand that you don't intend to commit?"

"Susan, you're drunk. I'll take you home. We can work tomorrow."

I didn't say a word and started undressing. He sat on the sofa and watched me take off the dress, my tights, my underwear. Then I went closer to him, and when he was about to touch me, I said, "No, don't. Just watch."

He smiled, pulled me closer to him, and tried to kiss me, but I turned away from him.

"What are you doing?"

"What are *you* doing?"

"I know you want it."

"Are you sure?"

I moved farther away and started putting my clothes back on.

"What are you doing? Why are you doing this to me?"

"How does that feel?" I asked.

He didn't respond.

"How does it feel?" I insisted.

He grabbed my wrist, and pulled me closer to him, over him, then under him, and said, "I get it."

"Do you?"

I had not exactly planned this. I thought I could control his desire, and maybe I could. I just couldn't control mine. Not strong enough to resist it.

"I do," he said, and kissed me. "I want you to have pleasure."

"I want that."

"Then just let me do it," he continued to move on top of me and I felt warmer and warmer. That intense physical pleasure becoming metaphysical, something you couldn't touch or describe. Overwhelming. It took over. He did.

"You know, pleasure comes with pain. Do you want some?"

"I want . . . yes, I want it."

"How is it?"

I wanted to scream, but he covered my mouth with his hand. I felt. Pleasure. And pain. The pain lasted a fraction of second, but it was intense, and I kept it with me for much longer than that. At times, I can still feel it.

I fell on the sofa, drained and even more disoriented. He followed me a few seconds later, or perhaps less. It was intense, and it was fast. But I could feel him throbbing inside of me until the day after, like a sin, like a knife, like something that had given me pleasure and pain, like something that cut my skin and the veins under it to free me of them. Like something, and in fact like the only thing that could give me the peace I was looking for. Like me. Like love, like a search for myself, like something that was expanding me, taking me out of my body, and making me float somewhere high up. And so I left; I left my lighter body close to his tired one. The ceiling fan almost seemed tired too, moving slowly above our heads and breaking the moonlight into silver beams that looked like a futuristic painting on the white walls. I saw all of this, except I wasn't there. Not anymore. I thought eternity must feel like this. How would I return into the world after this? So much silence, and it lasted, but not enough. He was staring at the fan and did not move for a while. Yes, I wanted to ask what he was thinking, but I didn't. After a while, he turned and looked at me. His eyes seemed confused.

"Should we work?" he asked. "I can bring the journal to bed. We have July 25 to review. Will you read?"

If space is what he needed to understand what was happening between us, he should have it. Any attempt to make sense of what was going on between us would most certainly fail anyhow, and whatever answers I could get to my questions would not change my feelings for him. Yes, I still liked what I saw.

I read.

July 25

I've not written for a while. I was working on my novel. Worked so hard, in fact, I'm almost done. I need to write the ending, but I don't know what to write. A happy ending wouldn't be truthful to the story, although I so want one. But I don't even know how the story of us should end and whether it actually ended. I felt you still loved me when you decided to leave. I know you always will. And even if we were eye to eye, one in front of the other, and you said you didn't love me, I wouldn't believe you. Ed called me the other day and apologized. He realized it was a stupid idea to try to fix me up with someone like that. I'm smarter than that, I said, and he laughed. I've returned to the place where I had sex with that prostitute and had sex with her at least every other day for the past two weeks. And so, yes, now I'm paying for sex, but I definitely believe the worst experience I had was the arranged date I described in Lies. I thought that story was perfect for the novel. A story of lies within another. Of course I know she lies to me when she pretends to like what I do to her. I lie to myself when I pretend that she's actually enjoying it, that paying for sex is just something I do for fun, that I could have a normal relationship with a woman if I only wanted to. And my friends lie to me when they say that, after all, it's OK to seek a stable relationship with a prostitute, which is actually what I have been trying to do. So many lies we tell . . . I asked Pam, the prostitute, to go out with me. "I thought you were just looking for sex," she said. "Of course," I replied. But that wasn't true. Since she said that she was happy when she saw me, I thought she might like to go out with me. She laughed and said she wished she could do that, but couldn't. Another lie. I showed her a picture of you and me, the one at the park, your favorite. She said you looked beautiful. I don't think she believed you were my girlfriend. At times I don't believe it either. Everything started and finished so quickly. I should complete the novel in the next few days, and then will show it to my agent. And you, once again, inspired it. I miss you. What's next? I'm worried. I'm worried about what will become of me next.

Nick turned and kissed me, and kissed me again, and we made love again. I don't remember what happened next. When it was late, I said I'd go home.

"I'll take you home."

"No."

"I insist that you let me do this."

"But I . . ."

"Just let me take care of you."

So I let him. He took me home.

DAY SEVEN

That day we would meet "M.G.," Andrew's friend who had contacted Nick.

"I'm curious about this guy," Nick said. "He wants to meet at three at our café downtown."

The café was the one Nick and I liked, the one I had discovered, close to my favorite bookstore. When we arrived, Matt was sitting at a table on the first floor, waiting for us.

"Matt?"

"Is this your friend?" Nick asked.

"Yes, Matt, this is Nick. Nick, Matt, my friend who writes graphic novels," I said. "I had no idea you knew Andrew."

"How would you? You didn't ask," Matt said.

"True. There was no time, I guess."

Nick and I joined Matt at his table, and we ordered coffee.

"So you think the author of this journal is Andrew Pratt."

"I'm positive."

"How so?" I asked.

"Emily was Andrew's girlfriend. She was a dancer, they had some issues, and the story the journal describes is their story. Plus,

Andrew's best friends are Ed and Joe, both graphic novelists. Before disappearing, he completed his novel and gave them a copy."

"You said he disappeared after completing his last novel?"

"Correct."

"A year ago?"

"Over a year. Ed, Joe, and I were having dinner. Andrew called and said his agent didn't like the draft. He was upset and wanted to know what they thought about it. Ed told him where we were. He came, brought the novel, dropped it on the table, and disappeared."

"Were you . . . are you close to Andrew?"

"Not particularly. I know Ed and Joe, and they often talk about Andrew, so I mostly know him through them. The four of us hung out together sometimes."

"Do they know about the blog?" Nick asked.

"Not as far as I know."

"Could you set up a meeting with them?" I asked.

"Of course."

"Do you know if the police are looking for Andrew? If they did?" Nick asked.

"His roommates called the police after he didn't return home for a week. They didn't do much."

Matt left to call his friends, and I remained alone with Nick.

"So this is Matt. Do you like him?"

"What do you mean?"

"Are you attracted to him?"

"I might be. Would that bother you?"

"No, of course not. You can fuck who you want."

That hurt.

When Matt returned to the table, he said Ed and Joe were on their way.

A few minutes later, they showed up. Ed was tall and skinny. Joe was of average height, with curly hair and big, heavy glasses—the glasses and the hair bigger than anything I could remember after meeting with him. They seemed to be siblings, but when I asked, they said they were not. Their demeanor and clothes were alike though. They both had the same style, slow, lazy, tired, vintage or probably just old. They seemed to be happy to see that we cared about Andrew, or just OK with it. Or perhaps too lazy to have any other reaction or opinion about it.

"Did you read *Lies*?" I asked Joe.

"Yeah," Joe said, "great stuff." He looked to Ed for approval.

"Oh, yes," Ed confirmed. "Andrew is a fucking genius. That agent doesn't understand shit."

Joe nodded but didn't say more.

"How do you know his agent didn't like *Lies*? Did Andrew tell you?"

"Was it the last time you talked to him?" Nick followed up.

"Yes," Ed said.

"No further calls? Emails?"

"No," Ed confirmed.

They both looked down. At that point, I wasn't sure whether they were more disappointed in Andrew, in our job, or in Andrew's readers. I couldn't stand their passive acceptance of whatever came to them, their attitude.

"Did you guys talk to the police?" I wanted to shake them.

"Yes, we did. Two or three times. They mostly asked us routine questions, didn't seem interested. They probably thought he decided to leave and so they didn't bother to do anything."

"We never opened that letter." I said.

"Which letter?" Ed asked.

"A sealed letter we found in the journal. There's an address on it, but no name. We'll take a look," Nick said. "Perhaps, for now, it's better to stop posting," he added, while looking at me.

"Do you guys have a copy of the novel?" He then asked.

"Yes," Joe said. "You could take a look if you want to. Where do you live?"

"Walking distance," Nick said.

"I'll bring it by tonight."

They exchanged phone numbers and addresses. We shook hands and left.

"Do you want to come home?" Nick asked.

I nodded, and we started walking to his place, mostly in silence. We were both probably thinking of Andrew's mess or our own. It was hard to say which one was worse. And as I was pondering it, I thought I was—we were—in the perfect place.

Downtown should be renamed the madness district. Exhilarating and depressing, comforting and scary, a little hell that you could confuse with heaven, or vice versa, depending on your mood. At times I'd been attracted to downtown like Emily was, but at others it repulsed me. I realized I never saw it. Now I was looking at it, and I could see something.

When we stopped at a traffic light, I was hit by an intense stench, pee or shit or both. When I turned to check where it came from, a man grabbed me and pointed a knife at my throat. It all happened so fast that I have to force myself to remember what actually happened. It all seemed unreal. I became paralyzed, unable to speak. I tried to scream or cry, but I froze.

"What do you want? You can have everything you want, but leave her alone," Nick said.

"She smells so good. She's a spoiled brat. Is she yours? I want her skin."

"Leave her alone, and I'll give you money. Everything you want."

"I told you what I want. I want a piece of her skin."

"I'll give you my skin. Just leave her alone."

"I don't want your dirty skin. I want hers," the man said, almost crying.

"If you hurt her, I'll kill you. I swear to God."

I stopped breathing, and that's the last thing I remembered. I lost consciousness and woke up in Nick's bed, my throat still hurting from the homeless man's grip.

"What happened? Where's the guy?" I asked.

"With the police. You fainted right before I punched him in the face. You woke up briefly and were still shaking. I gave you something to sleep and put this on." He showed me his fist, still bleeding through the bandage he had put on. "You couldn't scream, huh?"

He gave me something to sleep? I didn't remember any of that.

"Scream? Yes, no. I wanted to, but I couldn't."

"You can't scream?"

"I think I can. But I couldn't . . . I wanted to."

He remained silent, staring at me with the same look he had when we first met. He was trying to get under my skin, he was looking for something.

"Come with me," he said, and dragged me out of the bed.

I did as he said, but I had no idea what he had in mind. I had only a T-shirt on, but I did not stop to think about what I was wearing and just followed him.

We took the elevator and reached the rooftop of his building. He pushed a heavy door open with both hands, and we stood in front of Los Angeles. It was early morning, the sun had not yet risen, and the city was enveloped in fog. The air was icy, almost painful on my skin. I was barefoot.

"I'm freezing!" I said.

"I know. I'm sorry. It won't take long. Think of something painful. Something buried deep down."

"What? Why?"

"Trust me."

"I can't. It's too cold."

"Susan, try. It'll only take a few seconds."

I couldn't think of anything. I looked at Nick, begging him to let us return to the apartment.

"Try harder."

I closed my eyes and finally stopped feeling the cold. I remembered something. My father telling me that my mother had died. I started crying.

"Don't cry. Scream."

I continued to cry, and I bent over because of the cold or the pain or the tears. He pulled me up.

"Just scream!" He said. "Scream!" He shouted.

"Ahhhhhhhhhhhhhhhhhhhhhhhhhh!" he screamed. "Ahhhhhhhhh-hhhhhhhhhhhhhhhhh!" he screamed again.

"Ahhhhhhhhhhhhhhhhhhhhhhhhhh!" I screamed.

"Louder," he said.

"Ahhhhhhhhhhhhhhhhhhhhhhhhhh!" I screamed and screamed.

"Louder!" he shouted.

And I finally did it. I screamed as I had never screamed, I cried as I never had.

"Ahhhhhhhhhhhhhhhhhhhhhhhhhhhhhhhhhhhhhhhhhhhhhhhhh-hhh!   Ahhhhhhhhhhhhhhhhhhhhhhhhhhhhhhhhhhhhhhhhhhhhhhh-hhh. Ahhhhhhhhhhhhhhhhhhhhhhhhhhhhhhhhhhhhhhhhhhhhhhhhhh!"

I screamed, vomiting out my pain, my anger, the lies I had been told, the ones that hurt me, my wounds, my insecurities, my fears, my harm. I screamed and screamed. I scratched, cracked that silent sky, my throat. Something started bleeding.

"It's OK, Susan. Stop. Enough. That's good," he said. "Stop. That's enough. Susan, stop."

I didn't.

Nick waited. He waited for me right there. And I screamed until I lost my voice, I screamed until I fell on the cold stone of that roof. Didn't feel the cold anymore. Didn't feel anything anymore. I had emptied myself. There was just pain in me. Nothing else.

I looked up, and the sky was now darker with my pain.

Nick took me in his arms, looked at me, and I fell in love.

DAY EIGHT

I woke up at eight in the evening and saw Nick standing in front of the window, looking outside.

"It's dark," I said.

"Yes, it is. Did I wake you?"

"I'm glad you did. I must have crashed at some point."

"You did. You looked exhausted. How do you feel now?"

"Better," I said, and meant it.

"Are you hungry? Would you like some food? Eggs?"

I smiled. I liked when he cooked for me.

"Eggs will be great."

"I was reading *Lies*," he said and showed me a copy of the book. "Joe brought this last night, while you were sleeping."

"Can I see it?"

He handed me the novel, and I started leafing through the drawings and the words sketched in the little balloons. Andrew's style was clean and pure.

"I like it," I said. "I want to read it."

"You will. Let's eat first." He bent, kissed my forehead, and then went to the kitchen. I could hear the fork beating the eggs. For a second, I felt as if I had lived that exact moment before. Many times over. I felt confused. It was my mother making eggs for me, my grandmother, someone, somewhere . . . I could not remember. Except that sound, its comforting warmth, felt familiar. I left my memories and looked for Nick. I could see his face from the bed. He looked upset.

"What's wrong?" I asked.

"I was just thinking about the story I read . . . so intense. And the lies theme . . . Do your lies ever seem real to you? They sometimes do to me. It's scary . . . Does it happen to you?"

Does it? Did it? I could not say.

He poured the eggs into the pan and, without taking his eyes from the food, said, "I think everyone's worried that Andrew might have killed himself. Do you think that's possible?"

"No," I said, and wanted to believe it. I needed Andrew to be alive. To continue whatever we had, for our search, for my own. Would it all be over if Andrew were dead? I was afraid.

Then Nick came to bed holding two plates with eggs and bacon, and we laughed when some of it fell on the blanket.

"Perfect. My attempt to seduce you miserably failed."

"Actually, I think it perfectly succeeded," I said, and pulled him toward me. He kissed me, undressed me, fed me, and we made love. Not exactly in that order. It all seemed to be happening at the same time, and perhaps it was. And this time it lasted longer. I was exhausted, and I placed my head on his chest. I could hear his heart-beat. It was loud.

"I don't want to own you," he said.

"What do you mean?"

"I don't want you to be with me because I'm your partner, boyfriend, husband. I want you to be with me when and how you want it. And I want to do the same. I want us to be together when and how we choose to."

So he wanted an open relationship. His words should have hurt me, but they didn't because they were just lies to me, ones he couldn't help but tell himself and me, somehow to protect us from something. They were just lies, yes they were, and so they didn't matter much to me. I knew what I had, I saw what I had. What I saw was real. It must have been.

I rose to go to the bathroom, and when I returned Nick was at his desk, reading the letter from Andrew's journal. Once he was done reading, he handed the letter to me.

August 3

My dear Emily,

I'm leaving. I've been waiting for your return but it seems that's not happening, so I'm leaving. I've finished the novel and my agent doesn't like it. It's not light enough, he says, it won't make people laugh, he says, and so, he thinks, it won't sell. I know I haven't sold much in the past few years, but I had the feeling this was different. I gave a copy to Ed and Joe, but at this point, it doesn't even matter what they think about it. I need to move on. I love you. I'm sorry for all the lies I told you. I wish I had added this truth to them. Maybe you would have stayed.

I turned the page, but there was nothing else, and so I turned to Nick. He was hoping to find something more in that letter and was disappointed. I wasn't. That letter gave me hope that Andrew was alive.

"We should go check this," Nick said, pointing to the address on the envelope. "It's an hour by car from here." Of course we had to. We cleaned, had some more wine, talked about Nietzsche and lies, and in the first hours of the day, we finally fell asleep. As soon as we woke up, we left, headed to the address on the letter.

"Do you want to know what happened yesterday? I mean, with the homeless guy?" he asked, as he was driving.

"No," I said. I really didn't want to. I wasn't afraid, angry, or sad. I just had the impression that what I had lived was a dream. Some of it had been dark. Some of it had been scary. Some of it had been poetry. And I wanted to remember the poetry now. Just that. I looked at his hand. The bandage was still there. "How's your fist?"

"Better. I can move it now. No big deal."

I placed my hand over his and lowered head to kiss it.

"Thanks for yesterday," I said.

He turned away and freed his hand from mine. Then he turned on the radio.

"Do you like jazz?" he asked. "This is Miles Davis. It helps me relax." He raised the volume and continued to drive.

The music did do that. I saw the muscles of his face slowly loosen up, and his eyes, following the music, reaching somewhere beyond where I could see. And even if I wasn't with him wherever he was, I felt I was moving toward it.

"This is the house," Nick said when he stopped, double-checking the address on the envelope. We had arrived. Almost too soon, I thought.

The house had two floors, a nice rooftop, and a courtyard with a basketball court on the left and an old turquoise Cadillac parked in front of a small garage.

"It looks like a family home," I said.

"Yes, it does."

We walked to the front door, and I knocked. We heard someone's footsteps approaching, and finally a lady in her late sixties came to the door. She smiled and studied us for a while, perhaps trying to remember if we had already met somewhere.

"Good morning, Mrs. . . . ?" Nick said.

"Mrs. Ross."

"Good morning, Mrs. Ross. I'm Nick Levitt, and this is Susan Blanc. I write a blog, and she's a psychology teacher. We are writing about Andrew Pratt and would love to ask you a few questions, if you don't mind."

"Andrew?" She looked deeper into our eyes, as if she were looking for Andrew too, right there, in our eyes.

"How is he doing?"

"We don't know. We thought that maybe you could help."

She studied us for a while, seemingly unsure of what to do, but then invited us in. She walked slowly, slightly bent over herself, as if she were carrying some heavy weight on her back.

"I apologize for my posture. All those years at the piano have left their mark."

She stopped in front of the living room, invited us to sit, and said she'd be back with some tea.

The room was beautiful. There were three big couches nicely arranged around a fine glass-and-marble coffee table. The couches had an elegant, flowery design made with velvet and cotton, and they seemed to be antique, but they were not worn. There was an upright piano in the corner of the room, close to two big windows covered by heavy curtains of a design and texture similar to the ones of the couches. And even though it was a sunny day, that room was almost dark. I loved the shadows and the intimacy they created.

"What a nice room, Mrs. Ross," I said, when she returned.

"This is where I used to practice piano for hours. Andrew loved it. Sometimes he would come and wait for Emily to wake up. He wanted to be left alone, and so I let him stay here, seated on the couch, the one where you are now sitting. He would work on his sketches and stories."

"So . . . how do you know Emily?"

She smiled.

"Emily was my daughter. As you probably know, she died of cancer last year."

She stopped to breathe, and then continued.

"It was brutal. We found out she had cancer in May, and she died in early June."

"What?" Nick looked at me, confused. We both were.

"I'm sorry, Mrs. Ross. Did you say Emily died last year in June?" I asked.

"Yes," she stood up and went to the piano to choose one of the photos she had placed there. "This is Emily. Wasn't she beautiful?"

Yes, she was. She had long, dark, straight hair. Her skin was pale and her lips red, just as Andrew had described. She had big and sad green eyes, and she looked fragile, elegant.

I looked at Mrs. Ross again but couldn't see the resemblance to her daughter.

"Emily was adopted," she said, somehow reading my mind. "But I loved her as if she were mine."

"So she died in June?" Nick asked, as if he still found it hard to believe.

"That's a month before Andrew started writing his journal," I said.

"What?" Mrs. Ross asked.

Nick told Mrs. Ross about the journal, and she listened without asking questions.

"Andrew must have suffered tremendously for Emily's death," Nick added.

"He did. We were all worried about him. He disappeared for a few days after the funeral, but then came back and visited me a few times."

"Did you notice anything odd in his behavior?"

She smiled.

"Well, Andrew was never an ordinary man. He's an artist, you know that. But there were a few things, something I noticed. Only I'm not sure whether I had simply not noticed those things before."

"What was it?" I asked.

She lowered her head, perhaps trying to decide whether she should share what she knew or not. She then turned to the window and began to stare somewhere beyond the room.

"Andrew would wash his hands as soon as he entered the house," she said, "and then again if he had touched any food. And then a few more times during our conversation. And then again, right before leaving. I believe he was casual about diet and sleep before Emily died, at least that had been my impression. But after her death he became obsessed with both things. My impression was that he was depriving himself of both. He quickly lost a lot of weight, not that he was overweight or anything . . . He didn't need to. I was worried he might be starving himself."

She took a breath and then continued.

"Sometimes I had the feeling he considered himself guilty for Emily's death. Hard to understand why."

She turned and hid her tears.

"And most of all, the strangest thing was that he would talk about Emily as if she were still alive, as if she had broken up with him."

So my instinct was right about Andrew.

"I talked to some of my psychologist friends," Mrs. Ross added. "They explained that sometimes these reactions are normal after a strong shock. They told me to leave Andrew alone for a while. They thought it was too early to consider treatment, and that he might feel better at some point. Emily's death was too big of a shock for him. He needed time."

She looked at me, seeking my approval.

"But I slowly lost contact with him," she then added. "He first came every other day, then once a week, then he disappeared. He mentioned a few times that he wanted to go to New York. I believe he said he had an offer from a publishing company to color their comics. You know he was from there, right?"

No, we didn't.

"He said he wasn't excited about the job, but thought that perhaps changing his environment might help. He wanted to go home."

She paused again and the continued.

"After Andrew disappeared, the police contacted me. Andrew had been reported as missing. I told them what I knew, what I'm telling you, and they eventually decided to stop looking for him. They thought he had chosen to disappear."

"They thought Andrew had left," I said, "but what do *you* think?"

"I don't know. I wasn't excited about Andrew leaving. Wasn't sure he was OK. I tried to persuade him to stay or at least postpone. He said he would do so, but then he vanished. Perhaps he did go to New York as he said he would."

"Did he mention anything about a new novel he was working on?" I asked.

"Yes. The last time I saw him he said he had just started working on it. He said it was about his story with Emily until the separation, as he used to call it."

"Apparently his agent didn't like the new novel, and Andrew might have left soon after," Nick said.

"And it would make sense," I added, "because he might have felt that his life here had become meaningless, that he needed to leave and start earning some money. Or, as you said Mrs. Ross, he just needed to go home."

Mrs. Ross's eyes moved from Nick's to mine. At times, she seemed to trust us, and at times she didn't.

"Do you happen to remember the name of the publisher he mentioned?" Nick asked her.

"No. But he said it was a big company that would pay well."

Nick checked the time and said we should leave.

"Mrs. Ross, thank you for helping us. It means a lot. Emily must have been a beautiful human being," I said, holding her hands in mine.

Mrs. Ross smiled.

"We'll keep you posted and let you know as soon as we find anything," Nick added.

"I appreciate what you're doing. In a way, you're also helping my daughter. She loved Andrew. They were different from each other, argued sometimes, but I know they deeply cared about each other."

Nick shook Mrs. Ross's hand, I hugged her, and we left.

It was almost Thanksgiving. Nick mentioned that on the way home, and I was surprised. I had completely lost sense of time. I looked outside the window, and for the first time, I saw some red and yellow leaves on the trees and on the streets. A taste of fall, a small one, offered as an unexpected gift to L.A. and its endless summers. How could I miss that?

"Have you planned anything?" Nick asked.

"You mean, anything with my family? No. My mother died when I was seven. My father might be in New York or travelling with a new girlfriend. I haven't talked to him in a long time." I kept looking outside the window. Yes, I really had missed fall. "What about you?"

"My father also died a long time ago. My mother lives in New York. Last year I promised her I would visit her this Thanksgiving, but I haven't decided yet. Quite frankly, I'd rather avoid that."

"Why? You—we—could go to New York and look for Andrew?"

"What? No, I don't think so."

"Why not?"

"Why should we do that?"

Because it'd be nice to go somewhere together, I thought.

"Because we started this and I want to take it to the end," I said.

He stopped the car.

"Are you serious? Do you really believe that there is any chance we'll find this man?"

I didn't know what I believed. I knew what I felt. He called Jack. When he hung up, he turned to me and said,

"We'd better find something worth writing about over there."

THANKSGIVING EVE

The last week of school went by fast. I finished my last class early and waited to see if anyone had questions. I didn't see John in class, and I asked some of my students if they knew why he had missed so many classes in a row.

"John who? I don't remember anyone with that name."

Nobody knew who he was. I went back to my office to check the roster, but there was no "John" in there. So . . . who had I met that day? Maybe he was in my class but then dropped? Nobody informed me though. Did the registrar send me an email? Did I miss it? I checked my emails but didn't find anything from, to, or about a student named John. Who was that guy? And why had he pretended to be my student? Had he in fact done that? Did I misunderstand what he said? I was very tired that day. I could still remember his face and his broken smile. Now that I thought about it, he seemed more mature than his colleagues, but I had had some older students in the past, so his appearance didn't strike me as odd.

I sat on my couch and tried to remember as much as possible of the meeting. In fact, he hadn't said he was a student. He merely said he had attended my lecture. So he might have been a visiting scholar, someone who was there to check on classes and teachers, perhaps before deciding whether to enroll. But if that was so, why didn't he tell me? Did I dream the meeting? After a while, I felt tired. I was about to turn off the computer and leave when Nick called.

"I bought two tickets for New York. We'll leave tomorrow morning. We should make it for Thanksgiving dinner. Perhaps a little late."

"Nick?"

"Yes?"

"I wasn't planning on spending Thanksgiving with my father. We don't need to be in New York for Thanksgiving."

"Well, we will be anyhow. Maybe you could come to my place and have dinner with my family. It'd be just my family."

Nick was becoming more and more real to me every day. I was excited, but I was afraid too. Hard to say why.

"By the way, why are you still at school?"

"Research."

"On what?"

"A student . . . or someone I thought was one of my students, but I haven't had any luck so far. In fact, I should do research on Andrew now that we know his last name."

"I looked for him on the internet but didn't find much. I have to go. My other phone is ringing. Let me know if you find anything helpful."

I took off my shoes and started looking for Andrew. After so much time talking about him and reading his most intimate thoughts, I wanted, needed, to see his face. When I found his picture on the internet, I was shocked. Andrew Pratt looked exactly like the student I had met that day in my office—John. Maybe Andrew was a bit younger than him, but he looked strikingly similar. I did more research and found out that Andrew Pratt was in fact named J. Andrew Pratt, that is, John Andrew Pratt. So he introduced himself without giving his full name. I wonder why he came to see me and my class? Did he know I coauthored Nick's posts? Is that why he came? I called Nick.

"I think I met Andrew. A couple of weeks ago. He came to my class and then to my office."

"Are you sure?"

"He said his name was John. But I did some research, and in the pictures I found Andrew Pratt looks identical to that guy, well, very similar. And, by the way, Andrew's full name is John Andrew Pratt. So that John was in fact Andrew. Must be. They look so similar. Can't be a coincidence."

"Did he ask you about the blog?"

"No, not at all. Our exchange was so brief. I thought he was one of my students. We really didn't talk much. It felt like he was studying me. Maybe he came to see who I was, see whether his journal was in good hands . . . maybe . . ."

"So he's not in New York?"

"Well, he wasn't when he was here."

"Did you find where he works?"

"No. The only information I found on the internet has to do with the last novel he published, *The Truth About Me*."

"Yeah, I know. I'll get us a copy."

Nick said he would come pick me up the next day. I was cleaning my office and starting to put my books into a box when someone knocked on my door.

"Are you leaving?"

"Matt? What are you doing here?"

"I've got a friend who teaches here. I mentioned your name, and he said I could find you here."

"I'm going to New York with Nick. We think Andrew might be there. We talked to Emily's mother yesterday. Did you know Emily's dead? Actually, she was already dead when Andrew started working on *Lies*."

"What? Andrew's girlfriend? No, I didn't."

We talked more about Andrew and my exchange with John or Andrew that day, and as I resumed packing he asked me whether I was leaving for good. I looked around. His question made sense. There was nothing left on the shelves or on my desk.

"I wish I knew what to say. I just feel I have to pack."

"So you're going to with Nick?"

"I am."

"Are you guys together?"

I didn't know how to answer that question either, so I didn't.

"I hope you'll come back," he then said. "I liked our time together, and you gave me great ideas for my work. Remember, after all, *The Girl, the Beach, and the Rain* might become a bestseller." He smiled.

"Are you seriously working on it?"

"Oh, yeah. I've got a third of it done now. I guess . . . I can't wait to show it to you. Can I . . . buy you a drink, pizza, or something? When do you leave?"

"I leave tomorrow and haven't packed yet. If you want, we could order pizza and eat at my place while I pack."

We called a taxi, and a few minutes later we were at my apartment.

"Nice place," Matt said, looking around.

"Thanks. I've never completely settled in, although I own it. A gift from my father."

"Why don't you have a good relationship with him?"

"It's a long story. Probably we never learned how to talk to each other. My mother died when I was seven. I grew up with my grand-mother. He never opened up to me, and, as a consequence, neither did I."

"Maybe this trip to New York could help."

"I doubt it."

"It's a shame, I mean, failing to fix things when we can do some-thing about them."

"I don't know if there is anything I want to *fix*. In fact, I don't know if there is anything that can be fixed."

I ordered pizza and started packing. He was seated on the sofa watching me throw things randomly in my suitcase and asking me questions that were not really connected to each other.

"Is there anything I can do?" he then asked.

Before I could answer him, the phone rang, and I picked it up. It was Nick. He was checking to see if I needed anything for the trip.

"Was that your friend, the journalist?" Matt asked, after I hung up.

"Yes."

"Are you sure he's not into you?"

"He likes me, but . . ."

"What about you?"

My light bulb burnt out, and we were left in the dark.

"Would you . . . kiss me?" Matt asked.

"Actually . . . I . . ."

He came closer to me.

"I love the way you smell."

I felt the warmth of his breath. He kissed my neck, and I felt disoriented, then uncomfortable.

"Matt . . . wait. I can't. I do, I feel something for Nick."

When his warmth left my skin, I felt relieved.

"I'd better go," he said, and turned away from me. And then I heard him close the door quietly behind him.

THANKSGIVING

A nd soon it was morning. Nick was waiting for me outside my apartment.

"Did you have fun yesterday?" He asked, after placing my suitcase in the trunk.

"What? With Matt, you mean? He helped me pack. We chatted. That's all."

"Was he really interested in *packing* . . . ?"

"Please. Nothing happened."

"Are you sure?"

"Why would I lie to you?"

"Right. Why would you?"

As we drove to the airport, we talked about Andrew's novels. Nick had found the last available copy of *The Truth About Me* at a used book store, and he had the copy of *Lies We Tell* Joe had given him. *Truth* was in the same style as *Lies*, except Andrew had used a shade of gray for its drawings.

"Somehow *Truth* feels darker than *Lies*," Nick said, leafing through the pages. "The blue-purple in *Lies* softens the darkness," he added, "makes the story more intimate, less cold and hopeless. But it's not just the color that gives me that impression."

No, it wasn't just the color. Sometimes the truth did look darker than the lies.

The Truth About Me described a few days of Andrew's life. In fact, the story revolved entirely around three or four days. But Andrew described every detail, every moment, through his own eyes, thoughts, and perceptions, thus incredibly expanding the time and space of each of those moments. His coffee and cigarette in front of a cartoon, his short walk to the trashcan every morning, his observing people, days spent in his pajamas, his reactions to the news, a phone call to Ed, his struggles in front of a blank page, some more cartoons, a porn movie, the waiting for Emily to come home, the modest dinner, the few exchanges with her. Emily was there, but she wasn't really. She was more of an extra than a true character. And the story was not about love as much as it was in *Lies*. In *Truth*, Andrew didn't seem to understand what Emily meant to him. I leafed through the pages and saw things more clearly. I saw Andrew, the man who had come visit me in my office. Then I looked outside the window and lost focus for a while. The clouds were thick white walls to my perception, there, even when I could not see them or wasn't even aware of them. And yet I had started seeing through them. Or at least it felt so.

"Wine?" Nick called to the stewardess. "I can't fly without drinking."

He drank all of his wine and then asked for more.

"So what happened with Matt?"

"Nothing happened."

"Then why aren't you looking at me when you answer my question?"

"Didn't you say you didn't care about whether I slept with other men?"

"No, I don't."

"Then you shouldn't ask that question."

"I'd like to know if you did."

"Why?"

He remained silent.

"All right. I did it. I slept with Matt. Happy now?"

He unfastened his seatbelt and walked away.

I could not tell how long he was gone, but it must have been a while. I lost track of the time, trapped as I was in a mixture of confused feelings, not all of which were about Nick, not all of which were about the present.

"I'm sorry, I needed something stronger than wine," said Nick when he returned, almost waking me up from my trance. "Why did you lie to me?"

"Is that the point? That I lied to you, or that I slept with another man? Do you actually care?"

The woman seated in front of us turned toward us and gave us a strange look.

"Don't be so loud," Nick said.

"Do you actually care?" I didn't lower my voice.

"I care. I care because we're friends, and I expect my friends to be honest with me."

"So that's what this is all about? Honesty between two friends?"

"Yes. Sorry if this is important to me."

"It's important to me too, Nick."

"Then why did you lie to me? First you said nothing happened, and now you tell me you slept with him?"

I looked at him and didn't know what to say. Should I be honest? Should I pretend?

"It's so hard. I don't even know what I should or shouldn't say to you. You're always uncomfortable when I talk about my feelings. I always have to censor myself with you, like there's a line I can't cross, a very thin line sometimes I can't even see."

"So you would have told me about Matt if you could talk to me about your feelings?"

"I didn't sleep with him, Nick. He tried to kiss me, and I stopped him because I couldn't. I didn't want to."

There was some silence, and then he poured his eyes into mine and the cold gray of the truth became light-blue and purple. Was it just lies? He kissed me. It felt warm. Everything did. And I liked it. I still did.

The hotel in New York was gorgeous, with a spacious lobby and elegant chandeliers hanging from the tall ceiling. There were carpets, big ones, everywhere, and many concierges ready to meet any of their customers' wishes and caprices, even the unexpressed ones. I was surprised by Nick's choice. I was expecting something modest, something that would fit a blogger's finances. Nick continued to be a mystery to me.

"Mr. and Mrs. Levitt, here's the keys to your room," the desk clerk said.

I smiled.

"One room, Mr. Levitt?" I asked.

"I thought you might not like it if I left you alone. There's just too much light for your tastes. Am I right?" He winked at me, and we took the elevator to our room.

The bed was large and soft. I sat and looked outside. We had a wonderful view of St. Patrick's Cathedral and so much space. Nick took off his jacket, sat on a couch, and remained still for a while, looking at me. I didn't notice at first, as inebriated as I was by the scent of the bedsheet and the room. And the view. And the dim light, the only one he had left on. But then I turned and caught his look.

"What's wrong?" I asked.

"Every time you and I are alone, I feel I have to make love to you."

I too wanted, needed, to make love to him every time we were alone, but I didn't say it. The clouds were still wrapped around me, and although I had started to see through them, there was something missing, something either he or I had decided not to share. Making love was all we had, and sometimes even that didn't seem to belong to us. It felt stolen. From whom? From what? I couldn't say.

He pulled off my dress and kissed me, and his kiss was long and made me want more. We made love, and it was slow, intense. At first I could hear the sound of the traffic coming from outside, but then that sound became softer and softer, and then it almost disappeared. Did we silence it? Had we silenced everything around us? I closed my eyes and imagined his arms around me, I almost felt they were there, except they weren't. He said something but his voice was becoming more and more distant. I could barely hear it from where I was. I felt as if I had just reached the bottom of the ocean, a dark-blue, peaceful corner of my ocean. From there I could see the surface and a slice of light coming from somewhere far off. I could see it, but I didn't want to grab it. I felt comfortable right where I was, did not want to move. I was lighter, at the bottom of the ocean, alone, while Nick was somewhere on the surface, waiting for me to return, to return to him. But then he became tired of waiting, came closer to me, and started kissing my breasts to wake me back to him, to take me back to the surface, and he succeeded. I felt desire again, he did too, and we made love again.

"My family's waiting for us," he then said, "we should probably go, just a quick visit."

I said that was fine, and I soon rose from the bed to reconnect with the surface as quickly as I could. We got dressed, called a taxi, and headed to Nick's mother's home. She lived on 66th and 5th, not far from our hotel. The building looked elegant and, from its façade, I counted six floors. There was green all around and, across the street, a small Italian restaurant— "addictive but expensive," as Nick described it. We rang the intercom and waited a bit. Soon a voice welcomed us. Nick pushed the heavy entrance door open and let me go first. We took the elevator and went up to the sixth floor.

"This is where my mother lives. She's always lived on top floors. She's afraid of being too close to the ground. And this is true in so many ways."

"What about your father? How was he?"

"A jerk," he said, when the door of the elevator opened.

"Who's a jerk?" an older woman asked, opening her arms to hug Nick.

"Dad. I was telling Susan about him."

"I'm sorry . . . Susan?"

"Yes, nice to meet you, Mrs. Levitt."

"Delighted. Please call me Ellen."

She smiled at Nick and then invited us in. We followed Nick's mother to the living room, where the rest of the family was. The room was elegant and tastefully decorated. There was a huge red carpet and many couches. In the middle was a large coffee table that was almost hard to see for all the half-empty champagne glasses resting on it.

"Would you like something to drink? Champagne? Red? White?"

"I'll have a glass of champagne," Nick said.

"That'll be fine for me too, thanks."

"Perfect," Nick's mother said, and disappeared.

Nick turned and introduced me to his family as "a friend from work." And then he introduced the family to me. "Susan, this is my brother Ethan, my sister Ann, my cousins Frank, Elsa, and Joel, and . . . oh, I didn't know you were here, this is Elinor. Elinor this is Susan. Elinor is . . . my ex-wife."

I froze, but then offered her my hand.

"Hi," said Elinor, as she got up and left the room.

"I'm sorry. I didn't know Elinor would be here," Nick whispered to me. "I'll explain it to you later."

I didn't know what to say. Nick had never mentioned that he had been married. But did he have to? Elinor was his *ex-wife*—ex, past, done. Maybe he just didn't want to talk about it. It made sense. Didn't it?

As I was trying to make sense of what was happening, Elinor returned with a glass of champagne. She was tall, thin, blond, and pale. She had short hair and big blue eyes that dominated her small face. She was so thin you'd fear breaking her just by shaking her hand. But the tattoos all over her body seemed to convey, or were meant to convey, the opposite idea. She was wearing tight pinstripe pants, black heels, and a black top that fell morbidly on her tiny breasts. She smelled good, something like citrus. Elinor reminded me of Emily. Hard to say how exactly. Probably Nick saw the resemblance too. When I first asked him about Andrew's journal, he said the description of Emily, her story, sounded familiar to him. Is that why he kept the diary? Was it his memory of Elinor or me that had brought us to New York?

As I was trying to answer my own questions, Nick followed his mother into the kitchen, and I was left alone with Elinor—or so it felt. She was sitting just across from me, silent, while the rest of the crowd seemed to all be excited about a board game that didn't interest her.

"What do you do for living, Elinor?" I asked.

"I dance, and teach classical ballet at a school nearby."

Right. A dancer.

"And you?"

"I teach psychology."

"How do you know Nick?"

I thought about how Nick and I first met, and I was a bit embarrassed to say that it had been at a nightclub, but I felt so confused that I couldn't come up with a better answer than the truth. In fact, I didn't even try.

"We met at a nightclub. I had never been there before and felt a bit awkward. I think Nick noticed and offered to have a drink with me."

"How polite of him," she said, while Nick was returning with our champagne.

"Who's polite?" he asked, as he handed me a glass.

"You, Nick. Susan was telling me about how you two met. So polite of you to come to her rescue."

"Very funny," he said.

Elinor laughed, and I laughed with her to lessen the tension between the two, or three, of us. I know I didn't succeed though.

"How have you been, Nick?" Elinor asked.

"Good, good."

"Good," she said, punching his eyes with hers. Then she abandoned her empty glass on the table.

"OK," she said, "I think I'd better go. I have an audition early tomorrow. Thanks for inviting me, Ellen," she called to Mrs. Levitt in the other room.

"Thanks for coming, dear," Mrs. Levitt responded from somewhere far off.

Nick waved to Elinor to say bye, and she evaporated in the hall.

Mrs. Levitt brought us some turkey and white wine she thought we might like. We stayed and chatted with the rest of the family for a while. Nick talked about the blog, our posts, their success, and the purpose of our visit.

"Are you guys . . . dating?" Ethan asked.

"No, we're not. We're friends," Nick said, looking at me.

So, no, we were not dating. We were just having sex, regularly, day after day. I faked a smile—or tried to.

We stayed there for a while. I mostly listened to their chats—sometimes present but most of the time absent—and when it was past two a.m., Ethan and Ann, the last two guests besides us still there, rose to leave.

"It's such an honor to have Nick in New York. Since the divorce, he does everything to avoid the city," Ethan said.

"And Elinor," Ann added, and laughed.

"You're drunk, sweetie," Mrs. Levitt reprimanded her. "Do you want me to walk with you to your apartment?"

"No, Mother. I'm fine. I aaaam fiiiine," she said, and turned to me. "It was such a pleasure meeting you, Susan. You have all my sympathy. Nick is not easy. But he's a good heart. I hope you'll be patient with him. My little brother really is a good heart." She hugged Nick and pretended to whisper something in his ear, which in fact all of us heard.

"It's so clear you two are dating. Why are you hiding it?"

"I agree with mom, you're drunk, Ann." Ethan said, as he dragged his sister to the door. "We'll see you later this week, Nick. Sleep well."

"Good night," Ann shouted from the elevator.

We said goodbye to Mrs. Levitt and left.

"I'm sorry you had to learn about Elinor like that," Nick said as soon as we were alone, back in our room. "It's hard for me to talk about her. We got married when I was twenty-four. She was twenty-two. It lasted five years, and then I caught her cheating with my best friend and . . ."

"And you decided to leave New York."

"Yes."

"Do you have kids?"

"No, of course not. I would have told you that."

Would he?

I put on my pajamas and got into bed. He poured himself some scotch, sat on a chair, and started leafing through the pages of some newspapers. I felt the distance between us and hated it, but I thought he needed I. Or maybe I did.

DAY ONE IN NEW YORK

New York is such a fascinating city, especially in November. It's cold, but not as cold as it gets in December or January, and it snows sometimes, but not as often as during those months. The leaves have changed their color, and sometimes it rains, but not hard. It's fall. I missed that in California.

The day after our Thanksgiving dinner we woke up late in the morning. I moved to free myself from the blanket and go to the bathroom. I didn't intend to wake Nick up, but I did.

"Good morning," he said. "We must have been exhausted last night. I don't remember much after my scotch. And you were already sleeping when I came to bed."

I didn't respond. It took me forever to fall asleep, and I did hear him when he came to bed.

"Are you hungry?"

I said that I was. We went to a bakery across the street, grabbed drinks and pastries, and walked to Central Park. Once there, we sat on a bench and watched kids playing baseball as we ate our breakfast.

"I love this park," he said. "It perfectly captures New York's poetry of hot dogs, street performers, dreamers, and businessmen . . . It's beautiful. Naked beauty."

"What do you mean?"

"It's honest, real. I don't get how people can miss this. I could never have enough of it." He pointed somewhere in front of us, but nowhere in particular.

While we were sipping our drinks, he pulled a notebook from his backpack. The notebook contained our notes on Andrew and many ideas, charts, and questions with no answers. After talking them over, Nick resolved to call Matt. Matt gave him the name of Andrew's agent, Pete Folberg, who lived in Montreal. Folberg had a nice website that listed Andrew at the bottom of a long list of published authors. For each author there was a link to another page with information about their life and major works. Andrew's page contained just a brief biography and a short description of *The Truth About Me*, apparently, his only "major" published work.

Nick called Folberg and stayed on the phone with him for quite a while.

"So what did he say?" I asked him when he hung up.

"He said that the last time he spoke with Andrew was over a year ago, when Andrew sent him *Lies*. Folberg told Andrew that the novel wasn't what he was expecting, and that angered Andrew. They had an argument over the phone, and Andrew said he'd publish the novel through someone else. But as far as Folberg knows, the novel hasn't been published. I told him I disagreed with his assessment of *Lies* and described how successful Andrew's journal was on the blog."

"And?"

"He listened to what I had to say, but didn't know how to get hold of Andrew. I asked him for ideas, clues on where he could be. He suggested we talk to the company Andrew was supposed to work for and gave me its name and address. He also said that Andrew loves old movies and often goes to theaters that show them. That might be another lead."

"What do you mean?"

"We should keep an eye on art-movie houses 'cause we might find him there."

"That's crazy. Do you have an idea of how many of those theaters there are in New York?"

"Fewer than you think. And in any event, it's better than nothing. Also, I think I have a sense of the movies Andrew might like," Nick said.

I remained silent and thought about what we should do next. At times the very idea of our search seemed hopeless.

When it was early afternoon, we left the park and started to walk to the publisher.

"Why did you say your father was a jerk?" I asked, trying to crack some of Nick's silence.

"I said he was a jerk because he was. He had many affairs, which he didn't even try to hide from my mother, and he was never at home. I have trouble remembering a single dinner with him. I remember my mother, my sister, my brother, and me sitting at the dining table and wondering where he was. At some point, we were so used to dining without him that if he showed up it felt like having a stranger at the table, and we would all stay silent most of the time. No laughs, no stories about school and friends, no chats about dreams and plans for the future. We didn't trust him. He wasn't family."

"What did he do for a living?"

"He was a journalist."

"Ah ... a journalist, like you. Interesting ..."

"Why *interesting*?"

"It's interesting that you chose the same career as someone you dislike so much."

"I think I had no choice. Reading and writing was my calling, and despite my contempt for him, I liked his job. I thought it was fascinating. When I was younger, we were close, and he initiated me into this vocation. He worked for a small independent newspaper in the city. He used to take me to his office, and sometimes he'd give me his drafts to read and comment on before publishing them. He liked my comments and edits, or pretended that he did. Who knows? But, at that time, I believed him. I felt important, happy, and I slowly convinced myself that I was good at his job. And then I became good, and his job became mine."

"What happened then? When did your relationship fall apart?"

"First, I think I disappointed him because of my grades in school. Then, there were his affairs. I hated him and his lies. At some point we stopped talking to each other, and then he died."

"When did that happen?"

"Right after my separation from Elinor. I was twenty-nine."

So that was part of his puzzle. And yet I felt there was more.

"And you? What's your story with your father?" he asked.

"My mother died when I was seven. My memories of her are confused. I do remember a few things we did together, some of her gifts, but mostly I remember the door of her bedroom closed to the rest of the house, and to me and my father. I remember her saying that she was 'tired' and needed to sleep. She would close the door to her room and would not come out for days. My father was working hard, and I spent much of my time with my grandmother, who lived with us here in New York. In fact, she still lives here, in the same house where we all lived. Haven't seen her in forever. Anyhow, after my mother died, my father became almost nonexistent. We didn't communicate, didn't know how to, and things haven't improved much since."

"What happened to your mother?"

I hesitated.

"You know, I'm not even sure. The official story, the one my father told me, is that my mother had an aneurysm and died. November second. But who knows whether this is what happened . . ."

"Why do you say that?"

"I don't know. I just feel that it's not what happened."

Nick looked at me and then grabbed my hand and held it as we continued to walk. I had to look twice to convince myself that it was actually happening. Then he squeezed my hand more tightly. Perhaps to reassure me that I was right. Or to work off his own pain.

"You see that theater?" he then asked.

"Yes."

"That's one of the oldest independent movie theaters in the city. They've been showing vintage films since before they were vintage. Let's see what they're showing tonight. Maybe we could come after our visit to the publisher or after dinner."

We looked at the marquee on top of the theater, which might have originally been white but now looked gray and dirty. The sign said, "*City Lights*."

"Have you seen it?"

"No," I said, and he looked at me in disbelief.

"Are you serious? It's a beautiful silent movie from the thirties. A movie Andrew might like. You might like it too."

"What's it about?"

"It's a love story."

A love story. Perfect timing, I thought. I smiled, and we continued to walk.

When we arrived in front of the publisher's building Nick rang the intercom and said we were reporters there to ask a few questions about one of their employees. Someone told us to go to the seventh floor. The door opened, we took the elevator, and went up.

The offices of the publisher were in a vast loft that had gray carpet on the floor and white desks spread across it, some of which were separated by little half-walls, but mostly they were open and visible. There were big windows, and the office looked luminous. I thought I might have found it hard to work there, as there was too much light, no intimacy at all.

A man in his late forties came to the elevator, shook our hands, and said he was the vice president.

"My assistant said you wanted to talk about one of our employees?"

"Yes, John Andrew Pratt."

"Andrew ... sure. Let's go to my office."

We walked across the room to the farthest end, where there was an office surrounded by glass.

"We love the light here," the host said.

"It seems so," Nick commented, perhaps sharing my feeling of unease.

"May I ask, before we talk about Andrew, why are you interested in him?"

"We like his work," Nick explained, "and we're interested in his backstory. We'd like to interview him."

"I see. How did you know he worked for us?"

"His former agent gave us your name and address and thought Andrew might be working here."

"He was. He was one of our best colorists. He worked here until last September, and then quit. He said he wanted to work on his own stuff. In fact, he mentioned he'd completed a novel. He thanked me for the opportunity we had offered him and said he wouldn't be coming back the next day. He'd finished his last assignments and wasn't going to accept more. Yeah . . . that was the last we saw of him. He stopped working for us the next day. It was quite unexpected, and shocking I'd say."

"Do you think there was something else that led him to quit? Did he look upset when he spoke to you?"

"Let's put it this way. Andrew never struck me as happy. His demeanor was always serious, thoughtful, sometimes dark, certainly not happy. And perhaps he felt especially uncomfortable here. Our people are usually extroverted and outgoing. We like to laugh here. I don't think he liked that. But he did seem to have something in mind, something he wanted to pursue outside of here. This job might have been an obstacle."

"Did you try to convince him to stay?" I asked.

"I did. I told him he was among our best colorists. I asked him if he'd be willing to train some of our employees and maybe work part time, but he refused. He really seemed determined to end his relationship with us. Although, I believe we always treated him nicely."

"Do you have any clue, any idea of where he might be?" Nick asked.

"Sorry, I don't."

We thanked him and left.

"Were you actually expecting to find something more?" I asked Nick once we were out. He seemed disappointed.

"I don't know. Maybe I was hoping he was still working there." He looked at me and added, "We'll keep looking. Maybe we should check with Mrs. Ross again. Sometimes people don't remember everything the first time you ask them to remember. They need time to think about your questions. But if you come back to them after a while, they might surprise you with incredibly helpful details they had forgotten when you first talked."

He checked the time and said,

"If you're still in the mood, I think we could walk back to the theater and see *City Lights*."

As we walked to the movie theater, Nick seemed distracted, his mind on something. I couldn't say what.

We arrived at the theater a few minutes before the movie started, bought our tickets, and sat in the back. There were very few people there. As soon as we took our seats, an organ rose up from below the stage. An organist wearing a suit that looked like it was from the 1920s started playing. A short, simple, happy melody. I had never seen anything like that. He played for a few minutes, then stopped, and welcomed the audience to the show. He said a few things about the film we were about to see, bowed, and walked off the stage. The red curtains went up, and the movie began. It was probably one of the most beautiful films I'd ever seen. It was silent, but I thought that even if there had been sound, the Tramp could have not told the blind flower girl much more than he conveyed without words.

We carried the silence and intensity of the movie with us on our way to dinner. We had probably talked about dinner options before, but I could not remember, or I was lost somewhere. The place was across from Washington Square Park, an Italian restaurant that looked enchanting from the outside.

"I like this place. It gives you the feeling of being in a charming European village," Nick said, and I wished we could take part in that kind of romance, although I knew we couldn't. The place just didn't belong to us. Its colors didn't. We were still light-blue and purple. Or, at least, that's what I saw.

When we entered, I noticed a fireplace in the middle of the room. I loved that. The atmosphere was intimate, with dim lights and lanterns spread around the room. It was almost full but not crowded and not noisy. Our table was all the way in the back, somehow shielded from the rest of the room by a wall with an open arch and violets nicely creating the illusion of a balcony. Perhaps one in Italy. The candles smelled like fresh orange. I felt inebriated by their scent, the wine, Nick—although I could barely see him in the dim lighting. The food was not great, just OK. But the wine was superb. I had a glass while waiting for my lasagna, and I got a little drunk. Nick ordered the same, and then a chocolate mousse for two and more wine. It was after the second glass that he started playfully reaching for my plunging neckline.

"People can see us," I said, although I'm not sure why, as I certainly didn't care.

"I can barely see you. Nobody can see us. But I think we should go. We need to."

We had barely touched our food. A bit later, we were back at the hotel. I left the curtains open since I didn't want to miss that beautiful view of the cathedral from our bed.

"Don't you want to close the curtains? The sun will wake us up tomorrow," he said.

"But we would miss the moon," I said.

He kissed me, and we made love. And then we fell asleep. The sun did not wake us up the day after, and I'm still glad for that loud spark of moonlight.

DAY TWO IN NEW YORK

Nick called Mrs. Ross in the morning. He told her what we had discovered and asked her if she had anything more to share with us. She remembered a friend of Emily's who lived in New York. Andrew might have contacted her. She gave Nick her name and her parents' address. They lived on the Upper West Side, right on the northwest corner of 72nd Street and Central Park West, in the Dakota Apartments, where John Lennon had lived and died.

Emily's friend was Christine Bass. Her father had been a famous writer, her mother an artist. Christine was no longer living with them, but when Nick called and asked about her, Mrs. Bass said Christine would be home for dinner, and we were both invited. Emily and Christine had been close, and Emily's death had been harsh on Christine.

"Do you know if Christine knew Andrew?" Nick asked Christine's mother.

"Emily's boyfriend?"

"Yes."

"I think so. She didn't say much about him, but I'm sure she knew him."

They talked a bit about it, but ultimately agreed that Christine would be the one to ask. Once Nick hung up, he suggested that we visit the Museum of Natural History before dinner. I had been there before, but not as often as Nick. Apparently, the museum was one of his favorite places in the city.

"What makes it so special to you?" I asked.

"It's peaceful. It reminds me of the mystery of life. That we're just a little piece in a gigantic puzzle we can't see. And it reminds me that everything changes. For better or worse."

We wandered around the animals and their reproductions spread across the room, Nick absorbed in his memories. We moved slowly among the galleries, carrying our heavy coats in our hands. We walked, stopped, walked some more, stopped again. I felt drained. Is that what he felt when he visited here? Is this why he came here often? To anesthetize himself? I wish I could ask him. But there was still too much distance between us, and I knew I couldn't cut through it so easily, nor could I ignore it.

"Do you want a hot dog?" he asked when we left. "You should try one of these."

We walked toward a little hot-dog cart that was parked near the stairs leading up to the museum.

"Nick!" called the man behind the cart when we were close.

"Do you know him?" I asked.

"Fred. Yes, of course I know him. I used to come here a lot, always stopped to buy a hot dog. He'd tell stories about customers, things he'd see from his cart. Fun and interesting stories."

"Fred!" Nick shouted.

Fred came out of his cart, and the two hugged.

"How've you been, man? I haven't seen you in ages. You disappeared."

"Nine years."

"Is that right?"

"Oh yeah."

"I must say, you haven't changed a bit. How is—" Fred looked at me and stopped right there.

"Elinor's fine," Nick said. "I saw her yesterday at my mother's place. We're no longer together. This is Susan," he turned to me and smiled.

"Pleasure to meet you, Susan," Fred looked back at Nick somehow approving his new choice, if that's what I was.

"Any stories to share?" Nick asked.

"Plenty, but look at that line." He pointed to the long queue of customers.

"Your business is going great as usual. Not surprising," Nick said. "Give us two hot dogs, and we'll come back another time. We have to be somewhere in an hour."

Fred gave us the hot dogs, and when Nick pulled the wallet out of his pocket, he said,

"These are on me. But promise you'll come back."

"Of course, I promise."

We thanked him and walked away.

"So you must have been good friends."

"Yes, we were."

"And he knew Elinor too?"

"Yes. This is where we had our first date."

"At the museum?"

"Yes, I took her here. I was a nerd when I met her. I was into museums, readings, cultural clubs. I was in my early twenties, and I guess I was trying to compensate for my failures in school. She liked the museum, so we became regulars. We loved walking in Central Park, and after our walk, we would come here to relax. She said she wanted to imitate nature's grace when she danced. She found inspiration here."

"Did the two of you talk much?"

"Yes, we did. It wasn't like Emily and Andrew. We were friends, partners, accomplices. At least for a while."

It felt good to hear his stories, to discover him slowly. He was becoming more real.

When we arrived in front of the Dakota Apartments, we rang the intercom and waited. A voice directed us to the fifth floor. We took the elevator, and as soon as the door opened we saw a woman waiting for us. She was thin and tall, with pale skin; dark, long, and straight hair; a tentative smile; and the posture of a ballerina. She reminded me of Andrew's description of Emily and a bit of Elinor too, but perhaps she was more fragile than Elinor.

"Hi, I'm Christine. Nice to meet you." She offered her hand from a distance. She wasn't cold though; she was charming.

"Hi, Christine. I'm Nick, and this is Susan."

"Hi," she said, "please come in."

Once inside the apartment, she asked us to follow her to the dining room, which had a beautiful view of the city.

"This place is beautiful," I said.

"Yes, it is," Mrs. Bass said as she joined us. The resemblance between her and her daughter was striking, Mrs. Bass just an older version of Christine.

"We inherited this place from my parents," Mrs. Bass added, "and it'll be Christine's someday, when we're no longer here."

"Mother, always positive thoughts, right?" Christine gave her older self a severe look.

A maid came in with glasses of champagne that had raspberries at the bottom. Elegant, I thought.

"Would you like some before dinner?" Mr. Bass asked. His look was sweet and didn't share the austerity of his wife and daughter. He had the bearing of an artist too, though.

"That would be nice. Thanks," I said, and he handed me a glass.

"This is more than we could expect. I am—we are—very grateful," Nick said.

"Of course," Mr. Bass said. "Emily was very important to our daughter. We thought she would like to share her memories of Emily with you, help you find Andrew." His daughter turned and then looked down.

"Have you seen him recently?" I asked Christine.

"I ran into him. Once. He wanted to talk about Emily. We met at a café. He asked me so many questions. It was hard to stop him. Thank God I had a rehearsal and an excuse to leave."

"Do you know where he lives?" Nick asked.

"Andrew? Oh, no. I have no idea."

"How did he contact you?" I asked.

"He came to my school and waited for me outside. In fact, he came for days before finding me. My friends told me there was this weird guy waiting for me across the street. He stopped them and asked about me. They said he'd been there for a week or two. I had been invited by a friend from Paris to dance at his theater and so I was away for two weeks. When I came back, my friends told me about him. I had no idea that he was Andrew. And then, a few days later, I met him in the hall of my school."

"Did you recognize him when you saw him? Had he . . . changed?" I asked.

"Of course I recognized him. I knew him well. He and Emily were together for four years. We met often. I mean . . . not that we went out together or anything like that, but I would see him after our performances, or at friends' parties." She took a breath and added, "No, he hasn't changed at all."

"So you don't know where we can find him?" I insisted.

"No."

"Any clue might help." I explained the reason for our search, but she seemed disinterested.

"He invited me to watch an old movie with him," she continued. "He said he loved old movies and had found a theater where he liked to go often. The Thalia Theatre, I believe . . . yes, that's the one he mentioned. He asked me if I wanted to go there with him. I said I was busy, but maybe some other time. I haven't seen him since then."

"When was that?" Nick asked.

"A week or so ago."

"Oh . . . so he must still be here?" I said.

"I suppose, maybe . . .," she said, shrugging her shoulders.

"Did he tell you if he was working?" Nick asked.

"He said he was drawing, painting or something."

"Does he work for anyone?"

"I'm really not sure. Maybe he mentioned he had received an

advance from a buyer or publisher and thought could live on that for a while."

The maid came in with the meal. Over dinner we talked about Christine and her next performances and how much she loved ballet.

"My ex-wife's a ballerina, and I think she teaches ballet too," Nick said.

"Where?"

"At Juilliard."

"Really? That's where I work. What's her name?"

"Elinor Clarens."

"Elinor?"

"Do you know her?" Nick asked.

"Of course I do. We have two ballets together this season."

"What a small world . . .," Nick said, filling his glass with more wine. But was it really? He had decided to keep the diary and to keep . . . me. Did I have anything in common with Emily or Elinor? With Christine?

"You guys should come tomorrow to our performance. We'll dance the *Nutcracker*," Christine said. "It'll be fun."

I had to figure this out.

Nick started to say, "I don't think—"

"Why not? I'd love to go," I insisted.

"Let's think about it. We'll be really busy tomorrow."

"What time's the ballet?" I asked Christine.

"Eight. Two of my friends can't make it, so I have their tickets. I'll give them to you just in case."

I took the tickets and thanked her.

We stayed a little longer and left when it was half past nine.

"Let's walk," Nick said. "I don't want to take another taxi. It's not that cold tonight."

"Why don't you want to go tomorrow? Does it bother you to see Elinor?"

"No, it's not that."

"I've never seen a ballet before, and it would be fun to see Christine and Elinor dance."

"If you insist . . ." He finally surrendered.

When we arrived at the hotel, Nick said he wanted to read, and so he sat on the couch close to the window, grabbed a book from his backpack, and disappeared in it. I'd lost him again.

DAY THREE IN NEW YORK

"What's the plan for today?" I asked while Nick was still half-asleep.

"More research. We haven't found much yet."

"What about that movie theater? The one Christine mentioned? Shouldn't we go there?"

"Yes, sure, we could do that." He brought me a cup of coffee while I was still in bed, and then he sat at the desk and opened his computer.

"I found it," he said. "The Thalia Theatre. It's an independent cinema that shows classic films."

"Maybe he lives in that neighborhood?"

"That's actually possible. It's in Sunnyside, which, despite the name, could be a good fit for Andrew. It's a middle-class area in Queens. There are many old buildings from the twenties and thirties converted into apartments. The type of buildings Andrew might like and be able to afford, I guess."

"You talk about him as if you know him."

"He's revealed a lot to us, don't you think?"

Yes, I did, but I also sensed there was much more we didn't know.

We got to Sunnyside at around noon. It was a sunny day, and the sun was loud. When we got to the theater, it was closed. We walked around. The area was interesting. There were many little stores and barbershops, an Italian bakery, a pharmacy, kids with their back-packs, perhaps just out of school.

"Do you like kids?" he asked.

"I ... sure."

"What I mean is would you like to have kids?"

"I haven't thought about it. I know it's strange at my age."

"No, it's not," he said. "I don't know if I want kids. My life is so messy. I don't think I have the stability to be a father and, quite frankly, I don't want to be a shitty one like mine."

I thought about what he had just said and realized that perhaps we had much more in common than I had originally thought. And that was probably how I came to be part of his small world. I had been fearful of committing to things, to someone, partly because I thought I'd be unfit, messy, unstable. And I was probably so in love with my instability that I wouldn't have given it up for anything or anyone. Becoming fit, stable, organized, dependable would probably mean losing who I really was, and I wasn't ready for that.

"This is a place Andrew frequents," Nick said, reviewing thoughts and ideas, the data we had been collecting for the past few days. "He likes to come here to watch movies. Maybe he likes this area. Maybe he lives somewhere close. Maybe there is a store he likes."

After an hour or so, we arrived in front of what seemed a garage open to the public. It was selling books—in fact, comic books.

We entered and browsed the shelves. There was an entire section for superhero comics. That was what the bookstore mainly sold. But then, a door in the left corner of the room led to a smaller room with a couch and two big shelves filled with graphic novels. We entered, and Nick noticed that the novels were organized by author, in alpha-betical order.

"A ... B ... C ... P ... hmm ... Pratt, here it is," Nick said, "*The Truth About Me.*" He pulled the book from the shelf and showed it to me.

"So?"

"I wonder if Andrew ever came here. If people here know him. Let's ask."

I had never searched for anyone before, and so, I must admit, sometimes I didn't follow Nick's logic. But I trusted him.

Nick approached the counter. A man with a long beard, heavy black glasses, and tattoos all over his neck and arms was entering data in an old computer covered in dust.

"Do you guys need help?" the man asked.

"We're looking for the author of this book, Andrew Pratt," Nick showed him *The Truth About Me*.

"Oh, yeah, he comes around pretty often."

"Does he live in the area?"

"Who are you?"

"I'm a blogger, Nick Levitt, and this is Susan Blanc. She works with me. We're doing a profile on him."

"I don't know where he lives. He does come here from time to time. Give me your business card and I'll give it to him if I see him."

"Didn't you say he comes here often?"

"Now that I think about it, that was an overstatement. Last time I saw him was . . . I don't recall. Three weeks maybe? But he does come here, and I'll give him your business card if I see him."

"OK, thanks," Nick said, and pulled a business card from his jacket.

"Sure. I'll do what I can."

We shook hands and left.

"I'm sure he knew more than he wanted us to believe," Nick said, as soon as we were alone.

"Why would he not share what he knew?"

"To protect Andrew?"

"Protect him from what?"

"Who knows . . . In any event, we should keep coming here, check the schedule of movies at the Thalia Theatre, hang out in the neighborhood. Maybe we're closer than we think to finding him. Or we are not."

We walked back to the subway and returned to the hotel to rest before leaving for the ballet.

"Are you sure you want to go?" he asked.

"Yes, I am. But we don't have to if you don't feel like it."

"It's not a big deal," he said. He poured some scotch and sat on what it was now *his* couch. That was the sign that he wanted to read or be left alone, so I took a nap. He woke me up when it was time to leave. We took a shower, got dressed, and left.

The theater was packed. Our seats were in the front row, central. I could almost touch the curtain with my feet if I extended my legs. I was curious, eager to see, learn, discover who knows what. I leaned back and waited for the ballet to begin. When it started, I immediately recognized Elinor. And then I saw Christine. Both had major roles. Their performances seemed perfect to me, and they were smiling, but I could hear their whispering to each other and the other dancers, commenting on one move or another, breathing heavily. I sensed that their smiles were hiding stress, perhaps unhappiness too. I was discovering Emily, and perhaps Elinor, Christine, Andrew, and Nick too. Their small world of which I had become part, clearly not by chance.

Christine had told us to wait for them after the ballet. She said there would be a reception for the artists and a few guests, and we should join them. Nick didn't seem enthusiastic, but after I asked, he agreed to go. When Elinor and Christine arrived, we all drank champagne around a tall round pedestal table with a long red-velvet tablecloth draped over it.

"Did you like it?" Christine asked.

"You were both fabulous," I said. Elinor eyed me with a smug look that made me almost sad or sick. Were we competitors? I didn't want that.

"Can I get you ladies another drink?" Nick asked.

"Champagne," said Christine.

"I'll come with you," Elinor said, and she and Nick disappeared into the crowd.

"Aren't you jealous?" Christine asked me.

"Jealous?"

"Aren't you and Nick together?"

I smiled and said, "Who knows. But, no, I'm not jealous."

"News on Andrew?"

"No big news, except we found a comic book store he seems to frequent in Queens."

"How do you know that?"

"A guy who works there told us, and he told us he would give Andrew Nick's business card and ask him to contact us."

"He'll never do that."

"Why not?"

"If he knows Andrew, he knows he hates journalists. He doesn't trust them."

"But a blogger is not exactly—"

"I don't think it would make any difference to him."

"How do you know?" I asked. I didn't have the impression she knew Andrew that well. The comment had surprised me.

"Oh . . . I remember Emily talking about it. When a journalist wanted to interview her, Andrew tried so hard to convince her not to do it. Emily didn't listen to him, and once the article was published, he didn't talk to her for days."

"So Andrew and Emily were in New York for a while before Emily . . ."

"Yes. She came here for performances and stuff. When that happened, he came with her. But most of the time we spent in L.A. That's where we trained."

"I see. Well, Andrew's aversion to journalists is bad news." I wanted Nick to hear that and looked for him, but I couldn't see him. He and Elinor had been away for longer than I expected. I told Christine I needed to use the ladies' room but, in fact, went looking for Nick.

When I got closer to the restrooms, I saw Elinor leaving the men's room, and a few seconds later, Nick came out as well. I let my purse fall to the floor. A man came close to collect it for me and asked if I was OK. Nick looked at me and didn't say a word. I didn't either. I left, called a taxi, and returned to the hotel.

As I was collecting my things and preparing to leave, Nick showed up.

"Where are you going? Can we talk?"

I looked at him, turned to my suitcase, and closed it. I really didn't have anything to say.

"I'm sorry," he said.

I took my suitcase, slammed the door to the room, and went down the street. I called a taxi and asked the driver to take me to any hotel far from there where I could spend the night.

"How far?" the driver asked.

"Far."

He drove for a while, and then parked in front of a hotel with big flags hanging from a balcony. I paid for the ride, and without even checking the place, decided to stay. I was too exhausted and drained to even think. The desk clerk told me there was a room available. I said I would take it before he even told me how much it was. When the man told me the price, I looked around and finally saw where I was. I must have looked cheap to the driver. Perhaps I was. And perhaps I belonged there. I decided to stay. At least I'd be alone. The man gave me my key and said that I would find the room on the top floor, the twelfth. Good, I thought. The farther from the ground, the better.

The price was cheap, but the room looked even cheaper. It was small and old, the kind of old that makes things look dirty. There was a single bed; a window at its edge; a closet on the left; and between the bed and the door, a cramped bathroom with a shower, a small sink, and a toilet. I placed my suitcase on the bed and opened it. I took a long hot shower, put on a T-shirt, and went closer to the window to look outside and wait until I'd be tired enough to crash. I felt exhausted, and I felt pressure on my chest. My heart was beating too fast for me to surrender to sleep. I looked for some alcohol, but there wasn't any. I lay on the bed waiting for peace, but I kept seeing Elinor and Nick in the men's room, having sex. I closed my eyes to find relief, pressed them shut harder, but I heard a couple having sex in a room below me. They were so loud they seemed to be everywhere. And a baby started crying. A woman, probably his mother, was yelling at him. That should be it, I thought. But then a drunk knocked on my door and asked me to open it. That night I could have confused hell with heaven. Or maybe I wasn't confused at all.

I checked my emails. There was a note from Matt.

I went to the beach today and thought about you. I hope you're having fun out there.

LOOKING FOR ANDREW

I woke up early that morning and checked my phone. There were no phone messages, no emails.

I looked at the hotel room. It was depressing. If I wanted to stay in New York, I had to find a better place. So I packed again, checked out, and left.

I went to a café close to the hotel, connected my computer to the internet, and started looking for apartments to rent. I felt I needed time to finish what I had started, although I wasn't completely sure what that was.

My chair was uncomfortable, and the music was too loud, irritating, but I managed to isolate myself, and after a while I found an apartment in the East Village that looked interesting. It was a studio, but it didn't seem too small. I called the owner and scheduled a meeting with her to see the place. A few hours later, I had agreed to sublet the studio until the end of January. Once the landlady closed the door behind her, I lay in bed and remained looking at the ceiling for a while, my coat and shoes on, my head and heart somewhere else. I hadn't thought this through. Staying in New York until January for what? For Andrew? Myself? Nick? What was I going to do for two months? I replied to Matt's email with a short message. I wrote that

Nick and I had stopped working together, but that I would stay in New York for a while. He replied right away.

What happened with Nick? Why are you staying?

I had no answers to those questions, so after trying to compose a reply two or three times, I left my new apartment in search of distractions.

I returned to Queens, to the comic book store where Nick and I had been the day before. I didn't want to give up on Andrew.

I arrived there shortly before closing time. The guy Nick and I had talked to was cleaning up and let me in "only for few minutes."

"I didn't come here to buy anything," I confessed right away. "I came to talk to you. My friend and I are no longer working together, but I still need to find Andrew Pratt."

He looked skeptical.

"I'm not a journalist. I'm a teacher," I insisted. "I teach psychology. Andrew came to visit my class in L.A. once, and we talked. At that time, I didn't know who he was. He came looking for me."

"Ms. . . . ?"

"Susan, call me Susan."

"Susan, I want to be honest with you. I saw Andrew this morning. He came to buy some books. I told him you guys were looking for him, but as soon as he heard the word 'blogger,' he said he wasn't interested."

"Yes, I know. One of his friends told me he's not exactly a fan of media, journalists . . . but I'm not a journalist, or a blogger. And he looked for me before, so . . ."

He looked down and around, undecided.

"Fine," he then said, "give me your number and I'll give it to him."

I wrote down my number and email address.

"Please tell him to call or write anytime," I said. I bought a copy of *The Truth About Me* and left.

I walked for a while, sometimes stopping at a store or little market, unsure of what to do, where to go. And then I found myself in front of the Thalia Theatre. At night, the theater looked more inter-esting than it did during the day, more intimate, a story box that enticed me. The movie that night was *The Big Sleep*, with Humphrey Bogart. I hadn't seen it and didn't have anything better to do, so I decided to give it a try.

The movie was dark and slow, I was confused and tired, and after twenty minutes or so I fell asleep. I still can't say what the movie was about. I woke up during the closing credits, and thought it was probably best for me to call a taxi and go home. As I was looking for a taxi, I thought I saw Christine and Andrew walking, hand in hand, across the street. I rubbed my eyes to make sure I wasn't dreaming, but they were still there. Andrew and Christine were, in fact, holding hands. I tried to follow them, first with my eyes, and then I walked, ran, toward them, but they disappeared inside an alley, and I was too tired to run anymore. So I lost them, or I lost whatever I thought I had seen. But if what I had seen was real, if Christine and Andrew were together, why had she lied to us? Why tell us about the Thalia Theatre and then lie about her relationship with Andrew?

I went back to my apartment and checked my emails. I had none from Nick. I felt lost and sad. The radio was playing Louis Armstrong and Ella Fitzgerald's "Summertime." I poured some wine and let my thoughts wander.

Summertime, and the livin' is easy . . . Don't you cry . . .

The words of that song didn't make any sense to me. The sound didn't evoke summer. it was not summer, and living wasn't easy. Everything now seemed nonsense, and I thought I should probably give up the nonsensical search for Andrew. My instinct was wrong, and my tears were louder than my screaming on that rooftop. Maybe that night Nick had just been trying to prepare me for this. Well, he had failed.

One of these mornings you're gonna rise up singing
And you'll spread your wings and you'll take to the sky
More tears. I felt cold.

When I woke up the next day, I realized I still had my clothes and shoes on. I freed myself from them, took a shower, got dressed, and returned to the bookstore. No, I probably shouldn't give up on that nonsense. I wasn't ready to.

"Any news from Andrew?" I asked the man I'd talked to the day before.

"No news."

"Do you know if he's dating anyone?"

"Andrew?"

"Yes."

"How's that have to do with a profile on him? Why do you care?"

I didn't answer that question as I couldn't.

"I've seen him with a girl pretty often." I lied, I tried. "But I'm not sure if they are actually dating."

"Is it a girl with black, long, straight hair, thin . . . tall . . . ?"

"Yes, precisely."

"Yes, I think they're a couple."

So they were a couple. I had not dreamed that.

"Thanks . . . ?"

"Dave."

"Thanks, Dave."

"Look, I like you. I didn't like your friend. Trust me, leave the man alone. If he feels like it, he'll reach out to you. Otherwise, let him go."

I nodded, thanked him, and left. I took a long walk in the neighborhood with no specific plan or idea. After a while, exhausted from my wanderings, I stopped at a café and surrendered to my memories, which were now almost intoxicating. They tasted like Nick. I must have ordered something, but when the waiter came with my order I was surprised. He asked me if anything was wrong with the food. I cried.

"I'm sorry," I said. "This is perfect. It's nothing. I'll be fine."

Someone called him, and he left.

Why did everything always have to be so complicated for me? A cockroach ran under my table. I moved my foot, and it froze and remained still for a while. Didn't run or move. Impressive, I thought. That little thing was playing dead to survive. Why do we act the way we do? Is it our instinct or is it our reason that moves us? Should we follow the first or the second? I had followed my instinct with Nick, and there I was, alone with a cockroach that now seemed so beautiful to me. I didn't touch it. Its instinct had been right to suggest it should remain still. Had my instinct been right too?

While I was lost in my thoughts, Andrew appeared.

I thought I was dreaming again, and so I kept thinking, or dreaming. He stopped in front of the café's window, just in front of my table, and stared at me. He was alone. We looked at each other, neither of us moving. Then my phone rang, and the sound woke me up from my trance. Andrew was actually there, I had not dreamed it. I called to him. He turned and walked away.

"Andrew!" I called again. "Andrew, please!" I called louder, and I left the café. "Please, stop!"

He accelerated, I started running toward him, but I fell. I should have gotten up and followed him, but I didn't feel like moving. I wasn't playing dead. I felt dead. He turned, stopped, and walked back.

"Are you OK?"

I looked up. Andrew seemed so tall. It was early afternoon, and the sun was so bright I could barely see his face.

"What are you doing here?"

I remained silent, unsure of what to say, but then I tried to explain.

"It's complicated. I . . . was looking for you."

"Why?"

"You know why."

"The blog? My novels?"

"Can we talk?"

"I'm not interested in the blog, I'm sorry. You can keep the journal, publish all of it, I don't care. Really, do whatever you want with it."

"Why do you say that? There's something you should know. We have posted some of your drawings and parts of your writing. People don't know who you are but are dying to know. They're crazy about your work."

Trying to make sense, to convince him to stay, with no energy left in my body was hard, but I added, "I loved *Lies We Tell*. I read a copy of it. It's beautiful. How could Folberg miss it?"

"Do you know my agent?"

"I was looking for you, I told you. I talked to Emily's mother, Ed, Joe, Matt..."

"What? How did you find them?

"Hard work. Luck. Both."

He studied me where I sat on the curb. Then something crossed his mind, his look changed. He seemed more understanding—or curious.

"Were you having lunch at that café? Maybe I could join you."

"That would be great," I said.

He finally offered me his hand, I got up, and we walked back to the café. I felt a sense of relief and closed my eyes for a second. Did I make it? Was I with him?

When we were seated, the waiter came to take his order. My backpack was still on the chair where I had left it.

"Why did you come to visit my class that day?" I asked.

"I wanted to meet you," he said, studying me. I must have looked different from the time we'd met in my office. I felt different.

"I go back to L.A. a lot," he continued. "Memories, you know. And my sister still lives there. I moved back to New York last year, but I've gone back to Los Angeles at least four times since then. I came to your class on one of those visits. I had read the blog. I looked for you, found that you were teaching psychology, and wanted to see who you were and whether I could trust you."

"And you let me keep your journal. So you did trust me?"

He didn't respond. There was some silence, and then I said, "I saw you walking with Christine, holding hands."

He suddenly looked suspicious or scared, and he moved his chair as if he were thinking of leaving.

"I know it seems like I'm stalking you, but I'm not. I was just looking for people who knew you. I needed to find you, but I'm not even sure why." I felt sick, vulnerable. I was probably just exhausted. I hoped he would have mercy for me and give me a chance.

"What about your friend?"

He did.

"Nick?"

"Yes."

"We're not doing this together anymore," I said. I wasn't going to say more, but then I felt he deserved to know more, to see me, to make up his mind as to whether I was worth his time. I needed him to think that I was. I needed to believe that I was. "We were together. But then he cheated on me with his ex-wife. I guess life rarely goes according to plans."

"Seems so." He raised his eyebrows and took a sip of his drink. "You said you wanted to interview me?"

"Yes, I do."

"Are you going to write about me? My work?"

Right. What would I do with my interview? I actually had not thought about it.

"I'm not a writer or a reporter," I confessed. "I mean, I've written in the past, but I don't know if I can actually . . ."

"Do you want to try?"

Yes, I should try, I thought. I should write my interview, finish what I had started, and then try to publish it somewhere. Why not? After all, writing about Andrew had been my idea.

"Can we do the interview tomorrow?" I asked. "I need to think about what I want to ask you, read your novels again. In fact, now that I think about it, I don't have *Lies* with me. I read it, but I need to read it again before we talk. Nick had a copy Joe lent him."

"I have one at my place. I could lend it to you. I live close by," he said, and asked for the check.

When we left the café I followed him through the alleys, and soon we arrived at his place.

"Let's use the stairs," he said. "I don't like elevators."

His place was a loft packed with drawings, some even hanging from the ceiling, some piled up on top of others on the floor. The drawings were throbbing with life and pain. They were so loud that they almost hurt. The portraits and sketches seemed to be screaming. And among them, I saw one that looked like me. It was a sketch I thought he might be using for one of his novels. The woman's eyes were crying with no tears, and she seemed trapped, compressed in what seemed to be a box. I stared at that drawing for a while. Her eyes, lips, face were mine.

"She seems to be crying, but she's not."

"She *is* crying," he said.

"But there are no tears."

"You know her, she speaks to you, so you know she's crying."

I remained silent and he added, "The tears you don't see are the ones that hurt the most, aren't they?"

He came closer, and we both stared at the drawing.

"What do you see in there?"

I thought about what I wanted to say, but then he spoke again.

"I'll tell you what I saw when I drew her. I made that sketch after meeting with you that day in your office. This is what I saw. But perhaps there's more of myself than yourself in her."

"What do you mean?" I asked.

He smiled, "I wish I knew. I'm still trying to figure it out."

I looked at that drawing again. It was disturbingly real. I couldn't take my eyes away from it.

"I'll give it to you after you finish your piece on me. Maybe we'll understand by then what was crossing my mind when I made it. You might help me figure this out."

I liked the idea.

"When did you do all these drawings?" I asked, looking around. So much art.

"I started drawing as soon as I arrived in New York, and now there's someone interested in buying my work for big money. Well, big money for me."

"You're no longer writing novels?"

"Not at the moment. After *Lies*, I wrote another novel, *How Did I Get Here?*, and found someone interested in publishing it."

"What's it about?"

"Me after Emily."

"Can I see it?"

"I'll give you a copy, but please don't share it with anyone, and it can't be part of your piece on me either. I need to publish it first."

"Of course."

He went to one of his shelves and pulled out *Lies* and his other novel.

"Here you are. We'll meet whenever you're ready."

"Sounds perfect," I said, looked at the apartment once more, and left. It seemed unreal, but I had just met Andrew.

ABOUT ANDREW

I ordered pizza and returned to my apartment to read and take notes for the interview. The streets were crowded, busy, noisy. I was alone. There was an old radio in my apartment. I checked to make sure it worked, and I tuned it to a jazz station. The jazz slowly silenced the noise so I could finally start reading.

The narrative of *Lies* was built around short dialogues, and the drawings were intense, evocative. Like his journal, *Lies* described Andrew's first meeting with Emily in that café. In his drawings, she looked like I had imagined her, a beautiful ballerina. Andrew looked more clumsy than in person. This must be how he saw himself, I thought. Or perhaps he had changed after Emily's death.

I read and saw Andrew's initial romance with Emily, their later misunderstandings, their silences, the things he thought but didn't tell her, Emily's performances, the parties after the shows, their fights, his sleepless nights after an argument, the time she left to sleep at Christine's place. And then Emily's strict diet, Andrew's obsession with junk food, her discipline, his disorder, her clarity, his confusion. The story didn't allude to Emily's death.

I looked at the clock. It was almost nine p.m., but it felt later. I looked outside my window. A couple, holding hands, passed by and made my solitude bitter. I thought about Nick, and I checked the phone to see if there was a message from him. I leaned against the couch, closed my eyes, and imagined receiving a text or a call. When I opened my eyes, there was even more emptiness than before. I poured myself some scotch and drank enough to numb my feelings. When the noise in my head seemed less loud, or at least softer, I started reading *How Did I Get Here?*

The story described his agent's reaction to *Lies*, how Andrew was upset and looked to his friends for support. But then, discouraged, he decided to leave and go to New York. The narrative proceeded slowly, revolving around a few significant events. Andrew with a woman who had no name other than "my love." This woman reminded me of Emily, but I knew it wasn't her. They met in front of her ballet school, talked about the past, and ended up in bed that very night. She was fragile, insecure, disciplined, demanding. Andrew was attentive to her. He attended her performances and the parties. He stuck to her diet and sleeping routine, read magazines and newspapers, watched documentaries. He appeared happy in his drawings, but that happiness seemed forced, faked. I thought those drawings described too many compromises with the person I thought he was. But the story also described his rediscovered passion for art, and that felt real. The last drawing was clearly for Emily: Andrew sitting on a bench in a park, smoking a cigarette, his gaze wandering into space. There's no one around, just him and his thoughts. He thinks, "I could have been a better person for you."

When I finished reading, I closed the empty pizza box with the ugly leftovers and trashed it. I opened the window to cleanse myself with some fresh air, and I stayed there for a while, enjoying the cold on my cheeks and forehead until it almost hurt. I put Janis Joplin on and raised the volume as high as I could. I screamed. Someone yelled at me from the street. I laughed.

I went to bed sometime after two. My LP was stuck on a passage of one of her songs. It was on the same passage when I opened my eyes. It was four. I drank what was left of the scotch and then trashed the bottle and my notes. I should have started writing a list of questions for my interview, but I was too tired. I sent Andrew an email and told him I had just finished reading his two novels and that I could meet him later that day. I didn't know what I would ask, but I felt ready. I had entered his chaos.

I wrote to Matt.

I'm OK. Don't worry about me.

I turned off the light and went back to bed.

I woke up at noon. The sun was piercing the window.

I checked my emails. There was one from Andrew confirming our meeting, and one from Matt saying he would come to New York in two days. He asked me if he could stay with me. I thought about telling him not to come, but I felt too sleepy to even think about an answer. I made some coffee and worked on my questions for Andrew. I stayed at my desk for a while, jotting ideas and notes, random thoughts, and I stopped only when it was time to go. When I arrived at the café Andrew was sipping coffee and reading a novel by someone whose name I didn't recognize.

"A new author," he said, showing me the book. "I like to support new artists," he added.

"Of course you do. Is it any good?"

"He has potential," he said and smiled. That was the first full smile I had seen on his face since we first met. From his journal and novels Andrew seemed incapable of smiling. But there he was, smiling.

The waiter came. I ordered some coffee and pulled the notebook from my backpack.

"Are you recording or typing?"

"I'll just take notes. I'm old-fashioned."

"Old-fashioned is my world. So you read my novels . . . What do you think?"

"Wait a minute. I'm supposed to interview you, not the other way round." I smiled.

"Yes, sure. I'm just curious."

"You have a way of pulling me into your life that is unbelievable. I walk with you, become one of your friends, I'm there sitting on the bench with you, sharing your thoughts. The drawings are art. I love your use of shading, your dialogues. Your work is exceptional. And it calms me down. Makes me breathe."

"Really? How?"

"By slowing down the pace of life, by making things look more natural, less fake."

I'm not lying to you, Andrew. Let me in, my eyes spoke. I think he listened. Then the waiter came with my coffee, and I started asking my questions.

"Ready?"

He nodded.

"How were you as a kid?"

"Solitary," he said, and stopped there, as if he were waiting for me to ask more, but I didn't. That wasn't enough. He knew. I waited.

"I lived inside my comics," he added, as if every word were painful. "I grew up reading *Peanuts* and thought life looked much better and more interesting in those cartoons than it did in reality. I spent my time reading and collecting comic books, and I isolated myself from my classmates, my family. My father taught psychology to grad students at NYU. My mother was interested in politics. I never understood that. We lived here, in New York. This is where I grew up." He took a deep breath and continued. "My mother volunteered here and there, taught students with disabilities, was often away. I always wondered why she spent so much time with other kids and families rather than with her own. She never *volunteered* with us. Ironic, no?

"I have a brother and a sister. Both older. I didn't talk much to my brother. I talked more with my sister, but not that much. She married when she was sixteen, and so I didn't spend my teen years with her. She was also very different from me anyhow. She was all about acting, on the stage and in real life. She was loud and extroverted. We probably talking more now than we did then. Not that any of us has changed. We're probably just lonelier now and need each other more than we did back then."

"Are your parents alive?"

"My mother died a few years ago. She was an alcoholic."

He didn't seem sad.

"We tried to help her, but it was impossible. She was a great liar. She'd go to rehab, tell us it was over, then start drinking again. I remember that stench of alcohol every time I went near her. She repulsed me."

His gaze wandered, and he seemed to have drifted somewhere else. I tried to imagine what he was thinking, where he was.

"What about your father?"

"He left her, remarried, had two children. His second wife died too. One of his sons has some serious mental issues. So his new life wasn't easy either."

"Is he still alive?"

"I guess."

"You don't know? Don't talk to him?"

"I haven't talked to him in years. I don't resent him or anything like that. I just don't feel anything for him."

Andrew answered my questions without questioning them. He seemed to have surrendered to me. He seemed to trust me.

"When did you start writing novels?" I asked.

"As soon as I learned to write and draw. Second grade maybe. My teacher told us to write a Christmas story. She said, 'Be creative, surprise me.' I made a series of cartoons. In my story, I ran away from home on Christmas eve and boarded a fishing vessel. The captain found me only after the vessel had set sail, and he let me stay and help in the kitchen. I spent Christmas on that vessel with the crew, and saw killer whales, sharks, and all sorts of big fish that I dreamed of seeing in an aquarium. That was my story."

"Wow."

There had been colors in his mind, and hope, and dreams.

"How did you come up with that?"

"I wanted my mother to take me to an aquarium that was far from home. She promised she would, but she didn't have a car, and my father was working. The next day my relatives would come to visit us for Christmas. I knew nobody would take me to the aquarium then, so I took myself there."

"That's beautiful."

He smiled. "Maybe."

"Did anyone finally take you there though?"

"No," he said, and looked into his coffee.

"Do you think you became more truthful to reality as you grew up?"

"Is there a truth? I'm not sure any more. I think I just try to be truthful to myself. Like in that Christmas story. Isn't that what matters?"

He was right, I thought. I became temporarily lost in my own thoughts as he continued.

"My relation with reality, with the present, is complicated. I'm fond of the past. It looks more real to me. It makes me feel safe. It talks to me about myself more than the present does. Interesting, isn't it?"

"*Lies* seems to be built on that idea too, the idea of a present focused on the past. Am I right?" I asked.

"In a way. Sometimes, when I was with Emily, I felt stuck in the past and it was hard to live the present with her. It was as if we were living on separate temporal planes. That created distance between us." A loud ambulance passed, and I lost him momentarily. Then he continued.

"I kept my struggles and my doubts to myself, and that was wrong. I felt I was the victim of a scam, that I was someone out of space and time. I built assumptions about people's behavior, about Emily's behavior, and I didn't really try to understand her. I blamed all our issues on her. I never compromised. She was wrong. I was right. And then she left me."

I wanted to ask him what he meant by that, but I wasn't sure he was ready to talk about it. Or perhaps I wasn't.

"Your agent didn't like *Lies*, but judging from your journal that mirrors the novel and from the comments of those of us who have read it, it seems that your agent missed a prize."

"I don't know about that. I never won a prize."

"The pages of your journal resonated with so many readers," I insisted. "Nick and I received hundreds of emails from people who wanted to talk about your stories, people who asked about you."

He listened but didn't seem interested.

"What do you think about *How Did I Get Here?*" He asked. He still seemed more interested in my reaction.

"It's disturbingly real, even when you don't fit my idea of you."

He looked like he wanted to ask me what I meant by that, so I asked, "Who's the woman in the story? Christine?"

"I'm not sure, actually."

"The woman in the story seems to believe in your art. What about Emily?"

"I don't know. I hope she did."

"Why not publish *Lies*?"

He didn't respond. We finished sipping our coffees, and then talked more about his life in New York and how it felt to be back.

"Did you have more questions for me?" he then asked.

"Not at the moment," I said. "I think I've got enough to work on, but I'll call or email you if I do."

"Could I read your piece before you publish it?"

"Of course."

We got up and walked to the door.

On the way home, I thought about the interview and what I should write, and everything around me disappeared. The Thalia Theatre was showing *Rear Window*, the Hitchcock classic from the 50s with James Stewart and Grace Kelly. I was too tired to work so I decided to stop there. I needed to let Andrew's story sink in. His family, his past, Emily, Christine . . . Had he completely rejected Emily's death? Was he in love with Christine?

"How many?" the guy at the box office asked.

"Just me."

He issued the ticket, I paid, and entered.

There were only a few people in the audience, each sitting far from the others, perhaps trying to create the illusion of being there alone. I wanted to feel the same, and so I sat at the back corner of the room. The movie was beautiful, a rip in time that reminded me of Andrew's novel. Their slow pace and its intensity were similar. I felt good, somehow safe from the chaos of the city. Maybe now I understood what Andrew had described. Feeling safe in the past. Life seemed so simple back then. Or perhaps it did, just because I wasn't part of it.

When I left the theater I decided to walk a bit before going home. I walked for a while, longer than I thought I would, until I was too tired to keep walking, until I lost sense of time. And when I realized I had, I looked around, and it was dark. When I passed by an Italian restaurant, I thought about that dinner with Nick at his place, and his story of the Italian chef. I suddenly felt colder. I walked fast to the subway, then fast from the station to my apartment, and soon I was home. I closed the door, crashed on my bed, and dreamed about neighbors, murders, dancers, pianists, and parties. A life that was simple compared to mine. Nick wasn't there. I had lost him.

LITTLE AND BIG LIES

The next day I stared at a blank screen on my computer for hours. Nick wasn't the reason. I wasn't ready to think about him, I didn't want to. There was something else. I felt there were missing pieces to Andrew's story, something I had seen, heard, read that didn't feel right to me, and I didn't know exactly what it was. So many questions were buzzing in my head in a confused order, with no thread and at times no logic, it seemed. Too many questions to be able to write. Perhaps some of those questions were not about Andrew and his story. But some were. Some were questions for Christine. I remembered she said she was working at Julliard, so I headed there, hoping I would meet her. I waited on a bench in front of the main entrance, but after a while I felt tired and stood up to leave.

"Who are you looking for?" a guy in his early twenties asked me.

"Is it so clear I'm looking for someone?"

"If you are, maybe I could help."

"I'm looking for Christine Bass."

"Christine's in my class. We've just finished today's session. Unless she stops to talk with someone, she should be out any moment."

I thanked the guy and waited. Christine didn't come out as soon as he had predicted though, and after waiting for her for quite some time, I left. As I was walking to the subway, she passed me by.

"Susan? What are you doing here?" she asked.

"Actually, I came to see you."

"Me? Why?"

"I have some questions about Andrew."

"I think I've told you everything I know."

"Like the fact that the two of you are dating?"

She froze.

"How do you know?"

I looked at her. She was truly thin.

"Andrew told me."

She was about to say something, but I cut her off.

"Why did you lie about that?"

She turned and started walking away. I grabbed her wrist.

"I need your help. Actually, I don't even know why I'm here. You lied to me. You'll probably do it again."

"I don't think I can help you, Susan. I'm sorry."

"Nick cheated on me . . . with Elinor." I didn't know why I said that. I wasn't looking for her pity or anything like that. I just wanted her to feel my misery. Maybe we had something to share. She turned toward me.

"What? That's not true. Elinor is not interested in Nick. She's dating someone."

"What can I say? Maybe she changed her mind."

"I'm sorry."

I didn't say a word.

"What about the work you guys were doing together?" she then asked.

"We're no longer doing it together. I'm writing the piece on my own. And I met Andrew."

"Why are you doing this?"

"I'm trying to help him."

"I don't think Andrew needs your help."

"Really? Has he realized that Emily's dead? Do you talk about it?

"No, but . . ."

"But what? Do you know that in his journal he keeps referring to Emily as the woman who *broke up* with him?"

"I haven't read his diary."

"You don't need to. I'm sure you know what I'm talking about."

"I . . ."

"You do, right?"

She looked down, and started biting her fingernails, or what was left of them. She looked at me, perhaps trying to decide what to do.

"Let's get a cup of coffee. I need caffeine."

I nodded, and we headed to a café a few blocks away.

"This is where Emily and Andrew met the first time. She always talked about that meeting," Christine said.

She ordered a double espresso and sat at a table outside.

"When Emily started dating Andrew, she and I were together. I mean, she and I were dating."

She stopped to check my reaction. I can't even say whether I was surprised to hear that. I guess I was more overwhelmed with her pain than surprised. She must have sensed that, as she continued.

"Nobody knew that we were dating, but everyone knew we had a special bond. Then Emily met Andrew, and we were over. But that was nothing compared to her death. At times I feel I died with her. You can't understand. I wouldn't know how to explain." She turned to hide her tears.

"When I saw Andrew again, it was like having her back. They had been together for four years, pieces of her were all over him, some of her sayings, her comments on people and food, her reactions to jokes. When I saw him, I saw her, or maybe I just wanted to see her. What-ever it was, I felt almost whole again. He flirted with me and I gave up, confused as I was. I haven't told anyone else about this because I know it won't last. I wish it could. It'd be so much simpler." She turned, looked somewhere far away, and puffed her cigarette.

"Does Andrew know about you and Emily?"

"No. She wouldn't want that. I would never tell him."

"Don't you think Andrew should know?"

She inhaled deeply on her cigarette, closed her eyes, and swung her head as if she were following some music I couldn't hear. And then she stopped and stared at me.

"I'm sorry for you, and I'm sorry for Andrew," I said. And I was sorry for myself. She looked straight to me, then turned, got up, and left. I didn't try to stop her. Didn't need to. I had had enough.

I walked for hours without any direction or plan. I walked until I felt my body was about to collapse. I think I wanted it to. I sat on a bench and called my father.

"Hi, it's Susan."

"Susan? What a nice surprise! How are you?"

"I'm fine. I'm in New York."

"You are? When did you arrive?"

"I've been here for a few days now."

"Are you here for work?"

"Yes and no. I'm writing an article about an author, but it's not for school."

"Then why are you writing it?"

I didn't respond.

"How long are you going to stay?"

"Maybe until January. I'm not sure yet."

"Why don't you come over for dinner tonight?"

"OK," I said, surprising myself. "Is your address the same?"

"Yes, I'm still here."

"Is . . . Are you and Evelyn still together?"

"Yes. She's here as well." There was some silence. I really didn't know what to hope . . . for him, for myself . . .

"What time should I come by?"

"Let's do five, but come before if you like."

"Five? That's early."

"Well, it's for the baby."

"A baby?"

There was more silence, and then he said, "We had a baby five years ago. Evelyn was pregnant when you visited last time, but she was only in her second month, and preferred to keep it confidential."

"I see. Basically she's been in her second month pretty much for the past six years or so . . ."

"Susan, wait."

I hung up, took the subway, and returned to my apartment. When I arrived, I lay on my bed and stared at the ceiling. I must have been there for a long time, since I saw the light in my room change from bright yellow, to lighter yellow, to dusk, to shades of pink, orange, and blue, darker blue. At first there was so much noise, confused images having nothing to do with each other, and pressing the sides of my head. They seemed not to want to let go. They seemed not to want to let me go. But then the room became dark, and exhausted. They gave up, or I did.

I think I was half sleeping when I remembered or dreamed about my mother. We were playing hide-and-seek in our courtyard and when she saw me, she jumped high with wild enthusiasm. But then the dream became confused. She looked sad, very sad. "Mom, why are you sad?" I asked. "I'm here with you." She didn't respond, and she disappeared. I looked for her everywhere in the house, and finally found her, hanging with her head bent on the side, her eyes half-open.

I woke up covered in sweat. It was early morning. I freed myself from the clothes of the day before, took a long hot shower, and thought about how my life would be if my mother were still alive or if I had better memories of my time with her. My past didn't feel safe, and I had been trying to run from it all my life. I made some coffee and checked my emails. There was one from Nick.

Hey,

How are you? Are you in New York or LA? I still have trouble figuring out what happened between us. I can't ask you to forgive me. I don't deserve that. I just need you to know that I miss you.

I sipped my coffee and read those lines again and again. I wondered whether I should answer. But what would I say? My email would be an outburst. And I didn't want him to know how I felt. Unfortunately, I wasn't doing that well. And, sadly, despite everything, I missed him too.

I stared at a blank screen for what seemed an eternity, trapping my hands under my thighs so as not to write. And then I pushed myself outside the apartment, hoping Nick, his email, or both would not follow me. But they did. I looked for distractions. Could Andrew or Christine help?

Despite my interview with Andrew and my chat with Christine, I still felt there were gaps in their story. I felt some important pieces of their puzzle were still missing. And yet I wasn't sure what they were, and at times wondered whether they actually might be pieces of my own puzzle. Had my story become so intertwined with Andrew's that I needed to figure it out before writing about him?

A MISSING PIECE

A ndrew had said his father taught psychology to grad students at NYU, and the more I thought about it, the more his name sounded familiar. Pratt. I didn't take a class from him, but I think he was there when I was a student. I did some research and found that Henry Pratt, Andrew's father, was still teaching at NYU. He was no longer full-time, but he taught a seminar in the fall. There was a photo of him on his profile page. Andrew looked so much like his father. A more artistic version of him. Or was it the tie in his father's photo that made the older man look more serious? I couldn't say. The profile photo had not been updated in years and showed a man in his late fifties. I thought Andrew's father should be in his eighties by now. His list of publications was scarce to say the least, mainly what appeared to be a few short essays on very technical themes. I looked for them online, but they were not available. One of them that was part of an Oxford collection on personality disorders, though, seemed to be available at the NYU bookstore. Partly driven by my curiosity, partly by my memories, I decided to go to that bookstore to check it out. I used to go to that bookstore when I was in school. I may have even worked on that Oxford collection, but I wasn't sure.

Once at the bookstore, I found Henry Pratt's article on personality disorders. I pulled a used copy of the collection from the shelf. Someone had written notes in the margins and seemed to have underlined sentences with a ruler, almost obsessively. There were also a lot of questions that seemed to be addressed to the author. I read the essay, then the questions. The questions were sharp, harsh, and sometimes they sounded personal.

I checked again to see whether there was more of Professor Pratt's work that I could read, but there wasn't. There was, though, a phone number and an email address. I stuck the book in my purse and decided to call him. I dialed the number, but nobody answered. I left a voicemail. I said who I was, mentioned his article and my interview with Andrew, left my phone number, and said I'd love to meet for coffee if he had the time. I doubted he would ever call back. I sat on a bench and read Nick's email once more. I had no response for him, but I knew he wasn't looking for one. That email was his way of saying sorry, although, I thought, perhaps what had happened was not really anybody's fault. We were simply not meant to be. A homeless guy passed me by, and my throat suddenly hurt as if I were in someone's grip again, like that time with Nick. I remembered Nick's eyes and their expression a few hours later. How could I misread his eyes? His feelings? The phone rang.

"Susan? This is Henry Pratt."

He had called.

"Hi, Professor Pratt. Thanks so much for returning my call."

"You said you talked to Andrew. How is he?"

"He's OK. He's here in New York. Perhaps you knew that."

"No, I didn't." I heard him breathing heavily.

"I could meet you for lunch today?"

He gave me his address, and we agreed to meet in front of his apartment building, a university building. I had a friend who lived there when I was in school. I knew exactly where the building was. I walked fast, excited to see him, and soon I was there. A couple holding tennis racquets came out of the elevator and blocked my view of him. He walked out behind them, slowly. But then the couple moved, and I saw him. A man in his eighties. Tall, pale, with a few strands of white hair on his otherwise bald head. So different from the photo on the school's webpage. His eyes had not changed though. They were exactly as in that picture and reminded me of Andrew. He shook my hand when he saw me, and he put his wool hat on. He seemed frail.

"It's so cold these days."

"It is," I said, and I realized I had not dried my hair that day.

He walked surprisingly fast. It was hard to keep up with him. He seemed to know where he was going. I tried to start a conversation about his work, but soon realized he was too focused on getting to his destination, and so I gave up.

When we arrived in front of a café he thought might work, he ushered me in, and asked if the place was fine with me. I said that it was, and a hostess came to ask us if we wanted a table for two.

"Yes, that one," he said, pointing to a table close to the window.

"That one's reserved," she said.

"How can it be reserved? That table's mine. I come here every day at noon. That's my table." He looked around seeking confirmation.

"Did you make a reservation, sir?"

"No," he said. "I've been coming here for almost thirty years, and almost every day. I don't need to make a reservation."

"I'm sorry," she said, but didn't sound so.

I looked to see if there was another table we could take, but he seemed to be obsessing about that particular table.

"Maybe you could give us that table and give another one to the people who made the reservation?" I tried. After all, there were several empty tables.

The hostess looked overwhelmed by my request, said she would have to check, and left. A man then approached us.

"Good morning, sir. The usual?"

"Yes," he said. "She was going to give me another table."

"I'm sorry, sir. Here's your table." He removed the "Reserved" tag and gestured for us to sit.

"I read your article on personality disorder in the Oxford collection," I said.

"Oh, that was a long time ago."

"It's a wonderful piece."

He sighed and seemed disinterested in talking about it. Perhaps he just didn't remember what the article was about, and I was just making him uncomfortable.

"When I started teaching, we didn't need to write much to get tenure, and I didn't have much to say anyhow."

"It seemed that you did, though. That article is full of ideas and original insights. I haven't read anything that original and humble in such a long time."

"You're too generous." He smiled.

He was so dignified, profound. And the more he spoke, the more I saw Andrew in him.

"I was more interested in thinking than in writing," he continued. "Once you write, what you write is locked. But then you may change your mind, see things differently, and you can't change what you wrote."

"I know what you mean."

"And then what do you do?"

"You stop reading what you wrote, I guess. Sometimes you even pretend you never wrote it in the first place."

"Exactly. But someone else might read it and rely on it. So what's the point?"

"Yes, that's a . . . that's a risk."

"That's why I stopped writing. Also there's enough out there. You don't need another article or book from me."

He smiled, looked more deeply into my eyes, and then asked about my work. I told him about my book and my dissatisfaction with it.

"It happens," he said. "We write to learn, so we often don't know much about the topic we write about, and most likely won't know enough when we complete our work either. So it's the search we fix in writing, not the truth. The readers, though, they are not interested in that. They want truths. And they believe they find them . . . in our work. Isn't that crazy?"

I had never thought about that. If I read my book looking with that in mind, maybe it would look less nonsensical, and maybe it would reveal more than I could possibly expect.

"I bet you have so much to share, the searching process, I mean, your search" I said. "I agree with you on writing and changing ideas, but I wonder whether there are truths that you own now, that you have built on over the years. There must be some other things you won't ever change your mind about, right?"

"I don't remember things as well as I used to. I have Alzheimer's. It's not that bad yet, but it'll get worse, and my fear is that I won't even notice."

Suddenly I felt immensely sad.

"Does Andrew know?"

"No, he doesn't. I'm sure he's busy dealing with his own issues. He doesn't need to hear mine."

"He looks so much like you."

"Yes, he does." He smiled and looked down. "He and I share more than just our appearance."

"I had that feeling," I said, and he looked at me as if he were wondering who I really was.

"You care about him, don't you?"

"I do. We're not together or anything like that. But I do care."

"You're studying him?"

"No, no. We just clicked," I said.

"I can see why."

"Really? What is it?" I asked, wondering whether he had some of the missing pieces in Andrew's puzzle or mine.

"Something about you reminds me of him. Andrew would probably agree."

Before I asked why that was, he asked a question. The meeting wasn't about me anyhow. He wanted to hear more about Andrew.

"How is Andrew?" he asked again.

"He's doing OK. His girlfriend died of cancer over a year ago. That was harsh on him."

"Emily, I know. I heard that."

"Did you know her?"

"I met her once. She came to New York for a show and looked for me. I thought she was lovely. She cared about him."

"Yes, I think so."

"She came to one of my classes too," he said, somehow looking deeper into his past, "and stayed until the end. She introduced herself and we spent some time together that day. She asked me questions about Andrew."

"What type of questions?"

"She said she thought he was sick and needed to see a doctor. She wanted to know whether he had been in therapy before, and what she should do. I asked her about his behavior, what concerned her. She described his obsessions, his isolation . . . I told her to let him be, that she shouldn't do anything.

"When I started my career as a teacher, I didn't know anything about personality disorders, but I thought I did, lost as I was in a theory of life of my own fabrication. I would have handled Andrew differently then. I would have sent him to a therapist, fed him pills, talked to him about his disease ad nauseam, made sure that he understood what his problem was, and ultimately tried to convince him that he was different, that he was sick. Now I see things differently."

"How so?"

"He doesn't fall into our traditional categories. He'll suffer, he'll struggle, but he'll see things that you and I don't see. And that's OK."

"What exactly do you think Andrew's problem is?"

"I can't use labels. Our colleagues love labels. We're trained to use them. It should be this or that. Labels would help us choose the right therapy, or so we think. But sometimes labels and therapy don't work." He was silent for a while, and then added, "My approach is different now. I don't see labels. I see the person, with her own issues.

I listen and think about what could help her live well with herself. But I don't try to change the person, make her like anyone else."

"So how would you describe Andrew?"

"He's fragile. He loves deeply, feels deeply, and will often be hurt by someone or something. There's nothing you and I could do to shield him from that."

"How long did he live with you?"

"Until he was ten. His mother and I broke up shortly after that." He took a breath, and said, "I couldn't take care of her. I had my own issues. I thought it'd be better if I left. So I did." He paused, and then added, "I remarried, but my wife died five years later of cancer. We had two kids, a boy and a girl. One of them has Andrew's issues . . . and mine."

Right. I had that feeling.

When the waitress came back, we finally looked at the menu and ordered. We talked about school, colleagues, boring workshops, terrible food, and winter in New York.

"I did write something else," he then said.

"What is it?"

"It's my reflections on Andrew, what I learned as a father, things I wanted to tell him and never did. The essay doesn't mention Andrew or me by name. Only Andrew would know I'm talking about us. Would you like to read it?"

"I'd love to."

"It's in my apartment. I could go back, get it, and return. You could wait for me here if you like."

I said there was no need for that, and that we could walk there together, as I'd love to chat more. We left the restaurant shortly after, and I followed him back to his place. I thought I'd wait for him downstairs in the hall, but he offered to show me his apartment, and that made me happy. The apartment was that of an artist. It had the same vibe as Andrew's place, but it looked more lived in. There was a huge living room at the entrance, with wide windows overlooking the city. And there were paintings all over. Mr. Pratt said he had inherited some from his wife's family, and some he'd bought when he was younger. Then he paused in front of one and said how much Andrew loved it.

"I should have given it to him when he was here. If I gave it to him now, he would never accept it."

I looked around. There was a sofa and a small coffee table in front of it, with newspapers and magazines spread around randomly. Some of them were opened and marked, some had sticky notes on them. And there were photos of his family everywhere. On little stands, on the walls. He showed me some. Photos of him with his wife and the kids. Photos with the new wife. Photos of Andrew and his sister when they were young. I said I loved them, and he showed me more. I didn't want to intrude, and I thought I should be ready to leave as soon as he looked like he might be getting tired. He left to get a copy of the piece he wanted me to read, and when he returned, he wrote something on it, and said I could keep it.

"It's for you. Don't give it to Andrew. If you do, I'd feel I didn't have to talk to him and explain the things I wrote. But I'd rather do that and not be a coward. So this is for you. Maybe it'll help you write your piece on my son. Maybe it'll make you question your studies. Or maybe it won't do either of those things. In that case, feel free to trash it." He looked sad.

"Are you happy?" I asked. I knew the answer to that question, did not need to hear it. My question was more about why he wasn't. That is what I wanted to know.

"I'm not," he said, without hesitation. "I feel very lonely."

"What about your colleagues?"

"What about them?"

"Aren't they friends?"

"I've got good relationships with them, but they're not really friends. I dated some other women. Nothing important, though."

"I'm sorry. I know what you mean. I think I do."

I looked at him, looked at the essay, and hugged him for what he had shared with me. I thought it was time for me to leave, but then he asked me if I wanted to see the rest of the apartment. We walked across a hall, and he showed me the other rooms, one of which was his other son's.

"I'm taking care of him as much as I can," he said. "I wish I had the cure. There isn't any really. But at times I feel he's doing better, and I feel I've succeeded. As a father, not as a professional."

I showed him the book I had bought that morning at the bookstore, the one with his annotated essay. I told him about the annotations. He seemed curious to read them, so I handed him the book. We left together, as he said he would walk with me a bit. When we said goodbye to each other, I felt he didn't want to let me go. And I didn't want to go either. I wish I had said that, but I didn't. After he turned the corner and left, I started feeling sick. Maybe it was because of the hair I hadn't dried that morning, or maybe it was the meeting. I started shaking. I called a taxi, and as soon as I was home, I went to bed. It was early afternoon.

THE DOG AND THE CAR

Matt called and woke me up the next day.
"Susan, are you free? I'd love to see you."
"I ... Are you in New York?"
"Yes, I am."

I checked the time and could not believe I had been asleep since the afternoon before. It was ten a.m.

He kept talking, though I wasn't sure I was fully listening. I think he mentioned he had a few meetings for work later that day and we could perhaps meet right after that or before.

"Unless you have other plans, of course."

"I don't have plans."

"Where are you living?"

"East Village."

"If you want I can come there. I might be there in an hour or so."

"Sure," I said, but I wasn't enthusiastic.

In his last email, he'd asked to stay at my place. I didn't feel like offering that, but then I remembered what he'd said about his finances, and I felt that I should.

"You can stay with me if you want. The apartment is small, but I've got an extra bed you could use."

"That would be awesome."

I pushed my head against the pillow and thought about my meeting with Andrew's father the day before. That meeting somehow had the intensity and the lightness, the beauty and the magic of a dream. Or it was just my wet hair in the icy morning that had made feel fluish and confused? It took me another half hour to get out of bed. I made coffee, put some clothes on, and soon Matt was at the door. He looked different than the last time we'd met.

"You look great," he said as I opened the door.

"Really? I don't feel like it."

"Why? What's wrong?"

I didn't want to talk about Nick, or me.

"I found Andrew," I said.

"Oh. Is he OK?"

"He's fine."

"How did you find him?"

"Luck, I guess. I was at a café in an area I knew he frequented, and he passed by."

"How is he?"

"He's fine. He's painting and has sold some of his works. He finished another novel, found a new agent, secured an advance from a publisher . . . He's a busy man. Has a new girlfriend too."

"We were so worried about him. He's probably doing better than all of us."

"I wouldn't go that far, but he's fine. Seems so, at least."

"So you are . . . done."

Was I?

"I'm writing a piece on him and might stay until January."

"A piece on Andrew?"

"Yes. I've talked to him a couple of times already and might meet with him again. I want to write about him, his art, try to dig into it."

We talked some more about Andrew, my efforts. I told him about Christine and my worries. He tried to absorb everything I said, but at times I felt it was too much.

"Why are you doing this?"

"I actually don't know. I guess I need to."

"Then I'll do whatever I can to help you."

"Why?" I asked this time.

"I care about you," he said.

He was sitting on my bed when he said that, his hands on his knees, his eyes lost somewhere. I went closer and hugged him. And then I kissed him. My kiss was first sweet, but then more sensual. And then more than that. I don't know why I did it. I was probably looking for Nick, trying to feel the same way Nick made me feel. But it wasn't just that. There was something about Matt that felt different. In any event, it didn't work.

"Not like this," he said. "It doesn't feel right. I'm sorry."

Yes, it wasn't right. I remained silent, then stood up and went to the window. He placed his arms around me and kissed me on my neck.

"I'll wait. I know love comes with time."

"Does it?"

I freed myself from his arms and went to the kitchen.

"Coffee?" I asked.

"Yes, please."

As I poured the coffee, I checked him out again.

"You look . . . different."

"Me? How?"

"I don't know . . . more confident perhaps?"

"It's possible." He smiled, taking the cup from my hands. "I was just offered a position here in New York. I'm going to be the CEO of a publishing company."

"You? What do you know about business?"

He laughed.

"I have a master's degree in finance, and a PhD in Economics. I worked for the *Economist* for a few years and then decided that wasn't the life I wanted for myself. So I became a poor artist. Didn't want a nine-to-five job."

"But now you'll have one?"

"Time for a change. In any event, I haven't made enough money with my art so far, and I know I don't have Andrew's talent. I can draw and have some good stories in mind. Nothing exceptional though. I'll earn some money, travel, keep writing. Maybe one day I'll have the right idea and the right connections. But now it seems that it's just not happening for me."

"Congrats!" I tried to show enthusiasm and excitement, but I didn't really feel any.

We chatted some more, and then left for a walk.

"Have you seen your father?" he asked. "I remember you mentioned he lived here."

"Yes. He lives here with his girlfriend and, apparently, a five-year-old son."

"Oh. You didn't know about that."

"No, I didn't. I don't even know at this point if it makes any sense for me to see him."

"You should tell him how you feel."

"Really? Why? I'm not even sure how I feel."

"It's your father. I would talk to him."

We walked some more in silence, and then he stopped.

"There's something I want to show you," he said, and pulled me close to him on a bench.

"These are a few sketches from *The Girl, the Beach, and the Rain.*"

I leafed through the pages and remembered that day on the beach. Seemed so long ago.

"What's the story?" I asked.

"You tell me."

There were only drawings, no dialogue. There was no need for words.

"It's a love story," I said.

"Yes, it is."

"Is it finished?"

"Oh, no. It hasn't even started yet," he said, and winked at me.

He told me about the phone call from the publishing company, their offer, his plans for the future. And then it was time for him to leave.

"I'd better go now."

"Where's your meeting?" I asked.

He showed me the address, and I recognized the name of the company Nick and I had visited.

"Those are nice offices," I said. "Too bright for my taste, but nice."

"How do you know?"

"Nick and I went there looking for Andrew. He's no longer working there."

"Do you want to come with me?"

"No, I think I'll go home."

"I'll come to your place once I'm done. I might be late, as I've got some introductory training to do."

"That's fine. I'll be there."

He kissed me on my cheek and walked away, but turned three times to check on me, and he waved before disappearing.

I started walking toward the subway to take it home, but then I changed my mind. I called a taxi and asked the driver to take me to my father's place. I hadn't decided whether I should see him, and when I arrived there I still wasn't sure. I asked the driver to stop a few blocks away, I paid, and before walking toward the place, I looked around. The area was quiet and green. It was almost three, and the sun was bright and shining. I walked along the sidewalk, looking at opulent mansions on both sides of the street. It was peaceful. My father's house looked exactly as I remembered. Huge. Almost a castle. Evelyn chose it because it looked fancy, and my father bought it to make her happy. My father met Evelyn through friends of friends. She looked like the soubrette of a cheap TV show, and she was not particularly smart. He once asked me what I thought about her, and I believe I said, "If it makes you happy, what I think doesn't matter." My father started dating her about ten years ago, and apparently they had been together ever since. Now they even had a child. I had not asked my father about the name of the child. But, after all, I didn't care.

"Benji!" a voice called from the house. I turned and saw a little boy playing with Legos on the grass. I looked more closely, and I immediately realized that that boy was my father's son. They looked identical, the boy just a younger version of him.

"Benji, your snack is ready. Come inside."

I didn't recognize that woman, but I assumed she was my father's maid. The boy didn't even look at her and continued to play. A dog joined him and seemed to demand his attention, but the boy didn't stop playing, and the dog ran away toward the opposite side of the street.

"Cooper!" the boy called. But it was too late. The dog was already crossing the street as a car was approaching. I don't know why, but my instinct was to jump and shield the dog. And so I did. The driver tried to stop the car, but he slammed into me. The impact was so strong. I lost consciousness.

I woke up in the hospital the day after. I didn't remember much, except the sense of having been hit by a huge truck, although I had seen just a car.

When I opened my eyes, I didn't have my glasses on, but I thought there must be a woman standing on the left side of my bed. When she said, "She's waking up," I recognized Evelyn's voice. How could I forget that voice? I hated it. I wanted to close my eyes and disappear, but my father came closer, so close I could almost see his classic examiner's stare. For a few seconds I felt like a teenager again. Should I find an excuse, something, to justify the mess I had made?

"Susan, how are you?" he asked.

I tried to say something, but then I felt like throwing up. So I just waved my hand to signal that I was OK.

"Benjamin would like to say something to you."

The little boy came close to my bed and, pushing his head against his mother's hips, said, "Thank you for saving Cooper. I like you."

I smiled and closed my eyes again. And then I remembered Matt was coming over.

"I have an appointment. I should go. What time is it?"

"It's noon," my father said.

"No, that's not possible. It was noon before."

"It's noon. You had an accident yesterday. The ambulance took you to the hospital around three, and you've been here ever since."

"But Matt?" I asked.

"Oh, yes. He came last night together with another friend of yours. Nick?"

I felt sick again.

"They said they would come back later today."

I tried to move but couldn't. My left leg was in traction, some wires were pulling it away from me, and others were pulling it up.

"What's going on? What's wrong with me?"

"You broke your shinbone. You had a bad fracture and dislocation."

I looked down and saw my life in traction.

THE TRUTH ABOUT MY MOTHER

I spent two weeks in the hospital. My fracture was apparently bad, and so after I was put in traction, I had surgery to insert some metal screws and pins into my bones. The pain was intense, and it lasted for days. I wasn't thinking of Nick anymore. He didn't come to the hospital after his first visit, when I was unconscious, so I hadn't seen him since that night at the theater.

Matt came every day. I gave him the keys to my apartment and told him he could stay there. He spent most of his days with me at the hospital. He brought a little machine that projected moving stars onto the ceiling in the dark. So every day when he left, I asked him to pull the shades and turn off the light, and I would lie still, looking at the stars floating in the room and sketching plans for my future.

"You still like shadows," my father said when on one of his visits to the hospital he caught me with my stars.

"How do you know?" I asked, trying to remember when and how I could have possibly shared anything so personal with him.

"After your mother died, you wanted me to get rid of all the lamps in the house. You wanted only dim lights. And that's all we had for quite a while."

"Really? I don't remember that. How old was I?"

"Seven. And you continued to ask for shadows pretty much until you went to college."

"Really?"

"Yes."

"I forgot."

"I'm sure there are many things you forgot . . . It's not your fault though." He took a breath and said, "I love the sun, I love light. The shadows weren't exactly my choice."

He went silent looking at my little fake little stars.

"Why do you think I like shadows so much?"

"They remind you of your mother. When you were born, she slowly slipped into a deep depression. She spent her days in almost completely dark rooms. She didn't use lamps or electricity, just candles or dim lanterns. She first made it look like a game to you. You played hide-and-seek, and that was fun. But then she lost interest in that too, and what was left was just the shadows. After she died, you kept asking me to 'make some shadows' because, I think, they reminded you of your time with your mother, the happy times with her."

That seemed right, and yet I had forgotten it. I decided to trust him. Perhaps I needed to.

I said, "I have to ask you about something that has been tormenting me for quite some time, and I need you to be honest. Have you been honest with me about mom's death? Did she really have an aneurysm?"

"Why do you ask?"

"'Cause I've started having confusing dreams about that. I keep dreaming of these two women at mom's funeral, talking about how sad it is that she had hanged herself. Sometimes I see her dying that way too."

My father froze. He sat on the chair close to my bed, and remained silent, perhaps thinking about whether or not he should lie.

"Does that matter? Why do you want to know how she died? She's no longer here."

"She was my mother. I need to know."

He lowered his head, and without looking at me, said, "She did hang herself. You probably did hear women talking about it at the funeral. I remember you running away in the middle of the reception and going back to your room crying. Later on, you asked what 'hanged' meant, but I obviously lied to you. How could I tell you the truth? You were only seven."

I didn't ask him why he had lied to me. I knew I had lied to myself even before he did.

"Did you know she was sick? I mean, when this whole thing started."

"Of course, I knew," he said. "She was ill when I met her, but I thought I could save her. Turns out I couldn't. At first, I felt guilty toward her, toward you. As your father, I hadn't been able to save your mother. But over the years, I realized that there was nothing I could have done to change the course of events."

He took a deep breath, and then said, "I'm sorry I wasn't a good father to you but, trust me, I tried. It's not easy to lose your wife and raise a child when you're in your thirties. Wasn't easy at all. There are things you understand only when you get older."

I didn't say a word. I was still thinking about my mother. So she had killed herself, and I always knew it. Deep down, I knew it, and I had completely buried it. Just as I had buried the reason why I loved shadows so much. I had basically been lying to myself all these years to the point that I convinced myself that the lies were the truth. I remembered what Nick said about lies and reality, and how scared he was when he thought he could be lying to himself without even realizing he was doing so. At the time, I had thought that was something remote from me. And yet I had done the same. I had lied to myself about my mother. What else was I lying to myself about?

THE WOMAN IN THE BOX

The days at the hospital were incredibly long. Matt had started working, and my father was busier than he had been before. He wanted to send Evelyn to the hospital to keep me company, but I begged him not to. I spent my days thinking, but my thoughts didn't always follow a logic. Or if they did, I didn't know what that logic was. My father insisted that once released from the hospital I stay with him and his family, but I said I preferred to keep my apartment, have my own space, although I promised I would visit them from time to time. I was told I would have to be on crutches for a while, and when I asked for how long, the doctor couldn't say, as that depended on my bones' response. And although I had spent days trying to sketch plans for the future, I realized—I knew—that my plans were as uncertain and unpredictable as my bones.

Not much changed once I left the hospital. I thought that being released would feel like being freed from a prison. But once I was back in my apartment, it wasn't so. It wasn't just the crutches that were limiting my movement, it was something else, something I couldn't see or touch. I was a woman in a box. Andrew had said I could have that drawing, but only once I completed my article. I should write it article, and I would have to do it from my box.

The box, my apartment, was as I had left it, except for a new couch and a footstool Matt had bought for me. He said he had imagined me writing there, and he liked that image of me. He had placed the couch and footstool close to my desk and turned them toward the window and the street. I laughed when I saw them.

"I don't plan on spying on my neighbors."

"You never know," he said, smiling.

I sat on my new couch, and he asked me about my article.

"Have you thought about it lately?"

"Yes, I have, but I need to give it more thought. There's more I need to explore," I said, and thought about the essay Andrew's father had given me that day. He wanted me to read it, but the title somehow made me resist: "On the Past and the Present." I was curious though. I stood up and looked in my bag where I had put the essay to make sure it was still there. It had been handwritten. I ran my fingers over the ink. The letters seemed to come out of the paper, as if they had been engraved on it, as if they had a life of their own. When I pulled the essay from the bag, I realized I hadn't read Henry Pratt's note to me.

To Susan, with my best wishes in your search for the truth. I hope you won't be disappointed when you find there isn't any.

What did he mean by that?

I leafed through the pages. The essay had been written ten years ago. It started with a hypothesis on the effects of the past on a person's present and future, and the idea that we distort the past to purge ourselves of our mistakes. He described the process and explained how the alterations of the mind aren't intentional, and so they are not technically "lies." They are the product of a series of variables affecting our perception of reality. It's like taking a photo of someone or something. The light, the distance, the sound, the noise, our mood, a weak press of the shutter, a decisive one . . . all these variables will affect it. Our photo will never be the same as anyone else's. And no matter how sophisticated the camera, it will never ever capture what is in front of it. our eyes won't do that either.

So there's no truth, if we call "truth" something objective, something everyone would agree on. Pratt said we would never be able to agree on each and every detail, nuance of an event, fragment of our life, no matter how accurate the instrument to capture, record, or reproduce it. We could agree on a simplistic description of it, still captured through a sophisticated instrument. The problem with that, though, would be the lack of nuance and details, the lack of depth, which could make a huge difference, sometimes dramatically changing the essence of what we saw. So it's not the past per se that affects our present, our life, he argued. It's our perception of it, the way we *alter* what we live and sense. We can try to assess it, we can look at the events under a microscope. But what we'll see will always be only our own perception of reality. Hence, he concluded, there was no truth to be found. I had been reading and thinking about the essay for a while when Matt called from the kitchen.

"Did Nick look for you?"

"What? No. Why would he?"

"Just wondering."

I resisted a bit, but then I couldn't hold my question. I had to ask.

"Did you really need to call him that night?"

"Yes, I did. I was worried about you and didn't know anyone here other than him."

I looked outside the window, and he continued.

"I feel sorry for him."

"What? Why? Why do you feel sorry?"

"I don't know. He seemed so sad when I met him."

I didn't comment on that.

"He told me what happened that night at the theater."

"Wonderful. That's truly something to be proud of, something to share with other people."

"I think he wanted to tell you that he's sorry."

"Did he ask you to do that? Tell me he's sorry?"

"No."

"Then why are we talking about him now?"

"I'm just trying to understand whether I should step aside."

I pulled him toward me to hide my tears, and we had sex. I didn't feel anything, and when it was over, I pulled the blanket on and felt cold. It was December.

The days went by slowly, like in one of Andrew's novels. I would feel everything so deeply, I would question everything, carefully study this or that detail looking for answers to questions that had nothing to do with what I was observing. I stayed home while Matt worked. And yet I wasn't waiting for him to get home. In fact, I would have rather spent my days alone. His presence was an opportunity to convince myself that Nick and I were done. Except we weren't. Or, at least, I wasn't. I wrote, read, watched TV, wrote more—but I wasn't happy with my writing. I blamed it on the leg, on the apartment that had become too small for two, on the noisy streets early in the morning, on the afternoon silences, on everything that could possibly cross my mind, and on everything that didn't. One day, as I was sketching ideas for my piece, I called Andrew. He sounded happy to hear my voice.

"Do you feel any better?"

"I do. The doctors said I should be able to walk without the crutches soon. So I'm sitting at my desk, watching outside, spying on my neighbors—"

"Like in *Rear Window*."

"Yeah."

After a moment, I said,

"I called to let you know that I haven't forgotten about your article. It's been hard to focus lately."

"You don't have to explain. I'm glad you called. I've got good news."

"What is it?"

"My new agent loves *Lies We Tell*, and we might have a publisher."

"That's so wonderful. I told you it was great."

I asked him about Christine.

"I haven't heard from her in a while. We broke up. Actually, *she* broke up with me over the phone."

"How are you doing?" I asked.

"I'm fine. Not great, but fine. Maybe breaking up the second time isn't as harsh as the first time. Or perhaps I cared less than I thought."

"Do you want to talk about it?"

"No. Not really."

"I promise I won't try to analyze you."

"It's not that."

I insisted, and he finally agreed to meet with me at a café on the ground floor of my building. When I arrived at the café, he was already seated, waiting for me. He seemed OK, relaxed.

He helped me sit down and was waiting for me to speak when I realized I wasn't ready.

"I talked to Christine. She was very close to Emily before you met her," I tried.

"I knew that," he said. "What's so special about this?"

How should I put it?

"Emily and Christine were in love. They were a couple before Emily met you."

"What?"

I remained silent. Had I been too abrupt?

"How do you know?"

"Christine told me."

He stared at me, his eyes in disbelief. He remained silent for a while, choking his napkin.

"Why should I know this?" he asked.

"It wasn't your fault if it didn't work out with Emily. She had conflicts bigger than you."

"How are you so sure about this?" he asked, perhaps trying to decide whether to thank me or punch me. "We'll never know what it was between them, between us," he added. "She's dead."

His eyes turned red. I watched him and his silence, and I realized that he was right. I didn't know anything.

"I don't know how you feel," I said, "so I won't say that I understand you, because I'm sure I don't. I wish I could though."

"I know you do."

He took a breath.

"Why me? Why are you interested in me? The journal?"

"I don't know."

"Right," he said, sounding hopeless.

The radio was playing "Summertime."

"This song is so full of contradictions," he said.

I smiled. Andrew's father was right. We really did share something, and maybe that was why I was trying to help him. And maybe that was why I had become part of his world. Such a small world. One of my own creation.

"When will the two novels be published?" I asked.

He hesitated and checked my eyes. Was the exchange about Emily over?

"Soon, I guess."

We talked some more about the drawings and the novels, and then I said, "I'm sure they'll be successful. And I'll write the article and publish it before then." I took a breath. "Andrew?"

"Yes?"

"Thanks for trusting me."

He didn't say a word, did his best to smile but couldn't, then looked elsewhere, and left.

Once I returned to my apartment, I put on some jazz, poured a glass of wine, and turned on my computer to start writing. I loved it when the wine and the music melded. When that happened, they made me feel warmer and loosened the tension in my body. I could almost feel the jazz and the wine in my veins. I thought about the woman in the box and felt sorry for myself. Then the intercom rang. I looked at the clock and thought it was too early for Matt. I pulled my crutches close to me and went to the phone to answer. The voice said, "Nick." I stopped breathing for a moment, stared at the phone, froze, hesitated, and then still unsure of what to do, I answered.

"What are you doing here?"

"Can we talk?"

I could have said no. I could have told him to leave. But I didn't. "I'm on the third floor," I said, my legs shaking.

I opened the door to my apartment, and there he was, staring at me. He seemed tired, darker. His eyes looked empty, almost anesthetized.

"Can I come in?"

I opened the door more and turned my back to him, heading to my couch. I needed to sit. He followed me inside the apartment and closed the door behind him.

"Does it still hurt?"

The fracture? You? I looked outside the window and didn't respond.

"Look, I didn't come here to apologize. I hurt you. I hurt myself. That's done. I can't undo that." He took a breath. "I came because I felt you needed me."

He was right, but I didn't say so.

"I wanted you to know that."

"I think you should go," I said, and stood up to take him to the door. When I passed by him, he grabbed my wrist, and I almost fell.

"How are you?" he asked.

My eyes betrayed me.

"Please leave," I said, without looking at him.

After he left, I closed the door behind him and cried.

AN EMAIL FOR CHRISTMAS

I hadn't seen Nick since that time in my apartment. I was trying not to think about him, but from time to time I did. He said he had come to see me because he knew I needed him, and he was right. He knew he was. In fact, he didn't come to confirm that he was. He came to let me know that he knew my feelings, and that he knew me. And my silence had probably been louder than any words I could have said or written.

My little box had become smaller and smaller, and so Matt and I moved to a bigger apartment. I kept the box, though, "for writing," Matt said. For myself, I thought. In fact, even if Matt was rarely home, the new apartment didn't feel as mine as the box, and from time to time I would return to the box. The box now had strangely expanded, or perhaps it just felt more comfortable. I was still on crutches, but getting around wasn't as hard as it had been, and sometimes I would even go out on my own to run little errands around the block, or a few blocks away. It hadn't started snowing yet, and the cold didn't bother me, or maybe I had become more used to it.

Matt worked hard. He said December was especially hectic at work because they had several deals to close and accounts and files to review before the New Year. I had started writing my article on Andrew, but I had also trashed an infinite number of attempts, as they were either too fake or too personal. It seemed that I couldn't talk about Andrew without talking about me. The sketches and drawings in his novels had swallowed me in. I had become one of them. Should I talk about myself in the article? Would I be able to? I tried, stopped, tried again, and then crumpled each new try. I kept hearing a voice in my head. It said that what I was writing wasn't good enough. But then another voice wanted me to continue writing and try to pierce the page using Andrew's art as my inspiration and story. I wanted my writing to scream as loudly as his drawings, but every time I reviewed what I wrote, it seemed antiseptic. I hadn't found my voice yet. Would it come to me? Should I wait for something or someone to tell me how to do this? Or maybe writing wasn't for me. But why did I want to do it so badly then? I stared at my last attempt for a while, then clicked "print," and a white page came out. I stared at that page in disbelief. I thought I had written something. Or maybe I just dreamed writing but hadn't done anything. I checked again, and I realized the printer was out of ink.

I opened the window, lay on the floor using the cold as my blanket, pushed my head against the soft floor, and closed my eyes. I felt so empty I could feel it in my stomach, and the emptiness started pulling my navel and sucked my tears. Andrew had said that "the tears you don't see are the ones that hurt the most." I got that now. He had also said that I could see the woman's tears in the drawing because I knew her and thus she "spoke" to me. Did I speak to Nick? Did he know me?

I checked my emails hoping to find one from him. I wasn't sure I would reply, but I knew I needed his email, him. Yes, I did. There wasn't anything, though. I shut the computer, put on my coat, and left.

It was Christmas Eve. Our apartment had no Christmas decorations as Matt was Jewish, and Christmas didn't matter for me. Or at least it didn't this time. I did miss looking for Christmas gifts though —in fact, I missed looking. So I told myself I should go out and look for something, something that would make me happy, inspire me, or even just distract me.

I thought about my dissatisfaction with my writing, and my sense that it didn't feel real. I had to feel what Andrew felt. And even if we had talked about it, and I had read his journal, and spent time with his novels, I knew I didn't know enough yet and thus couldn't write about it in any way that was meaningful. True, we were similar. We shared much. But I couldn't replace his story with mine and convince myself that it was fine because, after all, we were so similar. I searched the internet for an art store nearby, then I called a taxi and went looking for inspiration.

The store was packed when I arrived. There were too many customers for the salesmen to take care of. Christmas Eve, of course. I should try to take care of myself. I paused at the canvases, the brushes, the colors, the pencils, the pens, the clay. I remembered Andrew's description of his attempts to capture Emily, first in his drawings, and then with clay. I remembered his description of his movements around the curves, the corners, the wrinkles, the shading, the eyes, the lips . . . and thought I should try myself. I bought charcoal, paper, and some clay, and returned to my box.

I opened the window wide but kept my coat on. I placed the paper on the floor, sat close, took one of the charcoal sticks in my hand, and started brushing it against the paper. My fingers turned black. At first the charcoal felt cold and sharp. But then it became fuller, softer, and my sketch slowly came to life. I pressed lightly, then harder. I drew a line, then another one. I pushed the point, then the side of the stick, and the lines became fuller. I looked at what I had drawn and thought it could be an arm. Maybe the arm of a woman. I looked at it again, and now I saw a woman, except the woman wasn't there. It was just her arm. So I thought about it more and added some other parts to that arm, the ones I had just seen. A hand on the arm, then another arm, then the chest, the neck, the lips, the nose, an eye, another one. Sad, I thought. The eyes looked sad. They should look sad. And then the hair, long, and straight, as Emily's, but thick and wide like mine. And then I gave her depth, breathing into her the thoughts of my day, the voices I heard, my struggles when writing, my questions, the silent tears that I wanted to see. I started moving my hands around her eyes and lips, making shadows around them, the neck, the space between her arms, legs . . . I wouldn't say it resembled Emily, or Christine, Elinor, me, my mother, or any other woman I knew or had known. But perhaps it was all of us. And yet she didn't have the depth I saw before drawing her. The depth I had given her wasn't enough. I felt Andrew's frustration. I was sad. And then I felt almost desperate. I tried some more, made more shadows, pushed my fingers more on the paper, made some more dark, some more angles, more volume. But the woman I had seen wasn't in that drawing. I moved to the clay.

I added some water to the clay and then started massaging it, hoping it would slowly take shape and curves and depth and life. I tried to make the woman I saw, give her more than what I was able to give to my drawing. But it wasn't the paper, and it wasn't the clay. The woman I had seen would not be there. I spent hours moving around it, looking at the light and how it hit it each part of her face. I moved and moved around it, pushed and pressed, caressed and pressed more, but the woman I had seen did not come to life. I begged her to, but she didn't. Where are you? I asked, then whispered, then called. Where. Are. you?

I pulled my crutches close, but one of them fell, and I fell too. I lay on the carpet again, my head pressing against it, my legs spread. The window was still open, but I had just started feeling the cold. Perhaps the excitement of creation, or my hope, had left me, and now I was alone again. Exhausted, I closed my eyes and fell asleep. A few hours later, I woke up and felt inspired. I went to the computer to start writing, but then I checked my emails and found something.

Thanks for letting me in the other day. I never got to tell you, but assuming I can say it, I'm proud of you for finding Andrew, and I'm sure you'll write a wonderful piece. Don't worry if you struggle. Writing may be hard when you start. But you have to be honest. Brutally and disturbingly honest. We know that can be tough sometimes. But if you manage to do it, your writing will set you free. It's Christmas. In case you're sad today, I hope you'll do some good writing. This is my Christmas wish for you.

Nick

I finished reading and stopped breathing. "I'm here," my gift said. I am here. I felt good, but I didn't feel like replying yet.

The phone rang. It was Matt, reminding me of our dinner with my father and his family. He said he might be a little late. I should take a taxi and we would meet there. I chose a nice red dress, put on red lipstick, and called a taxi. When I checked the phone in my purse, my address book opened to Henry Pratt's name. I thought that was strange, but I gave that address to the driver. I had some time and thought that maybe it was a Christmas suggestion I should take. I remembered I had seen a bakery close to Mr. Pratt's building when walking with him, and I asked the driver to make a little detour and stop there. While he waited, I bought some cookies. I placed them in a little gold bag, returned to the taxi, and we drove to Mr. Pratt's address. I pushed the intercom's button and, when he answered, I said I had something for him. I went upstairs. He opened the door, a little boy hiding behind him.

"That's Noah," he said. "My grandson."

I said hi to both.

"I came to give you this," I said, and handed him the cookies.

"Why?" he asked.

"To thank you for sharing with me the way you did. Your essay was wonderful."

"Thanks. I thought you might like it."

He asked me to wait at the door, as he had something to give me too.

He handed me the book I had given him the last time we met, the one with the handwritten notes, and he said I should keep it.

"No, I don't need it," I said.

"I think you do."

I didn't insist but took the book, smiled, and hugged him. As I started to enter the elevator I remembered I hadn't asked him about the notes.

"What did you think about the comments and questions?"

He smiled.

"I wrote some answers," he said, and the door of the elevator closed.

I placed the book in my bag and headed to my father's house.

AN EMAIL TO LOOK FORWARD TO

When I woke up the next day, it was Christmas. There were still no decorations in the house, but I felt it. Matt was sleeping in the corner of our bed the farthest from me. I got up, made coffee, and turned on my computer. It was snowing. I read Nick's email once more, sipped my coffee, and let myself go. I wondered where he was. I tiptoed out of my pajamas and into the shower then to the bedroom to get dressed. I left a note for Matt, and said I needed to leave for a few days. I asked him not to look for me. I said I needed some time for myself and my writing. I took Henry Pratt's essay, the charcoal, the sketchbook, a few changes of clothes, and soon I was out the door. The streets were silent and empty, but I heard echoes of the parties from the night before. They reminded me that there had been life somewhere close. It was still dark.

When I arrived at my studio I turned on the desk lamp, my computer, and the radio, and I looked for a jazz station. Some music I didn't know started playing. I sat at my desk and typed *Lies We Tell* on the top center of the page, still unsure of whether I was going to write Andrew's story, mine, or both. Then I closed my eyes and saw the first line of the story. I typed it. I closed my eyes again and saw more. And then I saw it all, or I thought I did. I remained with my eyes closed for a while, and then looked outside and prayed. I hadn't prayed in a long time, and I didn't remember how to do it. I asked for help from whomever could hear me. I hoped I could make my story live, write what I saw—exactly what I saw, the life that I experienced it. I took a deep breath, and I started.

The sun rose and set, the noise outside became louder and then softer, and then it was silence again. I raised the volume of the music to keep from hearing the silence. I continued to write until the next morning. The radio was playing something I wanted to dance to. I went to the window, held onto the bars, and started moving following the music, my crutches on the floor. The woman in Andrew's drawing was still in her box. I had left. I saved what I wrote and sent an email to Nick.

You were right.

And I'm struggling.

What do you mean by "disturbingly honest"?

I haven't forgiven you.

Susan

I took a beer from the fridge and opened the window wide to breathe in the snow and cool my heart down. I started shaking. I opened my mouth to have more of what I couldn't see. I stopped breathing, then breathed again, and felt alive. The clock on my nightstand said 3:02 a.m. Would he be awake now? I checked my emails.

I know you won't. I won't forgive myself either. Disturbingly honest. Don't filter your writing, even when what you're writing hurts, and even if you can't hold your tears or you're laughing too hard as you write. Try.

I was hoping to be right, and I am happy that I was.

Nick

Yes, he was awake, and he'd done it again. He'd made me stop breathing again. Every time he talked or wrote was like a punch to my stomach, right in the center of me.

I turned off the light and went to bed.

And then it was morning, and again, and again.

I didn't leave my apartment for days. Then Matt looked for me, and we talked. The usual "it's not you, it's me" litany, just with different words and no effort on my side. We saw each other for coffee and lunch occasionally, but I asked him to give me time, although I said I couldn't promise anything.

I spent my days on my own, or sometimes with my father. He and I would go for walks, sometimes taking Benji with us. We didn't talk about mom or the past, just the persons we had become. I didn't know much about him, and I thought he didn't know much about me, but at times he surprised me, revealing things of myself I myself didn't even know.

"He really looks like you," I told him one day, holding Benji on my lap.

"You do too," he said. What did he see that I didn't?

I hadn't seen Nick, but we continued emailing each other, and I looked forward to his emails. They were usually short, but at times I felt that my writing, my would-be memoir or fiction, was expanding with each and every line I sent him, with pages and pages of stories he might remember or otherwise know.

That day, after a walk with my father, I returned to my apartment and reread Henry Pratt's essay. I hadn't looked at the annotations and comments since I'd first seen them. I lay on my bed and read. When I opened the book that contained the essay, many handwritten notes fell off the pages. A rain of thoughts. Andrew's father had numbered the reader's questions and comments in the book and had written answers to each of them on sticky notes, so it wasn't hard to put them back in their proper order. I read them, sometimes silently, sometimes whispering them, sometimes a little louder. Nick said how important the sound of writing was. Those questions and comments had their own sound, and their sound was familiar.

Comment no. 27

I wish you had been more honest and real. This is too abstract. What is the past that you know and how did it affect your and your loved ones' present?

Henry Pratt's Note 27

If you decided to read and comment on the essay, perhaps I was honest enough to reach you.

Comment no. 43

You say there are no truths. I feel that when you love someone, you own her truths.

Henry Pratt's Note 43

I loved, deeply loved, and yet I don't think I ever owned the truths of the ones I loved. And I don't think I ever owned my own truths. I'm not saying you're wrong. Perhaps I didn't know how to love, and maybe I didn't love myself enough either.

I looked at the handwriting on the margins of the used book to see if I recognized it, but I couldn't. The more I read the comments, though, the more I imagined Nick writing them. Was I just looking for him? I responded to his last email.

I think I understand what you're saying. I'm trying to write in a way that is disturbingly honest. But I often question my writing. I wish I could share it with someone.

I met Andrew's father some time ago. I brought him a collection of essays that had one of his essays in it. The book was secondhand, and there were handwritten comments and questions on the margins. Some of those notes seem like they could be yours. Are they? I know it sounds weird, but I thought I should ask.

I continue to love writing. I'm sure you do too.

Susan

I felt he was looking for me every time he sent me an email that wasn't just in response to mine. This time I had done the same. I wasn't just answering his questions. I was looking for him.

Weeks had passed since my accident and surgery, and finally it was time to get rid of the crutches.

"Your legs need to remember how to walk again," my doctor said. "You'll need some therapy. She'll tell you what to do," he added, introducing me to a colleague.

What if I didn't want to walk the same way I did before? What if I didn't want to remember?

My doctor and his colleague talked for quite a while, explaining to me the procedure, the "routine" as they called it, but other than "routine," I didn't hear another word of what they said. Perhaps that word was exactly what shut my interest down. I made up my mind. I would walk again, but I would recover my own way. I would start with short walks, maybe first with one crutch, then none, and then perhaps I would start jogging. I had always seen people running and thought I should try it, but I never felt quite ready for it. All of a sudden I did. The irony of it was, I could barely walk.

Interesting, the story of the writing in the margins. Yes, I used to read many psychology books before dating Elinor. And I used to annotate them and sell them, hoping some random stranger would buy them and answer my questions. I never signed my name under my notes though. I thought it shouldn't be too easy for the stranger to find me, or for me to remember that I was the author of those notes. Wouldn't it be nice if you had found my annotations?

I must confess that the idea of writing notes in books hoping someone would read them wasn't mine. It was my father's. He used to do that. He also loved philosophy and psychology books. Who knows, maybe one day you'll feel like showing that book to me.

I loved the rain today. Have you noticed the color green is greener when it rains? Whenever I tell people that, they laugh or want to argue with me that it isn't possible. When it rains there's less light, so how come the colors are brighter then?

I would love to read what you write, but don't send me your work before it's done. Send something else. If you feel like it, you could write about our first meeting. I always wondered what you thought about it, but never dared asking you, and now it's even harder than it was before.

How are you? How's your leg?

Nick

Punch.

Nick was looking for me too, and his questions at the end of each email were saying, *Talk to me more, don't leave.*

I had started walking without crutches. At times my leg hurt badly, but other times I felt almost no pain. Every morning when I woke up and put my feet on the floor and stood on them, I felt uncertain, as if they would not support me. But then when they did, and every time they did, I felt grateful. I continued to write and when I felt too tired, I left my apartment and went for walks. I never had a precise itinerary in mind. I just went. And it didn't matter if it was raining or cold. I walked. First my walks were limited to Central Park. But then I went farther and farther, until I was able to walk around Manhattan, from bottom to top and back again. It took me the entire

day to do it, as I stopped here and there, for drinks and food, sometimes at libraries, and finally at movie theaters. But I loved it, and at
times, I felt like I needed it. I had started going back to the Thalia
Theatre. I felt close to that theater and drawn to it. And so I would
plan to go or just find myself there without having planned it. I
brought my sketchbook with me during my wanderings, and from
time to time I would stop and draw what I saw. Discovering I could
draw was inebriating.

> It's going well. I've started walking, and walked for hours today. I walked
> around Manhattan, the entirety of Manhattan, from top to bottom and
> back. It was nice, especially because it rained, as I love the rain too. And,
> yes, green is greener when it rains. Of course, it is.

> The writing is exhilarating, intoxicating, obsessive. I love it.

> I've started drawing. Andrew would probably find my drawings
> rudimentary, but I like them.

> Our first meeting: It wasn't what you said. It was the way you looked at
> me. Your eyes are all I remember. They silenced the noise around me and
> that inside of me. For a few seconds I felt at peace. You didn't speak, and
> yet you said, "I would like to talk to you and would like to listen to what
> you have to say." Perhaps this lasted only a few seconds, but to me it was
> forever. And then everything continued to be as it had been before. Except
> it never was.

> Susan

I had also described our first meeting in my story—my piece or
book or whatever it was—and I could have just cut and pasted what I
had written to avoid thinking about it again. But I was thinking about
it anyhow, and writing it was actually a relief. I didn't review what I
wrote. If I had, I would have probably erased those sentences,
censored my feelings, the naked truth. But what was the point? He

knew what I felt anyhow. Disturbingly honest. So I wrote, didn't review, and pressed "send." I was free.

My story was now pages and pages long. I liked to pause and review passages, read them aloud, sometimes while looking outside my open window. I watched my words trace lines and paths of their own, beyond my control, deep down hoping they would reach those they wanted and could reach, as Andrew or his father might have put it.

Of course you love the rain. I thought you could see what I see.

Yes, that was our first meeting. You just described it better than I could. But that is what it was.

Keep writing.

Punch.

His short emails could sometimes punch me harder than his longer ones. At times I wondered whether they were drawing imaginary circles around him inside of which I wasn't allowed. I liked them though, as much as I liked his long emails. They made me look forward to more. One line from him was all I needed.

But then there were no more emails for days. The last email had been his, but I didn't feel like replying. What if I was right? What if his last email had traced that circle?

I had to stop thinking about it, get distracted, and so I started jogging. At the beginning I could run for only a few minutes, but after a month I would run for thirty minutes. The first time I did, when I stopped, my heart was beating so fast I could barely breathe. It felt good.

Weeks later, he wrote again.

I went to the Thalia Theatre today on my own. I never told you, but I saw you there one day. You went to see The Big Sleep, but then fell asleep soon after the movie started. I was sitting right behind you. You didn't see me.

I'm planning on going this Saturday. They'll be showing Stolen Kisses *by Truffaut. It's at 2.15PM. Elinor won't come. I'll get two tickets in case you would like to join me. Maybe you could show me your book with the handwritten notes.*

Nick

Punch. Punch.

I didn't respond and didn't go to the theater. Nick was back, and I had left.

I CAME TO SAY GOOD-NIGHT

One morning it was March. I had extended my lease because I was finding it hard to leave. Writing was my refuge, and my apartment its perfect frame.

I found a letter in the mail. It was from my school. They had accepted my request for a leave. I had discussed this with my father, and he thought I should use the money in the trust he had set up for me. I hadn't known there was one, and I didn't know whether I would use it or not. But I really needed to disappear for a while, so I was grateful for the opportunity.

I had been in New York for several months now, but New York wasn't my home. I tried to think of where home was, but I couldn't identify any place that truly felt like it. I had memories that tasted like home, but I knew that if I now returned to the places in them, I'd feel a stranger there. Sometimes I even felt a stranger to myself.

I had no email to look forward to anymore. I had kept Nick's last email in my inbox for a while to remind me that I could write if I wanted to, but after weeks I decided I would not. I had nothing to say. I really didn't. Elinor did not want to go to the theater, but she was home waiting for him. I deleted Nick's last email and went for a run.

The void seemed smaller when I ran. If I ran fast enough perhaps I could run away from it. Maybe one day I would.

It was raining that morning. I passed by a bush that seemed to be the walls of a house I couldn't see. What a nice screen, I thought. The bush was green, and the green was so intense I could almost taste it in my mouth. It was refreshing. I stopped and ran my fingers through it. Then I brushed my cheek on it, and the bush cried on me. I ran for a while, and when my mind was tired, I stopped at a café. As I was seated I saw Andrew's father walking by. I ran toward him and called to him.

"Mr. Pratt!"

He turned, smiled, and continued walking.

"Mr. Pratt, wait!"

He stopped and looked at me but seemed not to recognize me.

"Did we meet somewhere?" he asked.

He didn't remember me anymore. I thought he had said his Alzheimer's wasn't that bad when we met, but perhaps he was wrong about that, or had wanted to be.

"How's school?" he asked.

Maybe he remembered now.

"I took a leave" I said.

"Oh, what was it? You didn't like your teachers?"

No, he didn't. I attempted a smile.

"Would you join me for coffee? It would be nice to chat with you," I said, hoping he would say yes. He smiled and agreed to follow me.

"How's Andrew?" I asked.

"He's doing fine," he said, checking me with his eyes. He paused and then added, "I know he was looking for you. He came the other day to visit me."

Did Andrew really go visit him? Did he remember me?

"Did he publish his novels?" I tried again.

"I think he should sometime soon."

Did he?

"I'm glad. I should finish my work soon," I said, and confused him again.

"How are you?" I then asked.

"Do you really want to hear?"

"Yes, I do."

"Lonely," he said. "I feel lonely. I don't remember much these days, and it seems nobody can understand me. My wife would have. I miss her."

"Andrew's mom?"

"Yes. You know she was my student? I never told anyone."

"Tell me about her."

"She was an artist, like Andrew. She quit school after we fell in love. She was sweet, fragile. Our families didn't want us to get married. They thought I was too old for her. But then we got married," he continued. "I wanted to give Andrew his name, she wanted to call him Frank. We flipped a coin and I won. I'm glad I did. When we told our parents, they were mad at us for picking Andrew's name the way we did. They thought it was stupid. We thought it was fun." His smile was so sweet. I had never seen Andrew smile like that. I wished he did, now that I knew he could.

Andrew's father told me more stories of his family, and more stories about Andrew, stories of him as he was growing up.

"He was such a sweet kid. He didn't talk much but would bring his sketchbook everywhere he went and communicate through his drawings. Everyone loved his drawings. He drew all the time and everywhere. So many drawings. His bedroom walls were entirely covered." He laughed. I wish I could see what he was describing. I tried.

He opened his wallet and pulled out one of Andrew's first drawings. It showed a boy on the bow of a vessel, wearing a captain's hat, his arms reaching to the sky, the ocean all around. I remembered that. Andrew had told me about it. This is exactly what he wanted to share with me when I asked him about his art growing up. I thought it was interesting that Andrew's father had chosen the same scrap of memory his son had chosen.

"He made this when he was seven, or something like that," he said. "I stole it before leaving. This is how I remember him. A boy on the bow of a vessel, ready to conquer the world. Happy." He folded the paper, which was as weathered as his hands. I placed my hands on his and dove into his discolored eyes, eyes that were almost fading.

"What else do you remember?" I asked.

"I remember Andrew."

"Tell me more about him."

"Hmm . . ." He took a deep breath and looked outside the window, searching through his memories.

"He was too young when I left. I remember his look when I took my suitcase and walked out the door. He didn't understand all of that, but I never tried to explain. I would have if he had been older. I did whisper, 'it's not your fault,' but I am not sure he thought it was, and I'm not sure he even heard what I said. I would have given anything to know what he thought. I wasn't even close. Ever. I'm sure."

He paused and continued to play with his napkin as I had seen Andrew do the last time we were together.

"I didn't leave Andrew though," he continued. "I never did, even after I left. I tried to follow him as much as I could. I went to his school and watched him arrive and leave. I talked to his teachers, his friends . . . He didn't want to talk to me, so I had no choice. Yes, I followed him, until I thought he was ready to be on his own. Maybe I got that wrong though. A child is never able to go on his own, right?"

I wasn't.

We talked more about Andrew, and his father's memories of him. Those memories seemed intact. He hadn't forgotten. He did remember Andrew. I wasn't sure he remembered me, though, but I tried again.

"I loved meeting with you months ago, and I love this time with you. You seem unreal. Sometimes I feel you are."

He smiled.

"Yes, it was special, and today is too." His eyes told me he had remembered. I believed him.

After we left, I walked with him to his building and then returned home.

I was no longer warm from my run and had started feeling cold, but I decided to walk back to my apartment. When I arrived there, I felt sick. This time I was sure it wasn't from the cold. It was my meeting with Andrew's father that was too intense to sustain. I hid under my blanket and stayed there for a while, staring at the window, my thoughts wandering without any trajectory I could grasp. I had no energy left. I closed my eyes and hoped I could see the fake stars on the ceiling again, but I had no machine to make them. I got up and sat close to the window to look for the real ones, but there weren't any. The sky was still cloudy from the morning rain. I went to my desk and wrote about my meeting with Andrew's father. I reviewed what I wrote and then tried to sleep, but I couldn't. I waited and waited. Then I looked out my window and saw Nick. I hadn't seen him in months, and yet he was there, looking up. I looked at him, but I'm not sure he saw my eyes. I was too far up, and he was too close to the ground. I ran down in my pajamas. We hugged each other and stayed close for a while.

"I just came to say good-night."

"I couldn't sleep."

"I knew that."

I opened my eyes and felt confused. What exactly had I dreamed?

SOMEONE WINS. WE LOSE

I had learned to live without Nick, and it was OK.

So on a Sunday in April, I agreed to meet with Matt. He said he had something to show me and wanted to take me to brunch. I had missed people, as isolated as I was in my little apartment. I wore my best dress and my best smile, and when I closed the door behind me to go to the meeting, I felt like I was closing more than that.

"You look great," he said when he saw me.

"You do too," I said.

"I've missed you."

"I've missed you too."

"How's the writing?"

"It's going . . ."

"When will I get to read it?"

When? I wish I could say. Soon, I hoped. To get some peace, to get released from the obsession, from the isolation, of the past several months. It would feel nice to close my story and move on.

"So one month, two?"

"I really don't know," I said.

"Well, I have something for you." He handed me a book wrapped in light-blue paper.

"What is it?"

I unwrapped the little box, and there it was. *The Girl, the Beach, and the Rain.* He had finished it, and the story looked beautiful.

"The first page . . . Isn't that the sketch . . . ?"

"Yes, you forgot to take it."

I had forgotten to take the sketch he had made for me that day on the beach, and it had then become the first page of his novel. I was happy to see that. Part of the story, though, was that I had forgotten to take it, and that made me sad. The sketch was so beautiful, I could almost touch his feelings for me in it. They felt so real. And yet they, the sketch, had not pulled me into his story, toward him. I felt sad and sorry for myself, sorry for being unable to see, live, something that was real, something that I could touch, trust, rely on.

"I'm sorry. But you finished your love story," I said, pushing my tears back. "That is . . ."

"I'm actually still waiting for it to start. I hope this is how it begins," he said, his eyes smiling.

We spent the day talking and then made love. It was sweet, tender. I went to my apartment the next day, collected my things, and returned to the place Matt and I had shared and to our life together. He said it was as if I had never left. I felt differently. Matt said I could use his office in the apartment for my writing, and so I worked there, and returned to my own apartment less and less.

One morning Andrew called. I was happy to hear his voice, although he sounded distracted. We talked about his last two novels. He said they were ready to be released, but before they were, he said, it would be nice to have my piece out.

"It's not actually a *piece*, anymore."

"What is it?"

"It's a book, a story, a fiction, or something. Hard to find a label for it."

"Is it related to my work?"

"More than I could possibly explain. But it's not what you're expecting."

"What's the title?"

I remained silent, unsure of what to say.

"I don't have a title yet, as my story is still incomplete. But I know it'll eventually come to me."

"Could you write something shorter for the *Times*? I told them you were working on a piece on my work, and they seemed interested."

"The *New York Times*?"

"Yes," he said, and maybe smiled. It sounded as if he did. "Just try to finish it as soon as you can, and give me something I can use."

I said I would.

"Andrew, I've got a question. Might sound weird to you, but . . . did you visit your father lately?"

"Why do you ask?"

"I don't know. I had a dream, or something."

"He died last week."

There was silence, and that silence hit me. I couldn't stop my tears.

"Why are you crying?"

"I don't know. I'm sorry."

"It's OK. I hardly remember him. Someone in the family called to let me know."

"Did you visit him lately?"

"Who? My father?"

"Yes. Did you visit him?"

"No, I didn't."

I left the house and went for a run. That day I ran for four hours, until I had no more tears to cry and could barely feel my body anymore. I ran and ran and finally arrived in front of Henry Pratt's building. The hall seemed more silent. The gate was open. I took the elevator to his floor and knocked on his door. His son came to the door.

"I was a friend of your father," I said.

His resemblance to his father and Andrew was striking.

"I heard he died and wanted to come and say I'm very sorry."

"Yes, thanks," he said, clearly uncertain as to how to respond.

"I'm also a friend of Andrew. I'm writing about his work. Your father told me about a drawing Andrew made when he was a kid, and I would love to give it to Andrew. He didn't see his father before he died."

"Yes, we didn't see Andrew at the funeral either."

"I think it would be nice to give him that drawing."

"I'm not sure what drawing you're talking about."

"I met your father last month and he showed me a drawing Andrew made when he was a kid."

"My father? Where did you meet him?"

"Somewhere close by."

"My father was in the hospital since early January. Did you meet him before then?"

"I'm sorry," I said. "I must be confused or something."

"Do you remember what the drawing was about or where it was?"

I told him about the drawing that his father had carried in his wallet, and he said he would look for it and call if he found it. I gave him my number and left.

When I got home, I turned the computer on and wrote "Finding Andrew." I wrote nonstop and finally put the last two sentences down:

For each lie we say there are so many untold truths. Andrew's story taught me that I should stop looking for the lies or the truths, and should rather look for myself.

When I finished reviewing my article and was ready to send it to Andrew, Andrew's brother called. He had found the drawing.

"It wasn't in the wallet as you said. It was in a book my father was reading. Anyhow, it's yours if you want it."

I went back, and he gave me the drawing. I felt so happy when I could hold it. Did I dream that meeting? The drawing was as I had seen it, as I remembered it. I was too exhausted to ask questions. I returned home, printed my article, and brought it to Andrew, together with his drawing.

"I think this belongs to you," I said when I saw him, and handed him the drawing.

"Thanks, Susan. You were faster than I thought," he said.

I remained silent.

His eyes froze when he saw the drawing.

"Where did you get this?"

"Your brother gave it to me. Your father had kept it for years. He said he 'stole' it before leaving. I think you should know this, and have it back."

He cried. I hugged him and left.

When I returned home, Matt proposed to me, and I said yes. We got married that June, but summer never came that year. The following spring I became a mother.

FALLING

Our baby was born in March. A beautiful boy. We named him William. It was Matt's choice, from the name of one of his favorite graphic novelists. I liked the name, and thought it was perfect for him when I held him in my arms. The baby looked very much like his father. He was blond, had blue eyes, and his smile was open and full. I spent my days with Will, and I had not written since I left my apartment. Sometimes I leafed through the pages of my manuscript and stuck notes and ideas in there. But when I reviewed them, I realized they didn't belong.

Will would wake up often in the middle of the night. He loved watching me draw, and so when he woke up, I drew and drew for him. Somehow watching me draw would make him slowly fall asleep again. I still used charcoal, and now there was charcoal everywhere in the house. One night I drew Nick's portrait.

Even though Will would wake up easily, he would just as easily fall asleep again, leaving me to wander around the house for a couple of hours or so before returning to bed. Almost two years had passed since my sleepless nights. I again had some private time with the night, but it was different. I was different.

One night, after putting Will back to sleep, I started searching through my photo albums, novels, and psychology books, and I found my thesis. I remembered what Henry Pratt had told me one day. He said that we write to search. What search did my thesis contain? That night I didn't go back to bed. I read and reviewed my thesis. I looked behind the chapters, within the lines. Moments of my life, thoughts and events almost forgotten, all mixed up with my garage/studio, my favorite music, my solitude.

Midlife transition. The feeling of being trapped in a career I wasn't sure of. The boring lectures of Professor Forg. I was completing my PhD, but I didn't want to be him, or at least I didn't want to be someone like him for too long. Could I transition then? At some point? And would I feel better if I succeeded? In my transition, I meant.

Daydreaming. When I was working on this chapter I went to the movie theater to see *Hearts in Atlantis.* I was alone. It was after Thanksgiving. Classes were over. I was only writing my thesis at that time, had no classes, and felt like I was sleepwalking. Why do we daydream? Was it OK to live your life as a dream?

Sadness. One of my teachers died. She hanged herself. I read the news in an email the dean sent out to the school. There was no photo, just a cold, dry list of her work and, obviously, no explanation of the reasons why she did it. Nobody knew that. Or did they? What was sadness? What caused it? Were there degrees of sadness?

Feeling restless. I wrote night and day and slept only for few hours. I would go to bed at midnight and wake up two hours later, eager to start writing again. I did it for weeks and then crashed. But I crashed only for a few days and then started writing again as insanely as I had before. Was it OK to constantly feel as if you didn't have time to waste? As if you could die any moment? Was it OK to constantly feel like you were trying to achieve something, and once you did, start searching for something else? Should I feel rested at some point? Would I?

Increased sexual desire and sexual affairs. I met a judo athlete who did strip shows to make ends meet. We met on a train. He approached me and stalked me with an excuse. I thought it was romantic. He probably didn't. I was reading *Siddhartha* on that train. Was the book what attracted him to me? We went out a couple of times. It felt weird. We didn't have anything in common. I had an increased sexual desire. I was his sexual affair. But he didn't know my truth, and I didn't know his. What did it mean to desire? Why would someone in a relationship seek and have an affair?

Increased or decreased ambition. One of my articles was published in a top scientific journal and even cited in several studies. The teachers at the school were ecstatic or jealous, I couldn't say which. And the school featured the news on the front page of its website for days, as that would probably help its ranking. I felt gratified but wanted more. And yet, days later, I no longer cared. Why? Where did this come from? Will I be swinging from ambition to apathy and back for the rest of my life? Will I be someone famous or nobody? Will I even care?

Those chapters were talking to me. It was early morning when I rested my head on the sofa, but Will woke up again.

"Will you take care of him?" Matt called from the other room.

I got up, and with my eyes half-closed went and played with him in his little crib. He was so sweet. He wasn't really crying, he was calling me. But even when he cried and I was tired, I loved to go and make him feel that I was there. Being a parent had changed my perspective on many things. I had certainly become less selfish. But I had not changed my perspective on Nick. Did he know I had a baby? Was he still in New York?

When Matt got up he started listing his appointments for the day and complaining about his workload to me. I listened—I always did —but that report took almost all our time together. It always did. I got one report in the morning when we had coffee together and one at night, at dinner when he returned from work. And during the weekends we would talk about problems he had at work. And then there was more work for him to do. So we didn't exactly talk. But quite frankly, I'm not sure I had much to talk about or share with him, other than Will.

That morning, even though I was tired and knew I should have tried to sleep a bit, I took Will to my father's and went to my apartment. I brought my computer with me and told myself I had to start writing again. I reviewed what I had written, looked at the lines, deeply into them, but it didn't take much effort to find the search in my story.

The phone rang, and it was Andrew. His books had been published, the first run had sold out, and they were already in the second printing. There would be a signing event the next day, and he had called to make sure I would go.

"You didn't reply to my last emails. Did you get them?" he asked.

He had sent me three emails, all about the event. And of course I got them and read them and thought about it. But I couldn't make up my mind as to whether I should go or not. I was worried that Nick would be there, or that he wouldn't. In either case, I knew I would feel horrible.

"No, I didn't," I said. "You know, with Will sometimes I forget to check." Will was my best excuse for everything at that time, especially for my absences. But it wasn't Will really.

"You know, I wish I had known before. Now it might be hard to come," I added.

"I understand," he said. "I hope you'll make it, though. It would mean a lot to me."

"I know."

"Have you finished your novel?" he asked.

I was holding my work as he inquired about it.

"Do you know when you'll have it done? Approximately? I'd love to read it."

"I haven't exactly been writing lately."

"You should. Incomplete stories are frozen butterflies."

What a disturbing image. What was a frozen butterfly? A cold one? A paralyzed one? One trapped in a large ice cube?

"You can't torture those butterflies like this. They're waiting. And you're waiting too."

I was ready to ask him what he meant by that and what did he know about writing, when I realized he knew more than I did, and I was afraid of his answer, whatever it might be.

"I'm sorry," I said, his image of the frozen butterflies still pounding in my head.

"Sorry for what?" he asked.

I didn't respond.

"All right, then. Take care of yourself."

When he hung up, I thought more about the frozen butterflies. Not that I had a choice. They had infested my head. I thought I should try to draw them. And I did. I used charcoal again. And when I was done, and I saw the charcoal butterflies in my drawing, I thought they looked exactly how I had imagined them, seen them. And actually, now that I had captured them in that drawing, they felt less painful. Perhaps they had left me. I almost liked them now. I felt bad for them though. If I could only warm them in my hands and make them fly again.

I moved to my desk and tried to write. I wrote and rewrote a chapter, but it wasn't working. I grabbed a bottle of wine, but there wasn't much left, and I threw it against the wall. The wine stained the window, the glass broke, and parts of it fell on the carpet. I sat and placed a piece of the glass on my hand and looked at it, through it. My frozen skin, my frozen me. I pushed the sharp edge between the thumb and the index finger. I didn't feel it. I pressed harder. I didn't feel anything. Blood filled the space between the two fingers. The line of blood that was staining my hand, almost separating my hand into two parts, was cold, and my hand didn't move. I pushed the glass harder, and I felt better. And better. And better. I wanted my hand to move. I asked it to move. I implored my frozen butterfly to feel, to live, and write again. But it didn't. I let myself fall to the carpet and fell asleep.

When I woke up, I had blood all over. On my sweater, my jeans, on the carpet. I didn't feel anything though. Initially I thought it was the wine. I remembered the broken bottle. There was still wine on the wall. But then when I tried to move my hand, it hurt. I was happy. Perhaps, I thought, I could write now. I should try. I turned my computer on and wrote the word "Falling" on top of a blank page. I wasn't going to write about something that was complete. So . . . *falling*. How much further down could I still go? My hand hurt. The blood stained the keyboard. I wrote some more, some sketches and a few ideas. I looked at them and saw they all belonged to the story. I was inspired again.

When I stopped writing I realized I had seriously injured myself, so I went to the closest emergency room. The doctors told me that I had cut my flexor tendon, the one between my thumb and my index finger.

"How did you do that?" he asked.

"I don't recall," and I really didn't. I remembered the glass, but my memories weren't clear.

"It might have been some glass."

Did I want him to know? To tell *me* what had happened? What had I done?

He scanned me, bandaged my hand, and didn't believe me.

"You're lucky," he said. "You won't need surgery . . . this time. Be careful with that glass."

No, he had not believed me.

"Do you feel safe at home?" he then asked.

Oh, right, he had no idea.

Did I feel safe at home? Safe from whom?

"Of course," I said.

He prescribed some drugs and let me go. I walked to a pharmacy and waited in line. That waiting was almost healing. It felt like something I could do, had no choice but to do. I just had to wait. But then, as I was waiting, I saw someone that looked like Nick. I stopped breathing for a moment, but when he turned I realized it wasn't him. He noticed I was staring at him, and after he paid he came closer to me.

"Hi, what's up? What did you do to your hand?"

"I . . ."

"Do you live close by?"

I didn't respond. I paid and left.

When I got to my father's place to pick Will up, my father told me Will was sleeping and handed me his carry-cot. He saw my bandage and looked worried.

"What happened?" he asked.

"What?"

"Your hand? And you look pale . . . ?"

"I was cleaning and some glass . . ."

"Is everything OK?"

"Yeah. I just damaged a tendon. But the doctor said I should be OK. No need for surgery."

"Are you sure?"

"Yes," I said, but looked away.

"Do you want to talk?"

"Oh, Dad, I'm so tired right now. I've been at the ER for two or three hours. It was draining."

He didn't take his eyes off my hand. He looked suspicious. But how could he know? Did he? I told him once again not to worry about me. I kissed him and walked to the door.

"Wait," he said.

"What?"

"Your grandmother asked about you. She asked me to give you this." He handed me an envelope.

"What is it?"

"There's a note she wrote for you and a copy of the keys to the house. You know she has a caregiver living with her now. But she said you can go visit her whenever you like. And here are the keys."

After I left, I opened the envelope. The note was short.

Dear Susan,

I hope you're doing fine. It would be nice if you stopped by whenever you have a chance. I would love to see you again.

Grandma

When I got home, I lay Will in his crib and looked at him for a while. How did I make something as peaceful as him? Where did his peace come from? Was there peace in my soul? Somewhere? I pulled the envelope from my purse and placed it in the drawer of my desk in what was once Matt's office. It was supposed to have become my writing room, but somehow it never did. And I had not used my apartment that much either. So I had two writing rooms but no finished, publishable writing yet. How sad, I thought.

When Matt came home, he kissed me, and went to the bedroom to change. He didn't even notice my bandage until we were seated at dinner. He then asked me about it, and I repeated the same story I had told my father. He believed it. No further questions asked. We quickly returned to his list of problems and appointments for the next day. And that's all I remember of our night together. He may have said something else, told me about his day, and I may have made a comment. I wasn't there though, and he didn't even notice. When I woke up, I decided I wouldn't go to the book signing.

"I'll be home early today," Matt said before leaving. "I've got some work to do, but I'm so tired I need a break from the office. Do you mind?"

"Why would I mind?"

Yes, why would I?

I said that I'd be waiting for him and we might do something in the evening. Maybe take Will with us. I tried. I did try.

I didn't do much the entire day. I looked at my pages and my sketches but felt like everything was twisted inside of me, my lungs, my stomach. I blamed it on the drugs the doctor gave me, but I knew it wasn't that. I had started so many things and completed none of them.

Matt came home after lunch. We had coffee together, watched a movie, and when he said he needed to return to his work, I told him about the book signing.

"Andrew wrote and then called. He said it would mean so much to him if I went," I said.

"You should go."

"I told him I couldn't as I hadn't made arrangements for it."

"But I'm here. I can watch Will. You should go."

"I really don't want to."

I tried.

"Why?"

"I just don't."

I did try again, but he finally convinced me to go. I didn't even change. I kept my jeans and sweater from the day on. I wanted to be invisible. Would it be possible to see Nick without being seen? I guess that would be hard, but it was my goal.

When I arrived Andrew was talking at the microphone. He saw me at the door and waved. He was happy I was there, and he said beautiful things about my work, the article I had written, our meeting, my artistic instinct, our friendship. Did I really help him? I hoped so. I thought I should look for Nick. I knew he was there. When Andrew finished his speech, I turned and saw Nick, standing there, pretending to be interested in something, anything other than us. Pretending, like me.

Andrew came to say hi.

"You made it," he said.

"I did."

"I'm glad you did."

"I'm glad too," I smiled, he hugged me, and over his shoulders I caught Nick looking at me. He was with a woman, but it wasn't Elinor. The woman was tall, blond, and had big, glittery lips and glittery makeup. She looked like a cheap model, a living Barbie or something. He looked sad. Our eyes met, and he looked down and then back at me. I chatted more with Andrew, and when he excused himself, I was left alone for a while. I thought I should leave, but then Nick came up to me.

"Hey."

"Hi."

"You look great."

I looked at him but didn't respond.

"What happened to your hand?"

"Nothing interesting."

"How are you? How's Matt?" he asked.

"He's doing great."

"Andrew said you had a baby."

I nodded and looked away. Could I go now?

"And the writing?"

I remained silent, and he tried again.

"I hope you didn't give up on that."

"I . . . didn't, but it has been hard lately."

"Why?"

There was more silence, and then he said, "I could read what you have if you wanted."

"What would you read?"

"Your book."

"I don't think it's a good idea. And it's not done yet."

"Well, how much of it do you have?"

"A good chunk. I guess I'm missing the finale."

"Oh, that's the hardest part to write. You don't want to rush it. It's good you're thinking about it. You shouldn't push it. It'll come to you. Let me read what you have."

Thanks, but I don't think it would be a good idea. I'd better go now. My husband and my son are waiting for me. That is what I should have said. Instead, I said,

"OK, I'll send it to you when I get home."

"It's been a while."

Yes, it was, and I was still falling.

NICK READS

When I returned home, Matt wanted to have dinner, but I wasn't hungry. I told him about the event and that I had seen Nick.

"Yes, I imagined that could happen," he said.

Really? Then why did you insist that I go?

"How did it feel?" he asked.

Do you really want to know? I can't tell you.

"He wants to read what I wrote."

"Your book?"

"Yes, my book."

"I think you should let him."

Matt and I hadn't talked much, but at least we had talked and we had talked about me. I felt grateful for the exchange and for his blessing.

Here's my work.

Susan

I attached my book and clicked "send." A few minutes later, Nick had already replied.

I'll read.

Nick

After dinner, as Matt was preparing for bed, I told him I would stay up to read. I needed some privacy, silence, the night. He seemed to understand.

"Could you take care of Will if he wakes up? I need to be alone tonight," I said.

"Will you disappear again?"

I wasn't thinking of physically disappearing, of going anywhere, but then I looked for the keys my father gave me and decided to go check out the house. I grew up there with my parents and my grandmother. Then my father met Evelyn and decided to give the house to my grandmother and move to a new place with his new girlfriend. I left the house too when I went to college, returned my set of keys to my father, and never went back.

I left a note for Matt, telling him I was going to check out my grandmother's house. We had briefly talked about it before, and I'd told him that I wanted to go, so I thought this would not come as a surprise, at least not a big one. I grabbed a printed copy of my book and left. I am not sure why I took the book with me. Perhaps it was because at times I felt like the book was the most precious thing I had, and I didn't want to lose it. And even though it was saved on my computer, every time I printed it the story seemed like it was now something that could get lost.

I wasn't in the mood for talking, but my taxi driver was. He probably thought it was unusual for a woman to go out alone at night, and he tried to make me feel comfortable. That thought made me laugh. When we reached our destination, I paid the driver and stood in front of the house for a while. There was light on in what used to be my bedroom. I wondered if it was now the caregiver's room. After a while, I noticed my driver hadn't left. He was probably updating his rides book or something. I waited for him to leave, as I wanted to be left alone. Instead he backed up, rolled down the window, and asked me if I wanted him to wait.

"No, thanks. This is home," I said, and when I said it, it hurt.

When the driver disappeared into the alley, I opened the gate, and entered. The sprinklers started to fire water all over, but I didn't move, perhaps waiting for the rain to push me in or out. But someone opened the door, making the decision for me.

"Who's there?" A voice dimmed by the night or the years asked. I saw my grandmother.

"Grandma, it's Susan."

"Susan? Is it really you?"

She turned on the light and came closer to make sure it was me. She hugged me and caressed my hair as she used to do when I was younger. That usually calmed me down, and it worked again. Yes, this was home. She was much older, maybe approaching her nineties. I hadn't seen her in so many years. Twelve or fifteen. I didn't recall. But her posture and demeanor hadn't changed a bit. And while I didn't have bad feelings for her, she reminded me of my past. And so I had long avoided her to feel better.

"Come in, sweetie, I'll make you some tea."

That's what she used to call me. She was the only one who ever did so. I wasn't a sweetie. I really wasn't. But when she called me sweetie, I tried to become one for her. And sometimes I succeeded, but I didn't want anyone else to see that happen.

The caregiver came to check on us, and my grandmother said we were fine. She proudly introduced me to her as her granddaughter, "the brain of the family," and listed my accomplishments so precisely that I don't think I could have done a better job myself. In fact, I had forgotten some of what she said. That made me sad. Not that I had forgotten, but that she hadn't.

She tried to pour the tea into my cup, but her hands were shaking so much she could barely hold the teapot. I placed my hand on hers and silently asked her to let me take care of it. She moved to make some room for me then lay her cane against the couch and held on to me while she lowered herself into her seat.

As she was watching me pour the tea, she noticed my bandage.

"What happened?" she asked.

"I cut myself. Nothing serious."

"Hmm . . .," she said, and smiled.

I didn't understand the meaning of that smile. Shouldn't she look sad? Worried? Ask more questions? Why was she smiling?

"I'm sorry I woke you up," I said, to silence my questions and make sure she wouldn't hear them. "I didn't intend to. I came here just to check on the house. I know, it's stupid. I thought I would come over tomorrow or maybe another day. To see you. At a better time."

"I'm glad you woke me up. I was waiting for your visit."

"Were you?"

"Yes, of course. I knew you needed your time, though, so I didn't want to push."

Yes, she never did. She always respected me, my silences, and my nonsenses, even when I myself would not have. And I remembered she would get mad at my dad when he pushed me to do anything I didn't want to do, as if I knew better than he or anyone else what was good for me. At times I felt she was trying to be a better mother for me, better than the one she had been for her daughter, as if she had been offered a second chance with me, the daughter of her daughter. Unfortunately, so many years had passed since the last time I had seen her. During the years of absence, and even before that, I felt like I didn't have a mother, either the original or a replacement. And yet, even though I wasn't responsible for the first loss, I was responsible for the second.

"Dad gave me your note."

She kept her eyes on mine.

"I was happy to get it. He actually gave it to me last night."

She sipped her tea.

"I'm writing a book."

"On your subject?" she asked. "Psychology?"

"No, it's a story," I said, and pulled the pages from my satchel. I was waiting for her to ask me what kind of story it was, and whether it was real or fiction, but she didn't. Sometimes I felt she knew more than one could expect, than I would expect. Or perhaps she just knew how to pick her questions better than anyone else. Hers was a careful selection, somehow resembling a graphic novel, one filled with drawings and events, but very few words. Like her, I also thought sometimes words didn't matter as much. I wanted to tell her that, but I didn't. She looked at the stack of paper that I introduced as "my book" and seemed impressed by its volume. I explained that I had written at least five times as much but had eventually deleted what I thought wasn't good enough.

"You have so much in your head, so many stories," she said. "I'm not surprised." She smiled and looked at me, into me. Then she immersed herself in drinking her tea again, before she added, "I always wanted to write a novel. I guess it takes courage to do so. I think I would have been tempted to tell my own story, but then I would have been naked in front of everyone else. You are braver than me. You're like your mother. I wish she had used her courage differently . . ."

"This story is not about me, Grandma," I said.

She rose, went to the kitchen to grab some cookies, and came back.

"Will you read it to me?"

"My novel?"

"Yes. I can't read anymore, and I usually ask Eva to read, but this is your story. I wouldn't want anyone else but you to read it to me."

"It might take a whole day."

"Or maybe one night."

"We would both fall asleep, Grandma."

She smiled and asked me to start. And so I did.

I read for hours, checking on her from time to time, bringing her more tea and more cookies. She never interrupted me or asked questions. When I asked her if she wanted me to stop, she just said "Continue," with a firm tone. From time to time I would see her eyes half-closed. But I knew she was still following the story, because she smiled, and moved her fingers on the couch as if she were listening to music.

"It's like a symphony," she said when I completed a chapter. "Your writing is. It awakens your senses, overwhelms them. Continue."

And so I did. I read and read, and then I got to "Falling."

When I was done reading that chapter, she started crying and pulled my hand to her knees, and I held it in hers. I watched her cry, but I was relieved. I had shared my story with someone I cared for, and she liked it. I wasn't alone with it anymore. I wasn't the only one who knew it.

"Thank you for listening to my story," I said, when I was finally done.

"The story is not finished yet. I will look forward to the rest."

She rose and asked me to follow her. The sun had not yet risen, but I said I would have to return home soon.

She took me to my bedroom. The light I had seen from outside was still on, but there was nobody in the room.

"I thought the caregiver was sleeping in my room now."

"Why?"

"I saw the light when I came, and so . . ."

"I leave the light on every night. I've done so since you left. The light's my prayer for you."

"I'm sorry I didn't come visit you all these years, Grandma."

"It wasn't the right time. I knew you would one day, and I never stopped waiting. Things come to you if you don't give up on them. Eventually they do. Sometimes it's just bad timing. But then the time is right."

We lay on my bed, holding each other. And when it was six, I said I had to go and walked to the door. We passed by what used to be my mother's bedroom, and for a second I thought I saw her at the door. I rubbed my eyes, kissed my grandmother, and left.

When I returned home, the note for Matt was precisely where I had left it. He hadn't seen it. He didn't even know I had been gone. The apartment was silent. They must be sleeping, I thought, and they both were, peacefully. I trashed the note, put on my pajamas, and got quietly into bed.

"How did you sleep?" Matt asked, after what seemed to be too little time had passed. "Did Will wake up last night?"

Did he? How would I know?

Before I tried to respond to his question, Will called, and I went to his room. He was smiling and playing with the little colorful animals hanging over his head. Will had slept tight, he hadn't woken Matt up, and now it was almost eight. Matt rushed to the shower and then to the door. He kissed me and quickly disappeared. I stayed in my pajamas all morning, playing with Will and his toys on our bed and occasionally revisiting the night with my grandmother. I decided she should see Will, so in the afternoon I took Will with me over to her place.

When Will saw my grandmother, he opened his eyes wide and started laughing with excitement. Once we were all seated, I placed him in her arms, and she looked at peace. She started lullabying him, moving her arms, following who knows what idea or vision. Will seemed almost hypnotized.

I rose to use the bathroom, but instead I went to my mother's room. I entered, closed the door, and sat on her bed. Everything was as I remembered. The heavy, dark wood of the bed frame. The white bedsheet. The white curtains. I could still see them slightly moving with the wind. The blinds half-down. The little craft trinkets she used to collect all over the place. The photos on the nightstand. There were photos of her at her wedding, photos of her with me. I hadn't looked at photos of my mother in so many years. I held one of those photos in my hands and studied it. Did her eyes, expression, lips reveal her disease? And what was it really? Was there a label for it? One that could capture what she had and who she had been? I looked more deeply into that photo. She was beautiful, but a flash of madness seemed to cross her eyes. She didn't seem trapped like the woman in Andrew's drawing, but she looked alone. I had the feeling she had fully embraced herself, her madness, and that had isolated her from the rest of the world. The other people in one of the photos seemed complete strangers to her. And yet I could recognize an uncle and an aunt, their sons, some family friends. I looked closer and noticed my mother had my hair, my way of smiling, my eyes. And the more I looked at her, the more I saw myself in her. Was I sick too? My hands began shaking and let the photo fall to the floor. The glass broke. I bent to pick up the glass and my other hand started bleeding from the tiny, little cuts I now had all over, none of which were intentional. Were they? I went to the bathroom, washed and cleaned the cuts as well as I could, and returned downstairs.

"I broke this, I'm sorry," I told my grandmother, and handed her the photo in the frame, now without glass.

"It's OK, sweetie. It's not a big deal, Eva will fix it."

"Grandma? Did my mother ever cut herself with glass?"

She examined me, and then looked at my bandaged hand.

"Did you?" she asked.

"No," I said, waiting for her to tell me the truth while I had just lied. But she didn't answer my question, so I broke the silence.

"We should go now," I said, and pulled Will from her arms. He started crying.

"Of course," she said.

I called a taxi and left.

As Nick was reading, I was getting ready to write again.

YOU LEFT YOUR DOOR OPEN

Susan,

I'm speechless. Your story is overwhelming, sublime. It makes it hard to breathe. It's chewing my insides. Maybe we could talk about it over coffee.

Nick

I took Will to my father's and went for a run, with one hand bandaged, the other cut. I looked for silence. The streets were crowded and there was noise everywhere, but I didn't hear it. I was alone. I needed to think. As I was running, I saw Nick entering a bar. I followed him. He sat at the counter and ordered a drink. I checked the time. It was eleven in the morning. The bar was deserted and almost completely dark. He was the only customer. The bartender served him a glass, then another, and another. He was making notes on a stack of papers. It must be an article he's editing, I thought. Maybe something he wrote. He used to do that. Obsess about his writing, edit and re-edit everything he wrote. Sometimes he seemed lost in it. I sat far from him and ordered a Coke. I was wearing my jogging suit. The bartender looked at me trying to figure out what I was doing there, but he didn't dare ask. I watched Nick drink another glass, and then another. Then after an hour or so, he paid, and left. He hadn't seen me. I left too, and I followed him. He wasn't walking straight, but somehow he made it to what I thought should be his place. He rang the elevator and went upstairs. I followed him. I don't know if I wanted to check whether he was OK. In fact, I wasn't event thinking. When I finally resolved to knock on his door, I realized that it was open. I pushed it slowly and entered.

His apartment was a mess of books and papers spread all over. It looked like his place in LA, but older and dirtier. I looked for his bedroom and found him lying there, already asleep, the box of zolpidem on his nightstand, close to an empty glass that still smelled of alcohol. I walked around the apartment searching for who knows what. And then, on the coffee table, I saw a stack of papers, perhaps the ones he had been working on at the bar. I took it in my hands and realized that it was my book. I leafed through the pages. His hand-written notes were all over it. He had added sentences here and there, erased words, replaced others. And he had written tons of questions for me. His notes seemed pressed against the paper as were the notes and comments I had found in Henry Pratt's essay. Was he the author of those notes as well? I sat on the sofa, ran my fingers through his comments, and read.

By three p.m., I was almost done reading. Nick was still sleeping, and I didn't want to wake him up. I pulled a blanket over him to protect his dreams from his mind. He looked so fragile, like someone who had been beaten down by life, his face covered by scars I could see more clearly now that he wasn't trying to hide them. I looked at the room. The light reminded me of Nick's apartment in LA, the first time we made love. I turned the last page and read his last question for me.

Can I help?

Just below it, I wrote:

You did. You left your door open and I came.

I closed my eyes to retain everything I had read, the close-up of him I had taken in my head, and left.

"SUMMERTIME" MAKES SENSE

And then June came. I hadn't seen Nick since that time at the bar, and he had not looked for me. I was writing again, sometimes at home, sometimes in my apartment, sometimes at my grandmother's place. I would go to her place after dinner, and sometimes I'd spend the night there. We had tea, looked at some old photos, and when she went to bed and left me alone with my thoughts, I would start writing in what used to be my room.

One night, after spending the evening with my grandmother, I went to my room to write. I opened the window wide. The night had its own sound, and it became louder and louder as I silenced my own noise. As I was playing with ideas to work into my story, my phone buzzed.

I'm here.

I checked the sender. It was Nick.

Here where?

I looked outside and saw Nick standing in front of the gate.

I called him.

"What are you doing here?"

"You think you're the only one who can stalk people?"

"That was an accident."

"Coming to my place and reading my notes was an accident? Whatever. I didn't find you by accident tonight."

"Really? Then why are you here?"

"To talk."

"Talk?"

"Yes. We should talk about your novel."

There was some silence, and then he continued.

"You read my questions, didn't you?"

I didn't respond. He insisted.

"Did you?"

"Yes."

"Have you thought about them?"

"I don't get this, Nick. What do you want?"

"I want to help."

"How would you help?"

He was silent for a moment. "It's so interesting you ask that. You remember when I asked you that exact same question? You wanted to help me write my piece the night of our first date. You said you wanted to help me. Do you remember what I said?"

"You said, 'How would you help?'"

"Right. And what happened next?"

There was more silence, and then I agreed to come down. I looked at the lamp on my desk and was about to turn it off, but then I backed off and left it on. I still needed that prayer.

"I brought you a copy of my notes," he said when he saw me. "I thought you should have them."

"I don't need them. I remember your comments."

"What did you think of them?"

"I liked them. I thought you were right. Most of the time."

He smiled.

"Would you like to go for a walk?"

"Here?"

"Yes, I think it'd be nice. It's summer. I can feel it tonight. Do you?"

Yes, I did, and I agreed to walk with him.

"How's the writing going?" he asked.

"I have moments of inspiration, followed by despair. Then more inspiration."

"This is how it's supposed to be." He smiled, took my hand, and dragged me into an alley. "I want you to see this."

That alley was magic. The houses looked like old castles, and there were autumn leaves on the lawns surrounding them.

"Autumn in June," I said, and looked for an explanation, something that made sense.

"I've got no idea. A charming nonsense." He had read my mind.

We both looked at each other, and I thought that the song "Summertime" now made sense. We continued to walk.

"Do you still have trouble sleeping?" he then asked.

"No. But I have nightmares at times."

"What are they about?"

"Death. One way or another. They never wake me up, but I always remember them when I open my eyes, and some of them stay with me for days."

"Did you figure out why you had insomnia before?"

"No. Perhaps I was just bored. Or I was afraid of wasting my life."

"Killing time, huh?"

I looked down.

"Have you ever killed time?" he asked.

"Yes, I think I have, and I hate myself for it."

"Maybe you needed to rest, to shut your mind down. You shouldn't punish yourself for that."

"Do you think insomnia was my way to punish myself?"

"I've thought it," he said, but he didn't give me the diagnosis I was hoping for. And he continued, "I loved your description of our first meeting. Did you really want to make love to me?"

"Yes, I did," I said, and smiled, somehow surprising myself with that truth.

"I did too," he said, perhaps thinking that it felt good to be honest. It seemed it did.

"I know," I said. "I read your comments."

"Right. Sometimes it's surprisingly easy to be honest . . ."

We both smiled.

"And you masturbated thinking of me?"

I looked at him and paused. I remembered his questions. He was going over them, one by one, as if he were following his script, careful not to miss any part of it.

"Did you come here to get your answers?" I asked.

"No. I came here to make sure you listen to them."

"I'm not following."

"You said you're having trouble writing your finale. I'm trying to help."

I didn't comment on that, but I thought about his words.

As we walked, the tension between us slowly disappeared and turned into curiosity. What did he know about my story? What did he know about my search that I didn't? If I had asked him, he wouldn't have told me. I had to go find the answer myself. He had left the door open. Again.

"Yes, I masturbated thinking of you. But I didn't think you would be doing the same, so that thought did not turn me on," I said, and thought about his question, one that was hard to forget.

I would have loved to see you masturbate that morning. I actually did the same thinking of you. Did it cross your mind that I could be doing that? Did it turn you on?

"Why did I make you uncomfortable?" Another of his questions I remembered.

"It was the unknown," I said.

"What do you mean?"

"What I didn't know about you made me uncomfortable. The way you looked at me. The thoughts that were crossing your mind and I didn't see. The ones that were crossing my mind and I couldn't share with you. Sometimes I felt I had to play the role that you had imagined for me. But it wasn't mine, and I felt trapped in your idea."

"Would you believe me if I said you made me uncomfortable too?"

It was hard to believe. I tried.

When we walked back onto the main street, I looked for the autumn leaves, but I couldn't find any.

"Look at the sky. It's not like in LA. It seems more distant from us."

Yes, it did. It looked unreachable now, and it probably was.

I remembered another of his questions.

"You wondered why I always tried to fix you?" I asked.

"Yes. Why did you?"

"I was hoping you would commit to me."

"Are you sure that's what you wanted?"

"You don't think that was the reason?"

"It's not convincing," he said. "I don't think you like stability. You're not stable. Like me. Instability is what you know and look for. Am I right?"

Was he?

I didn't know the answer to that.

His questions and my answers or silences were generating more questions. I got it now. He was helping me. But I needed him to push me, I needed him to ask the questions he had written for me, otherwise I would have forgotten or convinced myself that I no longer remembered them.

"The red lipstick . . . Why did you use it that day?"

"I think I wanted to be fucked," I said.

"I thought so."

"But you didn't fuck me that night."

"I didn't," he said. "I couldn't. I would have made love to you, and I was scared."

We walked more in silence, sometimes looking at each other, sometimes looking somewhere else.

Elinor was a hard topic.

"Do you still think about that night at the theater?" he asked.

"Yes, I do."

"And what are your thoughts?"

"It's not about the cheating anymore. It's more about me, my fear of losing my mind."

"What do you mean?"

"That night I felt like the pain was poisoning my brain."

"Your description of the hotel was scary."

"It was a scary place, but you know what? I thought it was exactly where I was supposed to be."

"Hell?"

"Yes, except that hell appeared more comforting than my mind."

"Was that the only time you felt so?"

I looked at my hands and said, "No."

"Do you want to talk about it?"

"I'll let you read that."

He took a breath, and said, "The night you left, I looked for you. Went to places where I thought you might be, asked my friends to help. I felt horrible."

It never crossed my mind that he could have looked for me. So many things I didn't know.

"I also lose my mind sometimes, and I like it," he then confessed, perhaps trying to make me feel better. "I like to drink myself to numbness."

I had seen that. I believed it.

"Did you ever think I could be a drug addict?" he asked.

"Are you?"

"Did you?" he pushed.

"I . . . No, I didn't think that."

"What if I told you that I am. Would that surprise you?"

I hesitated.

"No, I guess it wouldn't."

"Why?"

"I don't know. Maybe because I know you, or perhaps because I don't."

He looked at me as if he wanted to say that I did know him.

"Why do you think I cheated on you?" he then asked.

"Because you didn't care?"

"I actually cared, perhaps more than you think."

He looked sad and turned away to hide it. I almost believed him. He breathed in that summertime air and we arrived back in front of my grandmother's house.

"Did you ever doubt that I loved you?" he asked.

After a long pause, I spoke.

"No. I guess deep down I never did."

"Do you still miss me?" he asked.

"Do you miss making love to me?" I asked.

"Is that what's blocking your writing?"

I looked at him, then opened the gate, and walked back into the house.

HAUNTED

Is that what's blocking your writing?

I heard Nick's voice asking that over and over again. And it became louder, and louder, until it started screaming in my head.

Ahhhhhhhhhhhhhhhhhhhhhhhhh! my head cried. Who would hear that?

I had been writing for hours when I checked the time. It was three in the morning. The night seemed silent. Where did all that noise in my head come from?

I reached out to the bottle on my desk to pour another glass when I noticed there was no wine left. But I had opened that bottle that night. Was that how much I had drunk? I stood up and went looking for more wine. I searched my grandmother's house, and finally found a bottle covered in dust. A label on it said,

Happy anniversary, Jasmine. Wayne. November 2, 1968.

My mother had died on the day of their anniversary? Nobody ever told me that. I thought about putting the bottle down, but I was too drunk to think rationally, and I missed her, and I was angry, at her, at my father, at Nick. I needed to drink. As I was walking back to my bedroom, I stopped in front of my mother's room. I stared at the door for a while, undecided on whether I should enter.

Is that what's blocking your writing?

I rubbed my eyes to think more clearly but I couldn't. I entered her room. Maybe I wanted to share the wine with her. Would she come visit me? Would she forgive me for opening her bottle then? Her room was so silent. For a while I thought the noise had left me alone. I felt relieved. The windows were open, and the white curtains were moving with the wind. I had never seen them still. My mother loved the wind, and everything was as she had left it. I drank a bit, then more. I closed my eyes, and when I opened them again I saw her. She was as I remembered her, that memory of her I had not revisited in years. I thought I had forgotten. But there she was. Fragile, pale, her long hair, wavy, thin, extremely thin. You could see through her. A living ghost.

"Play with me," she whispered.

"I don't feel like it," I said.

"Why not? Nobody will see us."

"That's not the point. I drank too much. I feel sick."

"Is that why you don't want to play with me, Susan? What are you afraid of?"

"Mom," I said. I had not called her that name in years, perhaps not even in my dreams. It felt weird. "I can't play with you."

"Remember when we used to play? You liked it."

"I didn't," I said. "I did not. I can't play."

Is that what's blocking your writing?

That voice was back.

"What's wrong?"

"I can't. I don't like this."

Is that what's blocking your writing?

"Do you want to hear my story?" she said. "You want to know why I killed myself?"
"Mom, don't."

Is that what's blocking your writing?

"You need to hear it."
I lay the bottle on the bed, and the wine spilled all over. The bedsheet looked bloodstained, and the blood smelled like hell.
"My head was too loud," she said. "I heard voices. Loud voices. They made me sick to my stomach."

Is that what's blocking your writing?

"One day I thought they were in my veins. Those fucking voices. I cut them. I cut the veins. I did exactly what you did, Susan. I cut my skin, then the veins, deeper into them."
She laughed. I cried. My tears were warm now. I lay my head on the wine. The wine wet my hair. My head started spinning.

Is that what's blocking your writing?

"I cut my veins, Susan. But the voices didn't leave me."
"What did your voices tell you?" I asked. I wanted to hear. Were they similar to the one I was hearing now?
"They said I was trapped. Had nowhere to go. That I was drowning."
"But you weren't, Mom. Were you?"
"How do you know? You're drowning yourself and you don't even see it."
I ran my fingers across my face and my tears tasted like blood and wine. I was confused. I implored her to stop, but she didn't.

Is that what's blocking your writing?

"Mom, stop," I asked her again, but she continued.

"They kept pounding in my head. Those stupid voices. They would never let me free. When I went to bed, when I woke up, in the middle of everything and everywhere."

Is that what's blocking your writing?

"Mom, please."
"I had to kill myself, Susan. I had to do it. I had no choice."
"You had a choice."
"Really? What was it? What choice, Susan?"
She came close. I saw her hands. They were still young, as I remembered them. But then she came closer, and I saw her head, cut, hanging to one side.
I cried.
"You're like me, Susan. You are exactly like me."

Is that what's blocking your writing?

Is that what's blocking your writing?

ADDICTIONS

When I woke up the next day, the wine's stench was so intense that it made me sick. I felt I had to throw up. I looked at the clock on the wall and its swinging pendulum. Its repetitive ticking amplified my nausea and forced me to stand up. It was almost six. The sun would be up soon. I had to be quick, I thought. I folded the bedsheet and headed to the bathroom to wash it before my grandmother woke up. I didn't want her to see that. I passed by a mirror and avoided looking at myself. But then I wanted to see. I went back and looked. What I saw disgusted me.

"Susan, are you awake?" My grandmother called from downstairs.

I said I'd be down soon. I pushed the bedsheet into the washing machine and wished I could have joined it. I could add some bleach, some softener, and come out whiter, cleaner, sweeter. I did what I could to hide the hell of the past few hours, but she was waiting, and I needed more time to fake a healthy smile for her, big enough to hide everything else. So I gave up. It just wasn't going to work. When I went down, I saw my grandmother seated at the dining table, holding a cup. I smelled the coffee and closed my eyes to taste it. She looked at me and smiled.

"What?" I asked.

"What?" she echoed me.

"Why are you smiling?"

She looked down and remained silent for a while.

"What do you see that makes you smile?"

She rose and went to the kitchen to place the cup in the sink. I waited for her to return and answer my question. When she came, though, she looked at me and said, "You're going through hell. Aren't you?"

"Yes. And that makes you smile?"

She became serious, her smile disappeared from her lips.

"You need to finish your story. We'll talk about this when you're done." She went up the stairs, turned, and said, "Close the door when you leave. I'll see you when you're done. Remember you promised to read the rest of the story to me." She turned again, and added, "Your fiction." I heard her soft laugh.

Her tone had changed. Her voice now reminded me of something I had seen, experienced, before, but I couldn't say exactly what it was. I left a note for Eva and asked her to take care of the bedsheet in the washing machine, grabbed my stuff, and left.

When I arrived back home, Matt was getting ready to leave. He scanned me, and before I even said anything, he spoke.

"Is this what you're doing at your grandmother's place?"

I knew what he meant, so I didn't ask him to explain or try to hide my misery. I wanted to talk to him, share with him exactly what had happened the night before, my nightmares, the memories that were tormenting me, but I didn't mention any of that, and just said, "I know. It won't happen again."

He didn't respond and returned to the bedroom to choose a tie for the day, one among the many he had. All in variations of blue, all of which I had selected. Every time I could almost predict the one he would pick. This time I expected the striped dark-blue one. I was right. I poured some of the coffee Matt had made and checked on Will. He was sleeping. Did he wake up last night? Did he call my name? I didn't ask Matt, and I took a shower. When I came out of the bathroom, Matt said Will had slept well. He asked me if I wanted him to take Will to my father's.

"You'll need some silence today. I bet you have a terrible headache."

I said there was no need, as I wanted to spend time with Will.

"I'm writing my finale." I tried to open up a bit.

"Hmm..."

He took his work bag, headed to the door, then turned and asked, "Will I see you tonight?"

"I'll wait until you return, but I will then go to my apartment. I need a few more days."

"Are you sure this is healthy? What you're doing to yourself?"

"I don't know."

He didn't say more, just closed the door and disappeared.

I thought about last night and felt drained and confused. I remembered Nick's questions, the ones I had read, the ones he had asked. I thought about giving him a voice in my story, but I wasn't sure I believed that voice, and so I wasn't sure it should be part of the fiction.

Do you still miss me?

Do you miss making love to me?

Those questions had remained unanswered, perhaps because they didn't need an answer.

As I sat immersed in the taste of my coffee and in my thoughts, still in my robe, my hair wet to give me a temporary illusion of cleanliness, Will woke up. I played with him, smiled for him, sang, watched cartoons, and drew smiling trees and trains with big eyes. I didn't fake any of that. I would dig into my darkness to find those trees and trains for him, and when I found them they seemed real, even to me. But as soon as he fell asleep or started playing on his own, those trees and trains disappeared, and the shadows would return. Those shadows had become darker and darker lately. I was afraid of them.

I spent all day suspended between the light me and the dark me, and I did not write. When Matt came home that night, we tried to talk, sort of.

"Do you want to talk about it?" he tried. I'm sure he had thought about it all day. I hadn't.

"What do you want to know?"

"What you are feeling?"

I looked for an answer that would tell him enough. Could I grab my feelings, hold them, display them in a window for him? Every time I tried to hold them all within my arms, tried to explain them to myself, they would flee, disappear somewhere.

"Unfinished," I then said, and wondered whether he would understand, as he didn't know about the frozen butterflies, the unfinished stories, Andrew and his comments, my sketches, and what I felt when I thought about all of this.

"Unfinished," I repeated. Would he understand now? Did it help that I had repeated it?

He looked at me, trying hard not to ask or say too much. I would have helped him if I could. I needed his silence now. But there was nothing definitive I could say that would make him feel better about me.

"I suppose you don't even know what that means, what *unfinished* means to you."

I looked down. The charcoal image of the frozen butterflies almost materialized on the floor. They looked like insects, like cockroaches, their wide wings closed and broken. I could see their faces. I could see them.

I knew my story needed an ending, but I wasn't sure what I meant by "unfinished." So he was right. I didn't exactly know what *unfinished* meant to me. At least not yet. And so I didn't respond.

"I hate to see you like this. And I don't feel like asking questions either. But it would help to know when you think you'll be done."

"Soon," I said, silently asking for his mercy and my own. "I hope you'll still be here when I'm done."

"Do you?"

"Yes."

"Then, I hope I'll be here for you," he said, and started looking for something.

"You left your sketch pad here," he added, and handed it to me. "I thought you might need it."

The sketch pad still contained my portrait of Nick and my drawing of the butterflies. I had trashed the rest.

"Did you see this?" I asked, showing him the butterflies, and trying to share more than my words probably could.

"Yes, I did. What does it represent?"

I didn't feel like explaining now. The nausea, the stench of wine rising from inside. I couldn't really talk and so remained silent.

"I wish you could explain to me what makes you draw and write like this. 'Unfinished' doesn't really do it for me."

"I'm sorry," I said, and I was.

"I'll be home tomorrow morning. I'm going to my apartment," I added.

I kissed Will, handed him to Matt, and left.

It hurt. Something did. Although I couldn't find the source.

When I arrived at my apartment, I closed the door and felt excited and worried at the same time. Excited for the writing. Worried to discover where the writing would take me this time. I turned on the stereo and let my head go, looking for inspiration. I thought about the wine I had the night before, but that disgusted me now. I looked for my phone, and texted Nick.

Where are you?

He didn't respond, but my phone said he had read my text.

I thought about sending another text but didn't. Instead, I wrote. I wrote about the night before, and that was painful. I raised the volume of the stereo and rested a bit. When I opened my eyes, it was after two a.m. I checked my phone and found a text from Nick.

I'm at the Perl. Come.

The Perl was a nightclub not far from my apartment. I thought about going but then realized that if I did, I'd like myself even less than I had the night before. I looked at the empty bottle I'd left on my desk the last time I had been in my apartment, and I thought it was time to end that addiction. Would I fall into it again? I went out and closed the door.

I started walking toward the club, but I hoped that something or someone would stop me on the way. It was an ordinary Friday night. People were wandering around looking for a club or trying to remember where home was after too many drinks. Sometimes the door of a pub or a club would open and liberate a wave of sound or people, or all of them at the same time. A few times I peeked inside and felt dragged in, as if losing myself in the crowd would help me feel better.

And then another door opened, and some loud music leaked out. I liked what I heard. I tried to check inside but couldn't, as there were too many people dancing. I thought the place might be perfect for me, and I walked to the entrance. The man at the door asked for my ID. I showed it to him, and he stamped a butterfly on my hand and let me in.

"Entrance for women is free tonight," he said, as I was checking my butterfly.

"Like it?" he asked.

No, I didn't. I just thought it was ironic. There seemed no way I was going to free myself from it. I didn't say a word and entered. I walked to the bar but didn't order a drink. Too easy, I thought. Instead I pushed myself to the middle of the room and started dancing. I danced and danced and sweated. And then I danced more, until I was exhausted and almost ready to collapse. But I still didn't leave. I stayed longer and only when I was dying of thirst, did I leave. A woman nearby me decided to do the same, and I let her and her date, or boyfriend, or friend, walk past me. She couldn't walk straight and seemed to be about to fall at any time. She must be in her thirties, I thought. She was wearing all white. Hard not to notice. The dress was too tight for her curves and too short for her legs. It barely covered her backside. This seemed to be her biggest problem at the moment, as she was all focused on pulling her dress down. What would people say if the dress showed her butt? That would be horrible? Her being wasted was OK with them, after all. What a pathetic, wasted beauty, I thought. Was I the same? I turned the corner, ducked into an alley, and threw up, perhaps because I had danced too much, perhaps because I hadn't eaten in two or three days—I didn't recall. Perhaps the woman or the thought of being like her had made me sick. My wallet fell on the curb and opened to my faculty ID. The photo had been taken years earlier. I was wearing all black and looked so professional. I stared at it. That photo wasn't me. There was nothing of me there. I cried. I had wasted all those years looking for myself. Had I finally found it?

Where are you?

I grabbed the wallet, pulled the ID out, and trashed it. There was a hundred dollar bill behind it. Where did that come from? I never carried cash. I thought I had to spend it. I saw a homeless guy leaning against a rusty newspaper box.

"Would you cut my throat if I gave you a hundred bucks?" I asked.

He asked me something, but I couldn't understand what he was saying. I closed my eyes, and the music of the club started buzzing in my head. And then I thought I heard my name. I opened my eyes and saw Nick coming toward me.

"Susan? What the fuck are you doing? What the fuck?"

I woke up from my trance, started walking away, and then I ran. But I was too slow, or he was too fast, and he caught me. He came close enough to touch me and then grabbed my wrist. I remembered the last time he had done that. Two years had passed, and I still remembered it so well I could replicate it in my mind. I was addicted to that memory, to him, and perhaps I was now going through symptoms of withdrawal.

"Are you on drugs or something?"

Yes, I thought. You. I'm on you. I remained silent and looked at him, my wrist still in his grip, or at least it felt so.

"Would you take me home?" I asked.

"Where exactly is that?"

"I don't know."

He called a taxi, and we left. While we were seated in the back of the car he came close and took my hand and held it. This time it was my pain he was trying to soften. I closed my eyes and felt suddenly at peace. Did I pass it to him? When the cab stopped, we got out and he took me in his arms.

"You're so tiny," he said. "You lost more weight."

I wrapped my arms around his neck and pushed my head against his chest so as not to hear what I already knew. He opened the door, and we went inside. When we were in front of the sofa he laid me there to rest. I tried to crumple myself and our story up and toss them into a corner. Wouldn't it be nice to be able to write a new story now? Trash the past and start all over? What had I done wrong though? It still wasn't clear. Would this one be better than the last? I still had my addictions, and he had his.

"I'll make you some tea," he said, and while he was waiting for the water to be ready, he came closer, caressed my forehead, and then moved the hair that was covering my eyes.

"You need to cut this soon. People want to see your eyes again," he said. "I want to see them."

I looked at him, into him. Then he stood up to check on the tea, and when he returned with a cup, he asked, "Have you been drinking?"

I said I hadn't.

"Not today," I added.

"What's wrong then?"

I remained silent.

"We used to be friends," he said, perhaps to make me feel safer.

In a way, we used to be, yes. He was probably the only friend I had made and lost too soon. Was it too late now?

"I have a story to tell you."

"I'm listening."

I told him about my mother, my grandmother, my nightmare, what I saw, his voice pounding in my head, my pain. I talked for a while, and he never interrupted.

"How do you feel now?" he asked.

"A little better."

I hid in my cup.

"Do you miss making love to me?" I asked.

"Do you?" he asked.

Neither of us answered.

He started undressing me, and then I undressed him. I could barely see his body. I ran my fingers through his hair, then his lips, then his chest. He kissed me and stole my oxygen, and then I did the same to him. I breathed again.

"Let me look at you," he said.

I looked straight at him to forget that I was standing there naked, that he was looking at me.

"Remember when you asked me why you made me uncomfortable?"

"Yes," he said.

"When we were together, I felt like this all the time. Naked, while you had your clothes on. Wet with desire, while you were probably still wondering whether I was worth another try."

He came closer to touch me, but I pushed him back.

"Wait. Tell me what you see."

"I see your desire and I love it. I know I'm the one who's causing it, and this makes me want to screw you so bad."

He went down on me.

"God, you're so beautiful," he said.

"Am I?" I thought about the drunk woman I had seen before, my photo ID, and I wanted to believe him, to see what he saw. I didn't see me.

He kissed me, pushed me onto the sofa, pressed his pain against mine, pushed himself inside of me, and I spread my arms wide to

keep as much as I could of him. And I felt suspended again, lighter
for a few seconds, almost weightless, as I thought one would feel
when falling down from somewhere high. I was giving in to Nick and
my addiction.

AGAIN AND AGAIN

I thought I would be OK, transgress one more time—one time only—and then stop. This is what I would do, I thought. And then I would return to my life. I would complete my book, close it, and go back to my roles of mother, wife, teacher. I would free my frozen butterflies, let them fly once, live their story, and then die. But it didn't happen exactly like that. My one-time transgression turned into my life. And we transgressed again and again. We couldn't stop. We had become each other's addictions. I hadn't told Matt about Nick, but he knew about us. We didn't fight though, or argue about it. He just let me go, each night. He did say I didn't know what I was doing, and he knew I would come back to him. Whatever or whomever was keeping me where I was, it would be over soon. Would it? It didn't feel like that.

And so I would spend the night in my apartment with Nick and my days at home with Will, crossing Matt's eyes each time I would come and go, and each time feeling horrible for what I was doing. But I couldn't stop. I had to do it.

My book was almost complete. I had the feeling I was writing its finale, although it wasn't clear yet what that would be. I felt pleasure and pain and fear. Pleasure with Nick. Pain when I saw Matt suffering and I knew that I was the one causing it. And I feared. I feared I could lose my child any moment. I got it now. The adrenaline, the pain, the fear, the pleasure, the pain. They were addictive. And intoxicating. And so poisoned, my soul finally free, I wrote and wrote and no longer struggled.

The ice had melted around the butterflies' wings, and now they were flying all over. But they had turned into moths. Their wings were draped down their backs or spread out to the sides, and they would fly and feed only at night. They were flitting insects circling my candle, the only one I had left to light my studio, close to my computer, my prayer for myself and my writing.

Nick would come to my apartment every night, and we would both write, both immersed in a story or the craft of it. I would write on the carpet while he would write on my bed. Or we would both write at my desk, or both on my bed. That little apartment had expanded in unpredictable ways, suggesting lines or ideas and creativity that we had to explore.

We made love to the words we were writing, sometimes reading to each other. We would make love to each other and talk about it during the breaks. And occasionally we would eat, some cheap Chinese or Mexican food that seemed the best food I ever had. It all looked perfect, a story I would want to write.

"Don't put your clothes on," he said one night after we had made love. "Write naked. I want you to feel what that means."

"What do you mean?"

He got up and brought me to my chair.

"I want you to experience what it means to be unfiltered when you write, connected to your writing, poured into your story without layers. And I want to watch while you do that."

I smiled and felt warm.

Less than an hour later, he pulled me from the chair, went to the stereo, put on Sinatra, and asked me to dance with him.

I bent to grab my shirt from the floor, but he stopped me.

"Please, wait. Just this song, and then I'll let you get dressed."

A few moves later I was on the floor again, my back against the carpet, his eyes on top of mine.

How did that happen? It wasn't long ago that I was standing right there and calling his name, missing him like crazy. And now he was there with me. I still had bruises, but I had not caused them this time. He had, by pressing me against the carpet every time we made love there. I ran my fingers over those bruises and thought I loved them.

"I love you," I said, one night.

He looked at me, turned away as though to retain what I had just said. Then he turned back and asked, "Are you sure?"

I smiled, and he pressed me harder against the carpet.

"I love you too," he whispered.

The nights with Nick had become like opium to me. They relieved me from the pain, they relaxed me, and they made me feel as if I were sleepwalking or dreaming, suspended from the ground at some undefined height. But when I returned home, and when Will went to bed, I would feel the absence of it. I could not eat, I was more and more anxious, and I found it more difficult to focus. And then I would leave again. And crossing Matt's eyes at the door had become harder each time. But this is what it was, day after day, again and again.

BROKEN

And then it was the end of July. It was so hot that night I could barely breathe. I had no air conditioning in my apartment, and I was alone, as Nick had to be somewhere for work. We had agreed to see each other the following night.

I felt alone.

I thought about returning home to Matt and Will, but that didn't feel right. Will was sleeping, and I would have to share the bed with Matt. I left the apartment, taking my computer with me, and walked. I had no specific destination in mind, but at some point I called a taxi and went to my grandmother's house. The light in my bedroom was still on. Would it bother my grandmother that I had come back before finishing my story? She had told me to come back when I was done to read the story to her. The story wasn't finished though, and yet I felt I needed to be there. I found the keys in my purse, opened the gate, then the big entrance door, and entered.

The house was silent. It was two in the morning, and everyone was sleeping. I tiptoed up to my bedroom and closed the door behind me. I lay on my bed and started feeling tired and sleepy, but I wanted to write. If not the finale yet, at least sketches of ideas for one. I pulled out a notepad and started writing. I wrote a few words, then a line, but nothing special was coming out of my mind. Bored and frustrated, I started looking around the room. I had not done that in years, and I barely remembered what the drawers and closet contained. I opened my closet and found some old dresses. I stuck my nose in there and smelled the past. Sad and bitter memories danced around happy ones, and then more sad ones. I looked down, and hidden under some boxes and a blanket I used to take everywhere with me, I found some old flats. I held the flats in my hands and looked at them closely. Then I closed my eyes, and for a few moments I was back in time, back in that sewer.

I remembered. I had damaged the shoes when I decided to explore a sewer on my own during an excursion with my class. I loved the feeling of being there. Underground. And I loved that I had been brave enough to escape from the group and explore that sewer on my own. I fell into the water, broke an edge of my shoe, and damaged my dress. But I was able to pull myself out and return to the group. I said that I had fallen asleep. A little or big lie? Who would decide that if not me? I concluded it was a little lie, forgave myself for it, and kept the damaged shoe as a trophy for the courage and the successful completion of the mission. I placed the flats back and dug more into the past.

I moved some more clothes and shoes, and hidden in a corner, piled on top of each other, I found my diaries. I pulled them out and looked at them. I remembered their covers. A different color for each year. I had been very careful in selecting them. I even remembered my reluctance about the purple one. There was no other color left at the little bookstore, and I had just finished writing my green diary. I still had more to say, and so I bought the purple one. The only one left. That year wasn't a particularly good one. I attributed that to the color. Of course it was the color. I looked at that rainbow of memories and laughed. And then there was another diary, but it wasn't mine. I knew that because I didn't recognize the cover. But it wasn't unfamiliar either. I looked more closely and opened it.

To Jasmine, I hope you'll keep on writing.

It was my mother's diary.

The first entries were dated from September 1980, twenty-six months before she died. Her last entry was September 29, 1982. I wondered if she had written more after that. Another unfinished story, I thought. I leafed through the pages, and something resonated with me. I remembered reading that diary. But so many years had passed, and my memories were confused. I was probably in middle school. A flash of memory crossed my mind. I saw my grandmother talking to me about it, but again, that memory was fogged, I couldn't see clearly. I remembered feeling sick one day and staying home from school. I was bored like I was now, and I was looking around the house to find some hidden treasure. And I found this one. It was in one of my mother's drawers. My father didn't know about it. By the time my grandmother caught me I had already read it two or three times and almost knew it by heart. Yes, that is what happened. I remembered that my grandmother panicked and asked me to return the diary to her. I hadn't seen it since then. She told me the diary was a *fiction* my mother had been writing. I loved it and hoped I would be able to write one myself, one day. As I revisited my memories, I let the diary fall from my hands. Was my story similar to my mother's? Were they both *fictions*? My grandmother said I needed to keep the diary and my discovery confidential, that I shouldn't say anything about it to anyone because she might want to publish it one day. Yes, I was in middle school, and that is what she had said to me.

I went to the door, locked it, and lay on my bed. I decided to leaf through the pages first. Maybe I could find something she had tucked inside. My heart suddenly stopped beating, and I think I felt like dying, as this is what I saw:

Night One
Night Two
Night Three
Night Four
Night Five
Night Six

I had not seen that diary in decades. What I had written was my own story. I knew it was. My hands started shaking. Was I losing my mind? Is that what was happening? My last spark of sanity or insanity suggested that it might be just a coincidence, a miracle, or a damnation. I started reading and I realized it was more the second than the first.

The pages described my mother's insomnia; the boredom; her meeting with Marc, a man she had an affair with while she was married to my father; her time with Marc stolen from her marriage and me; the story of her mother, my grandmother, apparently suffering from the same mental issues my mother had; the letters she exchanged with Marc; the time Marc came to the house to see her; the time she slashed her veins. I felt so sick to my stomach that I threw up. Our stories were not identical, but they were too similar. Each a distorted version of the other. The time she went to his place and watched Marc sleep, her obsession with "Summertime," her ghosts and her nightmares, the drugs she used, her affair, and his breaking up with her. *Broken.* When I finished reading her diary, I let it fall on the floor and went to the mirror to stare at myself. The mirror was broken, and I now saw myself more clearly. I was broken.

THE DRAWING IS YOURS

When I had recovered a little bit of balance, I placed the diary in my purse and left. My grandmother was still sleeping, and I was glad of that. I returned to my apartment and called Matt. I told him I might have a temperature. Lie. That I had been throwing up all night. True. And that I didn't want Will to catch it. Somehow true, as I started wondering whether it might be bad for Will to be close to me before I took care of whatever was wrong with me. Matt didn't believe me and asked if I'd been drinking. I said I hadn't, but I also said that he might have been right about some other things. He didn't ask more, but said, "I hope you'll be home soon."

"I hope that too. I miss you and Will. I really do."

I hung up and cried. I let myself fall onto my bed, took some sleeping pills Nick had left on my desk, and shut my mind down. When I woke up it was dark. Nick was sitting close to me, reading a book.

"Good morning, or should I say good-night, my dear . . . sleeping beauty."

"What time is it?"

"It's after nine . . . p.m."

"Your pills," I said, and yawned.

He smiled.

"You're welcome. I know. I like them too," he said, and kissed me. He started undressing me. He wanted to make love, but I didn't.

"Sorry, Nick, I don't feel like it."

"What's wrong?"

I'm not sure this is real. I might have created you, I might have created this, and you believed it. I feel sick, I might be. I need to see a doctor, look into this more closely. I might need to be alone for a while. That is what I should have said.

"I think I might have a flu or something," I said instead.

"Oh, I'm sorry, babe." He kissed my forehead and got up to make some tea. Soon he came back with the tea and sat close to me. I was still in bed. He asked me about my day, and I told him I had been at my grandmother's place the night before looking for some fresh air, as the apartment had become too warm.

"It won't be the same tonight. The temperature's dropping, and it might rain."

I didn't feel relieved.

"I ran into Andrew today. He asked about you."

"Oh. How is he?" I faked my interest to distract him from me. Nick knew me well, and lying to him wasn't easy.

"I think he's doing fine. He was worried about you. He said you guys had not seen each other since the signing event. I told him you're almost done with the book and he said he owes you a drawing."

"Oh, right. The drawing."

The woman in the box. I thought about my mother, her diary, and that heading in her diary.

"He said he'll give you the drawing when you're done with the book. And he invited us for a drink tonight. He has some new drawings and paintings he'd like to show us. He'll have some guests over for dinner. I texted him earlier while you were sleeping, and he said we could join them at any time. Would you like to go?"

"Tonight?"

"Yes. I think it'd be good for you to get out of here. You've been here for too long. I'm worried about you."

I thought about my discovery and felt worried too. He might be right. Leaving the apartment and meeting with Andrew that night could be good and, perhaps, even necessary. I took a shower, and we left.

"Did you tell Andrew about us?" I asked Nick when we were in the taxi heading to Andrew's place.

"No, why would I? There's no need to tell people about us. You said you want to resolve your situation with Matt, and there's Will, so . . ." He looked at me as though he found my question strange. And indeed it wasn't the type of question I would have asked before. I was trying to make some distance between us. He now seemed too much a part of the insanity I wanted to shed.

"Right, there is no need to tell people," I said, and moved away when he tried to kiss me, faking a cough.

"This might make you feel better," he then said. He pulled his phone from his bag and handed me the earphones. "I know you like 'Summertime' so much. I heard this on the radio today, and thought you would like it."

I put the earphones on and raised the volume. It was Janis Joplin's version of that song. It lifted me up and threw me to the ground. I pulled down the window of the car, let the warm air hit my forehead, closed my eyes, and listened to the song again and again until we arrived at Andrew's place.

"Aren't you tired of it?" Nick asked when I returned his earphones. "I thought you might like it but you listened to it, what? Five times? Six in a row? It's insane."

"Right," I said.

We went up the stairs. The door was open. Andrew was talking to some friends and showing them some of his latest works. As soon as he saw us, he came to the door and hugged both of us.

"Susan, you're disappearing. Is it the book that's doing that to you?"

"Maybe. Yes. The book."

"I know you don't like this question, but I can't help it. When do you think you'll be done with it?"

"Tomorrow morning," I said. "In fact, I have to go now. I'll bring the book to you tomorrow morning."

"Are you serious? I can't wait to read it."

"Yes, me too," I said.

"Well, in that case . . ." He walked to another room and returned with my drawing.

"The drawing is yours," he said. "I promised it to her," he added, looking at Nick.

"Oh, I can see why. Did you pose for him?"

I remained silent and looked at them as if they were strangers, as if the only thing I could recognize now was myself in that drawing.

"Thanks, Andrew."

"I have to go now," I added, and looked at Nick.

"Where should we go?"

"*I* have to go. I have to go to my grandmother's place and finish the book. You'll both have it tomorrow."

He looked at me, surprised.

"Are you sure you're OK?" he asked.

"I will be."

I kissed Nick on his cheek, hugged Andrew, and left.

AN UNFINISHED STORY

I called a taxi and went to my grandmother's place. It was after eleven. I looked up and saw the light in my bedroom was off. I used the key to open the gate, I pushed the door, and ran to her bedroom. She was reading.

"You found the diary, didn't you?"

"You put it there."

"I thought you had to know."

"Why didn't you tell me when I read the first part of my story to you?"

"You had to write it."

I looked at her and couldn't restrain my tears.

"You did, right? You're done?" she asked.

"You tell me."

"Why don't you read it to me? You promised."

I was shaking, but I sat and started reading from where I had left off. At sunrise, we were done.

"So is your story finished?"

No, it wasn't. Matt would have said that I had not even started. But the fiction was done. At least, I hoped so.

I wrote the last line of the book; chose its title, *Frozen Butterflies*; printed it; and brought a copy to Andrew and one to Nick.

On Andrew's copy, I wrote:

Thanks for seeing me.

I left a copy of your father's essay inside the book.

I think the questions on the margins are yours.

Your father answered.

Susan

On Nick's copy, I wrote:

Nick,

Here's the book.

I wish this hadn't been a fiction.

I'll have to take care of myself now.

Maybe when I'm back

I'll meet you in real life.

Susan

THE END

A GIFT TO MY READERS

Releasing a story into the world requires an audience who understands it and is willing to read, hear, feel, respond, as if that reader could send that story back to its author, and send it louder, so that there is a meaningful exchange between the two, the very reason for publishing.

I occasionally send newsletters with details on new releases, special offers, and other bits of news on the stories I write, to share more, or soliciting feedback, reaction.

If you sign up to the mailing list, you'll become part of my literary club and you will receive a copy of my novella, *Like Still Water*, as well as samples of all my books (current and future ones).

You can get all of this, **for free**, by signing up here:

http://simonawrites.com/gift

DID YOU ENJOY THIS BOOK? YOU CAN MAKE A DIFFERENCE

Reviews help so much! When I decided to fly "solo," I understood the challenges and risks of doing so. A big publisher would have taken care of the marketing, paid for it, helped me spread the voice about my stories. But it'd have also imposed its own rules on the stories, their characters, the editing, cover...something I could not accept. I could not afford not being truthful to my stories, hence my choice was unavoidable. But without your reviews my stories will not be able to fly.

Honest reviews help bring my books to the attention of other readers, help the stories fly, and keep me writing.

I would be so thankful if you could just spend five minutes (or less!) leaving a review (it can be as short as you like) for *Frozen Butterflies*.

Thanks from my heart,

simona

ABOUT THE AUTHOR

Simona Grossi was born and raised in a small town in Italy, surrounded by books and music. She studied piano at the Conservatory and then attended law school and joined a prestigious law firm in Italy. After litigating for several years, she moved to the U.S. and joined academia. In addition to her addictions to her husband and to writing, she is addicted to piano and is currently graduating in classical piano from a Conservatory in Italy. She also loves cooking, traveling, and spending time with her friends. Simona has published two novels: Looking for Clara and Frozen Butterflies. Both have received stellar reviews on Amazon and Goodreads.

f facebook.com/simonawritesbooks

◎ instagram.com/simonagrossila

a amazon.com/author/simonagrossi

BB bookbub.com/authors/simona-grossi

g goodreads.com/simonagrossi

ALSO BY SIMONA GROSSI

LOOKING FOR CLARA: A NOVEL

Her life has become a single, low note. Will an Italian escape strike a joyful chord in her soul?

Clara Smith seems out of tune, drifting through one empty day after another. Alone in LA for Christmas and uncertain about her new boyfriend, the pianist-turned-lawyer feels as fake as the snow. But when her firm dispatches her to Siena, Italy to lead a major project, the rhythm of the daily grind gloriously changes tempo.

Bonding with her charismatic eighty-year-old neighbor over his large collection of photographs, she uncovers a picture of a mysterious woman.

And a breathtaking cross-country adventure, in search of the framed beauty who shares her name gives voice to Clara's long-silenced passions.

Can a melodious tour through vineyards and sun-drenched landscapes restore her sense of harmony?

Looking for Clara is a heartfelt journey into women's fiction. If you like deeply drawn characters, vivid settings, and romantic secrets, then you'll love Simona Grossi's life-affirming novel.

Buy *Looking for Clara* to listen to your heart today!

ACKNOWLEDGMENTS

I am indebted to many people for this book. First, my best friend, mentor, and editor, Allan Ides, for holding my hand as I was going through some tough times, doubts, and moments of despair in the creation of Frozen Butterflies. He read more than an infinite number of versions, each time with the love and dedication that only someone who truly loves you and cares about you would do. Without his guidance and editing, Frozen Butterflies would not be what it is. I want to also thank my husband, and the love of my life, Aaron, for being by my side as I'd spent hours writing, reviewing, and rewriting, for respecting my need to isolate myself as I was going through this literary journey, for loving me unconditionally no matter what. And there are so many friends I need to thank for reading my stories, for giving me precious suggestions, for supporting me, for believing in me. I will be forever grateful for their love and support. And thank-you my Reader! I hope this story enriched you as it enriched me, I hope it made you feel as deeply as I felt, and I hope it offered different angles and perspectives to realities and stories that are sometimes hard to comprehend. Frozen Butterflies was inspired by Federico Fellini's work and by my desire to go deeper into myself and decipher parts of me and of some people close to me that I sometimes struggle to understand. It was inspired by my belief that dreams are part of reality and that we can shape reality, sometimes without even realizing we are doing so. I wanted to create musical and figurative paintings and show the beauty in the darkest corners of our lives, like in Susan's, Nick's, Andrew's, Harry's. Those people are not perfect, but despite their flaws, and what might otherwise seem unreal, I think they are real and beautiful. Thank you for reading. From my heart.

simona

Made in the USA
San Bernardino, CA
30 January 2020